The Surprising Power of a Good Dumpling

The Surprising Power of a Good Dumpling

WAI CHIM

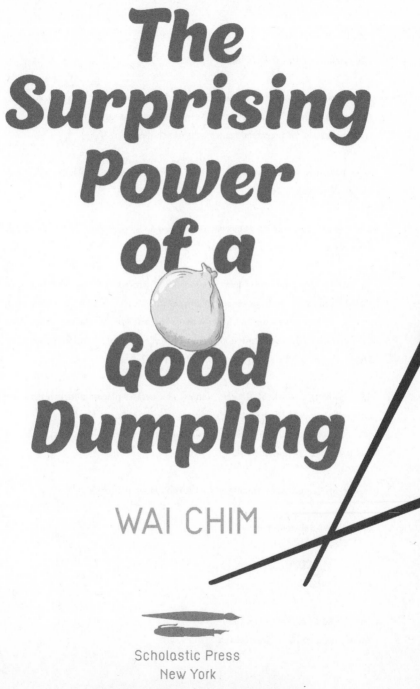

Scholastic Press
New York

Library of Congress Cataloging-in-Publication Data available

ISBN 978-1-338-65611-4

1 2020

Printed in the U.S.A.

First US edition, November 2020
Book design by Baily Crawford

For family,
whatever form that may take

A Note on Phonetics from the Author

This book uses the Jyutping romanization system for Cantonese language, which includes numbers that represent tones (inflections). Like many of her Western-born contemporaries (including myself), Anna Chiu speaks and understands colloquial Cantonese but doesn't know how to read or write the much more complex Chinese characters. I've selected Jyutping as a way of representing her use of her Chinese tongue.

Mom
Maa1

I need to tell Anna about the big black dog.

Anna, my precious daughter. I saw the dog the other day. It was snarling and snapping, chomping through its broken chain, frothing from the mouth.

Wo wo. Wo wo.

Anna, I have to tell you about the dog. Big as a car, ferocious. A beast. It barked and it howled, high-pitched like a demon.

Wo wo. Wo wo.

I need to tell you, Anna. So you will know, and you will understand. Its eyes were red and glowing like the devil.

Wo wo. Wo wo.

Chapter One
Jat1

February

THE SHADOWS OF THE LEAVES on the wall bend to the right, like gentle waves coming to shore. *It could be a good day.*

When Ma stays in bed, our mornings are a game of fortune-telling where I'm forever looking for signs. The search begins when I try to coax her up with a cup of herbal tea. I shuffle down the hallway, looking for a shadow that looks like a smiley face, waiting for a shock from the doorknob, or trying to miss the creaking board on the floor. These signs tell me something about what to expect behind Ma's closed door.

I can't say if they work or not. There was definitely a day I missed the squeaking board and Ma ended up throwing the tea I brought her against the wall. *Bad day.* And then there was the time I thought the shadows outside Ma's bedroom door looked like a kitten playing with a balloon. That day, Ma went out and bought me and Lily new iPhones because she said they were on special. *Good day.*

Today's shadows look promising and the knob doesn't shock me. The ceramic lid of Ma's special teacup rattles in my trembling hands as I push the door open. In here, the shadows look menacing; the thin slats of sunlight threaten to break through the barrier of darkness that engulfs the room. *She's still in bed, bad sign.* One for one.

I set the cup down on the bedside table. Ma's tiny form is lost in a swath of thick blanket so only a matted black nest of her hair pokes out. I know she's not sleeping. My heart sinks.

She's been in bed for two weeks now. It's not the first time, and I know it won't be the last, but I still can't smother the plumes of disappointment when she gets like this. When she stops being our mother.

Out of habit, I push my glasses up against the bridge of my nose. "Ma. Caa4." *Tea.* I can still detect the tinge of hopefulness in my voice.

She doesn't stir. A small breeze makes the blinds tremble and the beams of light shiver, but nothing else in the room moves, certainly not my mother.

"Ma." I put a hand on the cushioned part that I think is her shoulder and shake gently. Only then does she move and that's only to flinch my hand away. I stay by the side of the bed waiting for another sign, some acknowledgment that I'm here. But she doesn't turn. As I leave, I shut the door as quietly as I can. This time, I think that maybe the waves in the shadows look more like spikes on a lizard, so not the good sign I thought they were.

Or maybe they're just bloody leaves.

I plaster on a smile and head into the kitchen.

It's eerily quiet, just the sound of the dripping tap from the sink. It's the only plus side to Ma being in her room. My little brother and sister have been on their best behavior in the mornings since Ma's been in bed.

The two of them are crammed together on one side of the tiny dining room table making breakfast. Ma threw out the toaster a while back—toast is too jit6 hei3 (*hot air*) and the darkened bits cause sore throats, she says—so we are eating butter and jam on plain bread. Lily is helping to spread the jam for our five-year-old brother.

Michael flattens his slice of white bread into a gooey patty and crams it into his mouth, jam and butter smearing all over his pudgy cheeks.

I grab a paper towel to wipe it off, but it just spreads the sticky mess around. Now bits of paper towel cling to his face. I shrug and reach for the tub of butter.

"How's Ma?" Lily asks.

"Sleeping," I say. Lily will know this is a lie, which makes it easier for me to say. I'm a terrible liar, and I don't like to argue with my sister. While some people argue to be right, Lily argues just to prove the other person wrong.

"Mommy's sleeping! Shhhhh, don't wake her up!" Michael says this way too loudly, so I shush him.

As expected, Lily is not buying. "Okay, so, like, talking to herself or not talking at all?" At thirteen, my little sister is more matter-of-fact and sarcastic than I've ever been.

"She's *sleeping*," I say again, and jam the butter knife into the hardened brick. I gouge out a piece, not caring that it looks like somebody has hacked away a piece of flesh from the middle of the block. I do my best to spread it, then give up and just fold the bread over. I eat my buttered bread in two big bites. The lump of butter melts slowly on the roof of my mouth.

"If Mommy's sleeping again, are you taking me to school, ze2 ze2?" Michael asks me, a snarl of paper towel still stuck to the corner of his mouth. His bowl haircut and perfect bangs make his brown eyes look even bigger. He's so cute, sometimes it hurts my heart.

"Lily is going to have to take you today."

Lily's outraged. "I have to meet with my CT partners before our presentation. *You* can drop him on your way." CT stands for *Communications Theater*; calling it "drama" is too pedestrian for the students at Montgomery High.

"You start at nine, Lily. If you get going soon, you won't be late," I say.

"*Uuuuuugh!*" Lily's complaining is overly dramatic, but it doesn't faze me. She is up and running to our room, her sticky plate still on the table. I sigh and pick up my hardly used plate along with hers.

I leave the dishes in the sink and wet another paper towel in a final attempt to clean my brother's face. He sits there and lets me scrape things off with my chewed-down-to-the-nub nails.

"Baba didn't come home last night." My brother frowns.

"I know. Things must have been busy at the restaurant," I say.

I've noticed this has been happening whenever Ma stays in bed, but I keep this to myself.

Michael reaches up to touch my face. "Look, Anna! An eyelash. You have to make a wish."

I smile and comply, closing my eyes and blowing on his fingertip, wishing for Ma to be out of bed, for Baba to be home.

For things to just be normal.

We smile at each other as the eyelash disappears, and Michael looks very pleased with himself.

"Okay, it's already past eight. Time to get ready for school," I tell him.

"But I need Mommy or Baba to sign my permission form." He waves a piece of paper under my nose. "Our librarian, Miss Holloway, is taking us to an art camp! But she says I have to get my parents to sign it or I'll miss out. Can't we just wake Mommy up?"

I remember Ma's shape in the bed, all bundled up and still. The last thing I want is for Michael to see her that way. "Tell you what, you go get ready, and I'll see if I can wake her up," I say.

His whole face brightens and the ache in my chest is gone in an instant.

"Are we going yet?" Lily emerges from our bedroom, already dressed. She has pulled her hair back in a messy ponytail. Her rail-thin body is almost comical with her oversized backpack hanging extra low and bouncing against her bottom. A water bottle dangles from a carabiner clipped to the side. "Hurry up, squirt. We have to go," she calls after Michael's retreating form.

She plonks herself down, backpack and all, onto one of our

metal folding chairs. The water bottle makes a loud thud as it hits the chair, but she doesn't notice, just crosses her arms and stares at me.

"She's not going to sign the form, you know." The know-it-all arch of her eyebrow is so perfect, I wonder if she's practiced it before.

"I *know*." I snatch a pen from the kitchen drawer and scrawl on the line on the form. It's not the first time I've forged Ma's signature, and I'm sure Lily's done it a million times, too. But we have an unspoken agreement between us: We protect Michael from Ma's tendencies, the bad ones at least, while we can.

Lily lets out a not-so-subtle huff behind me. "You know, if I get another lecture from Lucy, I'm going to tell her it's my *sister's* fault. I'm not taking the fall."

"Sure, whatever. And don't call your teachers by their first name."

I place the butter in a used Ziploc bag and put it back in the freezer, where Ma insists on keeping it. The bread bag I tie up tightly and then knot it up in another plastic bag and stick it in the freezer. Everything in our house is tied up in plastic bags of some kind: All our food containers, cleaning supplies, even the picture frames on the shelves are sealed in clear plastic. Ma hates dust but she doesn't like dusting, so every few weeks, she just replaces the plastic bags because they're cheap. Any eco-warrior would be terrified stepping into our house, but no one ever comes over, so there's no worry.

"*Lucy* tells us to call her that," Lily retorts. "She says that children are human beings and deserve to be treated with the same respect as adults, so I can *express* myself to my full potential."

I try not to roll my eyes. Thanks to a scholarship, Lily attends a rich private school just outside Glebe. With a natural penchant for melodrama, Lily's sounding more and more like her well-off peers. I just hope they don't rub off *too* much.

"Ze2 ze2, I can't find my other sock," Michael calls out to me from his bedroom.

"Do you want me to help you?"

"No!" Michael is going through a phase of being very particular about his privacy, especially with his sisters. He won't let us in when he's dressing or bathing, and will only let Mommy see him naked, which is making things harder for me and Lily, as Ma's good moods are getting fewer and fewer. I miss the little guy who ran around naked with his half-done-up diaper trailing behind him.

Lily rolls her eyes again. "Oh gosh! I'm *never* going to get to school."

"Be quiet." I call through the closed door, "Michael, you have five seconds to come out of there or I'm coming in!"

"Noooo!" The door bangs open and Michael is standing there in his school shirt and shorts, a striped sports sock on one foot and a gray knee-high sock on the other. I walk into his bedroom and get on my hands and knees to look.

I snatch at what I hope is a gray sock, but it turns out to just be a giant dust bunny under the bed. *Yuck. If Ma saw this, she'd lose it.*

"Anna, I need my socks." Michael stamps his feet.

"*Aannaaaaaaa! I have* to go!" Lily's screeching makes me wince.

"Sorry, squirt, no time." I beckon him over and fold the knee-high sock over a few times to try to even the two out.

I help Michael into his shoes and then put on his backpack. It's almost as big as Lily's, and he bends backward slightly from the weight. "And good news, Ma signed your slip!" I wave it in front of him.

He frowns as he takes it from me. "Really? But you said she was asleep."

"Ah, she was. But she woke up for a bit and then went straight back to bed. I think she's really tired."

My lying is pathetic and isn't fooling anyone, not even a five-year-old. But there's no time to argue. I grab my own schoolbag, an over-the-shoulder messenger bag that I bought with the money I saved from the one-and-only paid babysitting gig I ever had, before Ma forbade me to babysit at strangers' houses. *"How do I know their house is safe? They could do drugs or sell the guns."* The woman paying me to babysit worked at the Woolworths down the road and was hoping to pick up an extra shift on the public holiday. But there was no use pointing this out to Ma.

Although these days, it doesn't seem to matter.

She's so often in bed.

As I leave for school, I pause by Ma's door but don't go in. The shadows are gone now. At least for today, there are no more signs to consider.

Chapter Two
Ji6

March

I'VE BEEN DREADING TODAY. It's my Pathways Advisement session, where students are made to talk about their future and what they're going to do with their lives. Pathways is something the school has been really pushing, and this year it's a requirement for all Year Elevens to check in by the end of first term, so they can "see how we're going."

I go to the office for my appointment. There are three other girls already waiting, taking up the bench so I have to kind of stand and lean awkwardly beside them. I don't know who they are but I'm pretty sure they're Year Twelves. They, of course, pretend not to see me.

"Oh my gosh, I literally stayed up studying allllll night. I didn't sleep *at all*. I'd be dead right now if it weren't for this coffee." One girl chugs her venti Starbucks.

"Girl, you're crazy to be doing fourteen units this year," another girl chimes in. "Why didn't you do it last year? Year Eleven doesn't count!"

"I know, uggggh, I'm so stupid," Venti Coffee moans. "Ugh. If I don't get a 99.7 on the ATAR exam, I'm going to kill myself."

I cast my head down and pretend to rub at a spot on my uniform. These girls are pretty much standard Shore Lakes High Asians—smart overachievers who take all the extension classes and get 99.99s on their ATARs. I know the type, with their tiger moms, classical piano training, and MD dreams.

"You know, these days it's sooooo competitive." One of the other girls tosses her silky black hair. "Like, you could get a 99.5 and still not get into the course you want. Like, what gives?" She puckers her Insta-perfect lips, and I rub harder at the nonexistent spot.

"Oh my gosh, can you imagine? You'd end up, like, a real estate agent or have to be a middle-aged barista or something."

What's wrong with that? I wonder, but another part of me is squirming because I know what a huge disappointment it would be if I ever said that to my own Chinese family.

"Anna Chiu?" I'm spared further ATAR exam drama when Miss Kennedy calls me into her office.

"Anna, please have a seat."

Miss Kennedy's office is all white, clean, and bright, accented with pastel stationery from kikki.K. I know the brand because I've spent too much time at the mall staring at the pristine notebooks and matching accessories. I have never lusted after anything like I have over cotton-candy-pink paper clips in a matching bird's nest dispenser.

"So how are we, Anna?" Miss Kennedy smiles, her plump lips shiny with gloss and not a brush of makeup out of place. She doesn't wait for me to answer as she pulls out my file—a crisp manila folder from a curved stack, arranged in rainbow color order. She studies its thin contents.

"STEM girl, huh?" She gives me a knowing wink that makes me grimace.

In Year Ten, we went through the obligatory skills evaluation to determine what coursework we would be most suited for. Boxing us in from the age of fifteen. So fifteen-year-old me was shitty at English and history and anything verbal, and was okay at math and less okay but acceptable at science and technology. So not only am I a boring, stereotypical Asian nerd, I'm a mediocre one at best.

I've been dreading this next bit, where we have to choose our HSC advanced placement courses and the career pathways available. Pathways. What a ridiculous term. Because they don't want to say they'll help us *actually* get into a university program or show us what to do. It's the educational equivalent of just showing us some overgrown jungle or the mouth of a cave and saying, "Off you go. We think this leads you to the responsible, fulfilling life that will testify to the success of the public education system. But we don't know for sure—it's not a road map or even a well-marked trail, it's a *pathway*."

I know some of the students are super ambitious and have high hopes and rosy dreams for their futures. Like Venti Coffee and her friends. And Lily will be like that when she gets to my age. She's smart without trying and she has discipline and focus, not to mention that stubbornness to be better than everyone else at anything.

Meanwhile, my high school career has been just me trying to take classes I can survive and that will tick the boxes for me to get through the year.

"How are you finding your classes this term?" Miss Kennedy takes the printed schedule I was told to bring with me.

"Um, they're okay." But I can tell she's not interested in how I've been finding Term 1 Stage 6 Chemistry at all. Instead, she pores over the schedule I've handed her, judging.

"Advanced Math, that's good. Standard English." She raises an eyebrow. "Do you think you should be challenging yourself a bit more?"

My face goes hot. I've always flushed easily and am terrible at being put on the spot. "Well, ah, I have chemistry, economics, and French, so that's—ah—that's the twelve units." I wonder why she's questioning my schedule now, as it's way past the point that I can actually do anything about my classes. We're already through most of first term.

"I see." Miss Kennedy pushes her lips out so she looks like a beaky Muppet. "You really need to push yourself harder, Anna. The HSCs are next year, and I don't think I need to warn anyone about how tough it's going to be."

"I—I know." My voice is shaky, and I swallow air.

"What about extracurriculars?"

"Um, I'm part of math league?"

She crosses her arms. "Math league meets only twice a term, and then there's a single competition test. That's not enough. What do you do after school? Any community service or volunteering? An after-school job?"

It's like I've swallowed three-alarm chili sauce. I push my glasses up against the bridge of my nose. "Um—I usually pick my brother up from school. And I help out at home." I feel my face turn the same shade as the cotton-candy-pink paper clips on her desk. It sounds pathetic, I know. *But she doesn't know about everything else.*

Miss Kennedy clucks her tongue with the disapproving tone that only adults know how to produce. "This is your second-to-last year, and if you don't establish good study routines and habits, you're going to find yourself grossly underprepared for next year. Find something you're passionate about. Your subjects—they're adequate, but you can be doing much more."

"Isn't it too late to add anything to my load?" Changes had to be finalized weeks ago, but I wonder if she can make an exception for me as the guidance counselor.

"I don't mean literally, Anna." She's looking at me like I'm a pitiful lamb for slaughter, smiling without teeth. "I'm just saying you need to start thinking long-term." She taps the side of her head with a lacquered nail.

Ugh. I hate this cryptic inspirational crap that adults always try to pull. I guess it also means I can't change my schedule. Some "pathways."

I don't say this out loud. Instead, I mutter a simple "okay," and take my schedule. I have to keep myself from balling it up into a thick paper pebble.

I'm halfway out the door when she calls my name. Her half smile is an attempt to be mysterious. "It's time for you to be extraordinary." She cocks her head toward the framed pastel print above her head that says that exact thing. She looks smug, like she's the Dalai Lama bestowing actual wisdom, not just ripping off some print of pretty typography.

I grimace again and nod. Once outside, I crumple the offending schedule and chuck it into the nearest trash can I can find. It pings against the sides too loudly, the paper taunting me with the same words already echoing in my brain.

Not enough.

Chapter Three
Saam1

THE BELL RINGS AND I bolt from my last class. I already have my books and everything I need from my locker, so I weave my way through the messy lines of students emerging from the hallway and am out the door.

I don't have time to wait for the school bus, so I rush to the public bus stop across the street and just manage to catch the driver's eye as he's closing the doors. He lets me on and I wave my pass before sinking into the first free seat.

The bus is mostly empty; I've beaten the usual school crowds. It's a winding twenty-minute ride to Michael's school, so I put on my Bluetooth headphones, a birthday present from last year when Ma had been in a good mood.

The poppy tune washes over me, and I fall under its hypnotic spell. Lily says my taste in music is tragic. She listens to everything K-pop, as well as unknown bands and trendy indie artists on Spotify, while I listen to the charts. But I like thinking that someone as cool as TayTay can feel lost and out of place, just like me.

For this little moment, drumming my fingers on my thighs and trying to discreetly mouth the lyrics, I pretend like I'm a somewhat normal teenager. Nothing to worry about at home. No mom stuff. A normal teenager thinking about the school formal that I can never go to because Ma says no dates with boys. Or looking up the latest news on the Kardashians or Real Housewives, which I've never even seen. I could be daydreaming about kissing boys or sneaking out after dark, even though Ma said she would break my legs and kick me out of the house if I ever tried either of those, and I know she's not joking. I know Miss Kennedy would look upon these thoughts favorably in a well-rounded teen life.

Exploring developmental boundaries, she'd call it.

In other words, *normal*.

I check my phone. Not much new since I'm not really on social media either, not compared to the other people my age. I have Instagram, but I don't post and only occasionally like other people's pics. I was on Snapchat when it was more of a thing, and didn't see the point since I don't have many contacts, and only used it to share silly things with Lily (and she claims she's above all that). I have Facebook (who doesn't?), but I only use it for Messenger.

There's a saying in Cantonese that I quite like. *If you say nothing, no one thinks you're mute.* That's my social approach—nay, my life approach. If I don't interact much, I won't have to worry about what people are saying or thinking about me. I don't have to deal with guys asking for nudes or all the account hacking and cyberbullying stuff that Ma is paranoid about because of what she reads in the Chinese newspaper.

"You and Lily, no use the Facebook. They take the girl away from her parents. Because of the Facebook," Ma had said to us.

"Okay, Ma." Neither of us had looked up from our phones.

At home, at school, and with all things social, I figure it's better if I can just fly under the radar.

I know it means I miss out on normal teen stuff, like parties and fun, but that stuff doesn't really matter in the long run.

(Right?)

A boy in his school uniform comes on board. He's dark-haired and tanned, half smiling, so I can see the dimple in his cheek. I don't recognize the crest or the school colors, so he must not be local. He gives me a small nod and his smile widens. I lower my gaze shyly.

The boy sits across the aisle, two seats in front of me, an arm draped across the back of the chair, taking up the entire seat. He turns his head, catches my eye, and lifts an eyebrow. I drop my head again, my cheeks blazing. I wish I had the nerve to look up and smile coyly, maybe bat my eyelashes through my glasses or toss my hair the way I see the girls at school flirting.

Instead, I spend the rest of the bus ride looking everywhere but at the boy, even though every single nerve ending in my body is aware of him.

I'm hopeless and clueless when it comes to boys—like, zero, zilch, nada. *Hopeless.* And it's not just Ma's threat to break my legs. The closest I have ever come to having a boyfriend was when I used to play with the Turkish boy named Berat from next door when I was six. Our family still lived in Gosford, and I was happy to finally have a friend. But then some of the neighbors joked that we would get married one day, and Ma quickly put a stop to that friendship.

Other than that, there's been nothing, not even a middle-school game of Spin the Bottle. I can't even look at the couples making out behind the buildings at school. I rush past them, red-faced, using my notebook as a shield. They don't stop what they're doing, though. It's like when it comes to matters of sex, I don't even count as an observer.

It's likely for the best. My parents have made it clear that I am not to have a boyfriend of any sort before I finish school. Boys are distracting, Ma reminds me all the time. In addition to the Facebook stories, she is constantly pointing out stories of pregnant teenagers who have ruined their lives and are working menial jobs because they were "tricked by a boy." Growing up, there were no parties, no sleepovers, or any real socializing outside of school and family. The normal kid stuff. It was just family, restaurant, study, Ma's moods, and Chinese stuff.

The bus pulls up in front of Michael's school and I rush off, not looking back at the boy. Only when I'm safe on the curb do I sneak a quick peek at the window, pivoting my head as if I'm just checking for the cars coming from behind. Yep. He's smirking at me and lifts the eyebrow again just as he falls into my line of sight. I pretend not to notice, but he's laughing as the bus pulls away.

Mortification bubbles under my skin, and I clench and unclench my fists as I hurry past the crosswalk toward the school gate.

Hopeless.

But there's no time to consider that. The bells chime in a poppy radio tune to signal the end of the day. Kids emerge from the buildings like tiny blue penguins, all oversized bags and floppy hats. They stream toward the entrance, which is already chock-full of impatient parents, peering over one another's heads to glimpse their tardy offspring.

I hurry through the crowds, keeping an eye toward the ground to make sure I don't trample a small body; I forget how little primary school children are.

I spot Michael skipping toward the office, clutching another boy's hand. I call out to him and he turns, and I watch his eyes light up.

"Anna!" Michael's chirrupy greeting is music to my ears. His schoolbag hangs half open, bouncing on his back. His smile is so wide, I'm wondering if that's how he maintains the cute little gaps between his baby teeth.

I ruffle his hair and reach to zip his bag shut. "Come on, let's go before we miss the bus."

"Wait, Anna. I want to show you something!" He takes my hand at the same time he drops his mate's. "See you later, Albert," he says with a quick wave. Albert is already calling after two girls who are starting up a game of tag. They remind me of six-year-old me and Berat. Friendships are easy when it's just about play. But when we get older, they become more about favors, support, and status.

Like family.

"Where are we going?" I ask. Michael's flying like a dart. I take long strides to keep up with him as he leads me through the school grounds.

The school library is a nondescript building at the back of the block. But the moment I step inside, it feels like magic. The space seems bigger on the inside, like the TARDIS from *Doctor Who*, and the lack of natural light adds to its whimsical ambience. It's all decked out to look like a real fairy-tale forest. There is an actual tree trunk in the middle, with thick branches that wend their way between the shelves and bear all sorts of plush forest creatures. A wise owl watches us from his perch, his big yellow eyes catching little bits of light so they look like twin moons. Fluffy clouds dangle from the sparkling ceiling, coated with fairy dust.

I'm absolutely stunned. That almost-adult part of me sees that it's all craft paper, glitter, and cotton balls, but my inner child is willing to suspend disbelief and accept that this is all real.

"Wow." I suck in a breath. There are a few children strewn about the space, tucked into corners, cradling books. A father sits with his daughter on the carpet, reading together.

"Over here!" Michael has raced to a far shelf. His faded hat stands out among the bright posters. I go over to read the display.

I STILL CALL AUSTRALIA HOME. The wall is peppered with paintings of people holding hands, playgrounds, living rooms, and kitchens. I recognize one drawing that is the big tree in the middle of this library. Everyday spaces, all of them unique. Once again, I'm surprised. When I did art in primary school, we all did the same exact painting of Uluru and Sydney Harbour. The more "creative" students (not me) added a koala on top of the Opera House or a kangaroo hopping across the bridge, but that was it.

"This one's mine." Michael points. *Wow*, I say again to myself. I recognize the scene, the jellyfish exhibit at Sydney Aquarium. We went there last summer break on one of Ma's good days. The dark rooms had been packed with families and strollers pinballing for space. Lily and I used our little brother to shamelessly shove up to the glass and gawk at the translucent fluorescent-pink and electric-blue blobs. Hard to believe they were part of the same world as us.

Michael has re-created the memory with heavy oil pastels on dark paper, scratching away at the oil so it really looks like you can see through the jellyfish. It makes a cool 3-D effect, like they're ready to spring from the page. It's avant-garde, stylistic, and very, very cool.

"Michael, you're still here?!" The singsong voice is bubbling over with energy even after a long school day. "Didn't I see you here for lunch, too? You don't live in the library, do you?"

"Don't be silly, Miss Holloway." My little brother shakes his head so that his hat teeters from side to side and his shiny mop of hair slides about. "No one *lives* in the library."

"What about the bookworms?"

Michael thinks for a moment and shakes his head again. "No, I don't think they're real. I've read almost every book here and I haven't seen one!"

Miss Holloway lets out a rapturous laugh. She's a bright, vibrant woman, her colored skirts swirling around her thick waist, and her head a mess of gray-blond that blends together whimsically, like elven strands. She fits in perfectly with the fairy-tale spectacle, the fairy godmother of the magical forest.

"This is my sister Anna." Michael laces his thin fingers between mine, and I give them a small squeeze. "She came to see my winning picture."

Michael never mentioned he won a competition.

I look again at his artwork, and sure enough, next to it is a smooth white placard that says, 1ST PLACE.

My heart swells with pride.

"Nice to meet you, Anna." Miss Holloway gives a little wave. "He's a very talented artist."

"I can see that. He's definitely the talented one in the family." *One of the talented ones*, I correct myself, remembering Lily's smarts. "He mentioned you went on an art excursion?"

"Why, yes." She shakes her head a little. "It's such a shame there's no art program in the school anymore. I always think reading and art go together so well and try to find new ways to engage the kids with stories."

I hadn't known this about the art classes. "He was so excited about the trip. Art was always his favorite class."

Miss Holloway beams. "Michael, can you do me a favor and sort the return books in the trolley, please?" Without further instruction, he goes to the trolley and starts piling up paperbacks and picture books. I smile; Miss Holloway has her helpers trained to a tee.

"I'm really glad you're here, actually. Although I was hoping I would get a chance to speak to Michael's mother?"

"Oh." The heat rises to my face. "She's very busy at work." The lie comes without a second thought.

"I see." Miss Holloway purses her lips. "Michael told me she doesn't work."

"Oh, not paid work," I say quickly. "But she's very involved in the community. You know, volunteering, church stuff." Ma has never set foot in a church all her life.

"I see." Her gray eyes flash behind the wispy lashes, and I do my best to look the right amount of apologetic, sheepish teen.

"The thing is, I'm very interested in putting Michael forward for a special art program. I think he'd be exceptional; he has so much talent."

"Oh, we can't afford private lessons." I remember the fight Lily had with Baba once about signing up for drama classes or even singing. Money wasn't to be squandered on "enrichment activities," Baba insisted.

"This would be funded by the program. It would be on scholarship." She presses a brochure into my hands. "It's an Inner West diversity initiative to foster young local talent, and I really think that Michael would be perfect for it."

My ears perk up and I study the paper in my hands. There's a stern-looking Aboriginal man in dotty black ink. "It's headed up by Paul Hookey, a local artist from Brisbane." She sounds very proud of this, so I smile and try to look impressed.

"Wow, that's great." There have been a few of these "diversity initiatives" of late. Programs and councils making sure to give minority voices a fair go. I never like to be called out as a "minority," but I guess the good intention is there.

"I think Michael would make an excellent candidate for the program, but he'll need parental permission to participate." She points to the bottom of the form, where there's an old-school printed perforation and signature line.

"No problem. I'll make sure our mother gets it."

"I'd still prefer if she could come in and I can explain it in person. Surely she can spare a few minutes out of her volunteering?"

I can feel her gaze boring into me. Her eyes make me nervous, like missiles homing in on their target. I know I'm blushing again and push at my glasses.

"I'll try. I mean, I'll ask her. I mean, of course she can." Miss Holloway arches an eyebrow, and I actually duck my head to avoid her prying gaze.

"We'd better go. We don't want to be late for dinner." I stuff the pamphlet into my bag and call out hoarsely, "Michael, come on." I'm already moving toward the entrance.

"Wait, Anna!" He catches up to me but then turns around. "Bye, Miss Holloway!" I can still feel her watching me, and I march on with steely determination.

On the bus home, I try to broach the subject about Ma. "What did you tell Miss Holloway about Ma staying at home?"

Michael shrugs. He's engrossed in a game on my phone. He's technically not allowed screen time until he's done his homework, but Ma's not here to enforce it and I want to be the nice big sister. "She asked me what my parents did, and I said Baba works at the restaurant and Ma stays at home."

"Right." I choose my next words carefully. "It's just better, sometimes, if you're more mindful about what you tell the teachers. Sometimes they won't understand stuff. There are some things we have to keep to ourselves." I say this last bit in my broken Cantonese, conscious of prickling ears on the bus.

Michael doesn't look up but gives me a faint nod. I sigh heavily, drumming my fingers against my thigh, and watch him play. Ma's moods seemed better after Michael was born, and Lily and I thought maybe that was the end of her erratic behavior and maybe, just maybe, we could be a normal family. But last year, she went back to bed at least twice and we're not even halfway through first term and she's already plunged herself into darkness. Despite us all pretending that Ma's just sick or tired, Michael has noticed something is up. Is that why he didn't tell us about his art competition?

The first time Lily and I realized we had to mind our teachers was not too long after Michael was born. Ma used to beat us with the end of a feather duster when we did something naughty. She only hit the fleshy bits, so I went to school with long sleeves covering the blue-and-green streaks.

Lily was the one who got us a visit from social services. Her marks were darker; she bruised easily and was generally less careful than I was about hiding them. She was in Year Three and I was in Year Six, so they called us both in to speak to the guidance counselor.

"I hit her," I had blurted when Ms. Lawn asked Lily to pull up the bulb sleeve of her school blouse. "It was an accident. We were just messing around."

"Anna, Lily has already told me what happened. With your *mother*," she added when she saw I was about to object. "Now, is this kind of thing common?"

"What? No! Of course not; it's the first time."

I watched Lily's eyebrows shoot up to the same heights as Ms. Lawn's. Mirrored expressions of incredulous disbelief.

"Anna." Lily had the disapproving tone of an adult. "That's not true. Mom uses the feather duster all the time."

I had clenched my fists in my chair. Now I really wanted to clobber her. I hoped they wouldn't believe her—I mean, who owned a *feather duster* these days? But there had been no such luck. Ma had been called into the school, baby Michael strapped to her in an old-fashioned Chinese-style wrap. The meeting was with her, Ms. Lawn, and the principal, and because there was no official school translator, they made me sit in as well. My face was red-hot as they made me go back and forth between English and Cantonese. Poor Ma. Her own daughter saying the shameful words of accusation.

Child abuse. Social services. Family violence. "But I don't know the words for that," I said.

"Just try your best." Principal Harris had a tall, thin nose that made her sound perpetually irritated.

"The school is upset because you hit us. They saw the bruise on Lily's arm," I said in Cantonese, after a beat.

"What? That girl said she was doing her homework, but I saw

her in the room on the computer. Of course I hit her! She lied to me. Tell them." Ma had been extra animated, bouncing the sleeping baby strapped to her front.

"What did she say?" Ms. Lawn asked.

I took a deep breath. "She said it's common practice in Chinese culture to discipline children this way." I kept my voice steady, trying to add a sense of authority, the way a teacher might sound.

"Your mother has to know this is unacceptable behavior here in Australia. We don't hit children, and we certainly don't hit them with whips or anything of that sort."

"It was a feather duster," I had muttered before turning back to Ma. "You can't do that in Australia. They say it's illegal and they could make Lily, Michael, and me live somewhere else. They can take us away."

Ma's eyes had widened in a mixture of anger and fear. "Wah! Are you kidding me? My own children and I can't hit them? No wonder their children all do drugs and become pregnant. Children need to be taught."

"Well?" The chair had squeaked in protest as Principal Harris leaned forward onto her clasped hands.

"She says she didn't know it was against the law. She promises she won't do it again," I said quickly.

The eyebrows had gone up again. She hadn't said a word but looked over at my mother, who held her fierce and steady gaze. Ma's small frame had been rigid, her jaw tight. I could almost hear a growl coming from deep inside her throat.

Finally, Principal Harris had relented. "This is a warning, and it's important that she know the rules are different here. She's in Australia. She has to follow our system or there will be consequences. Tell her. Make sure she knows."

"What did she say?" Ma had demanded.

"She said—she said we can go home," I had replied. My weary body had crumpled against the chair. Principal Harris had been busy shuffling papers on her desk, having already handed down her final judgment and decision.

Ms. Lawn had jumped in. "Anna, I want to see you and Lily in my office once a week for the rest of the school year. Is that clear?"

I had nodded. At least if Lily and I were kept together, I could be sure she wouldn't stray too far off script.

Ma had stood uncertainly, her expression wary. Baby Michael had started to cry, but she didn't look away from the principal until I nudged her toward the door.

"I don't like the look she gave me. This woman has malice in her heart and they put her in charge of kids?"

We never said anything else about the meeting ever again. But after that day, Ma retired the feather duster and only occasionally opted for a soft indoor slipper for discipline instead. Meanwhile, Lily and I were careful about what we said to our teachers and school officials.

Michael's so innocent and young, I think now, stroking his hair as I watch him fly through the game levels, snatching up pixelated coins like a greedy old Scrooge. He's still my baby brother. *Though maybe not so baby anymore.*

"Why didn't you tell us you won the art contest?" I ask. "I'm so proud of you!"

He shrugs again, not lifting his eyes from the screen. "It doesn't matter, does it? Ma still won't come."

His words splinter my insides. "Don't say that. Ma . . . Ma is very proud of you. She's just tired is all." Finally, he looks up. His eyes are dewy. I swear some days he's a living anime character. "Ma's not really tired all the time, is she?"

"What do you mean?" I grimace. "She's just feeling a little under the weather."

He shakes his head. "Albert's mom doesn't stay in bed all the time. None of my friends do." He looks at me with those luminescent, heart-wrenching eyes. "Is something wrong with Ma?"

I sigh heavily. There's no point pretending, but I want to hold on to his innocence a bit longer. "I think sometimes, it's just a bit . . . too much for her."

He crinkles his nose. "What is?"

I shrug. "All of it, I think. Everything."

His eyes widen. "Are *we* too much for her?"

"No, honey, you're perfect," I say automatically, but he doesn't look convinced. I pull him close and lean my chin on his smooth, shiny hair. "It's just for a little while, you'll see. She always comes back."

"I miss her."

"Me too." I'm not sure how much truth is in that reply.

Chapter Four
Sei3

LILY IS STUDYING IN OUR room when Michael and I arrive home. I say *our* room, in that we both sleep in it, but really, she claims it as hers. I've let her have most of the say in what we do with the space—she spends so much time in it, so I figure she deserves it. It's the big sister thing to do, give way to my mui6 mui6.

So Lily's the one with the posters over three-quarters of the walls, K-pop bands that I know nothing about. I've hung up a couple of old movie posters I pilfered when Blockbuster finally shut down. Lily has the giant corkboard with study notes, schedules, and retro Polaroid selfies of her and her friends; I have a single picture of our family by my bed. It was taken outside the Jade Palace in Gosford a few years back and we're all smiling, Ma, me, and Lily and two-year-old Michael. Even Baba is showing his teeth.

It's the happiest I can remember us being. *Almost normal.*

Ma's door is still shut. I grit my teeth and gear myself for the task of rounding up dinner.

I set Michael up at the dining table to do his homework and peer into the fridge. There's nothing except bread and milk and jars of sauce. No greens, no meat. I sigh heavily. I'll need to go to the store.

I put the rice cooker on so at least that's going and grab my keys and bag, then pull on a thin sweater that belongs to Baba. "I'm going to the shops. Be good," I tell my brother.

"Get some toilet paper!" Lily calls from our room.

I swear that girl has supersonic hearing.

I pause by Ma's door, my heart ticking faster. After a moment's hesitation, I push open the door and peek inside.

She's a lump of blanket and darkness.

"I'm going to the shops. Do you want anything?" I ask softly, hopefully.

No reply. I pull the door shut and pull my headphones on.

Ashfield is a bustling suburb that Baba says is a lot like the New Territories in Hong Kong where he and Ma grew up. I haven't been to Hong Kong, even though we still have family there, but all the images I've seen of the picture-perfect harbor city look nothing like the streets of Ashfield. I can't imagine the characters from *Crazy Rich Asians* using two-dollar sunshields meant for cars in their flat windows to block out the afternoon sun.

Liverpool Road is pretty quiet. Most people are already at home, tucking into their weekday dinners. The setting sun lines up perfectly between two buildings, which I take as a good sign. I don't bother with Ashfield Mall, but go to one of the corner shops, their veggies piled in boxes out front.

The girl behind the cash register doesn't look up from her phone as I grab a shopping basket and peer over the choy sum. Baba taught me how to pick produce, eyeing the freshness of the leaves, the wholeness at the ends of the stalks. Split ends mean the plant has been cut too long ago and is drying out. I pick an okay-ish-looking bunch of greens and look for a protein.

There's not much meat in the fridge, and what's left is covered in freezer burn. I go to the freezer and pull out a bag of frozen dumplings. *Michael will want noodles*, I think, but I've already put the rice on. I stand in the middle of the dried goods aisle, wondering what I can do with rice—maybe add some Chinese sausage and shiitake mushrooms to make a lunch or something.

A peal of feminine laughter from the front of the shop makes me look up. There's a gang of girls gathered there, and I recognize them from school. They're out of their uniforms already, dressed in jeans and short skirts. I duck into an aisle of sauces to keep myself hidden from view, my heartbeat sounding in my head as I silently pray to whatever gods there are that the girls won't see me.

If you listen to the teachers, they use words like *diversity* or *intersectional* when talking about the school, but the reality is that the students are all pretty cliquey and grouped up based on our heritage. The Asian kids hang with the Asian kids, and the Lebanese kids all band together. When we were young, the boys and girls stayed pretty separate, but by Year Ten, hormones meant the sexes gravitated together like galaxies circling each other. I'm not really in any of those groups. My used-to-be best friend Emily moved to Melbourne in Year Nine, and we sort of lost touch after a while.

I didn't make enough of an effort to find someone else, and what with everything at home, I don't really have that much time to do normal stuff with people anyway.

"Dude, I'm starving! Can we get bubble tea or something?" I recognize the girl named Wei. She's in one of the popular Asian groups in Year Eleven, where the girls are all skinny and pretty and the boys act like wannabe gangsters.

"Oh my god, can you stop with the boba? That shit's so bad for you! You're such a cow." I shrink back farther when I hear the voice. Connie Zhong is the leader of this group of girls and thinks she's the prettiest. Without looking, I know her dark eyes will be rimmed in thick winged eyeliner and her highlighted hair pulled back into a tight high ponytail, a classic Asian Baby Girl (ABG). Normally, she wouldn't know me from a block of wood except for the fact that her dad runs an import-export business and supplies our restaurant with all of its sauces and dried goods. Her family invited us to some big show-off banquet at a swish restaurant all the way in Chatswood, like they were rich Chinese moguls. Ma got too anxious with all those people in the room, and we had to leave halfway through the soup course.

Wei scoffs. "You're such a bully. I'm getting a drink at least. Don't leave without me."

She's heading into the store. I panic and look for some way out, eyeing the forty-pound sacks of rice as a potential hiding spot. But it's too late and Wei spots me.

"Hey, Anna." She comes over with a cheery smile. I force a smile and wave. "What are you doing here?"

"Um, shopping. Dinner. Stuff," I rattle off quickly.

Good job with the words, genius.

"That's nice. Hanging out in the hood." She nods, and I'm surprised she's being so friendly. "We live in Burwood, but I like coming out to Ashfield. It feels more authentic, you know what I mean?"

"Wei, who are you talking to?" Connie's voice travels unwanted through the air like passing gas. "Oh my god, is that Anna *Chiu*?"

I want to disintegrate into the sack of rice as Wei gives me an apologetic shrug.

"Hi, Connie," I say through gritted teeth.

"How *are* you, Anna? It's been aaaages," Connie coos even though we just saw each other in class today. Her shimmery-rimmed eyes home in like a hawk's, and she winks at her friends. "Hey, your mom shops at Aldi, right?"

I wasn't expecting that question. "Ah. Yeah, sometimes." I don't know why she would bring Ma up; it's definitely not a subject I talk about. Something inside rubs the wrong way, like sandpaper.

"I thought so." Her grin is fake and saccharine sweet. "My mother said she saw her at one of those Aldi deals a while back. Apparently, your mother was buying out the shop of walnuts." She winks at the other girls and they snicker. "She tried to make my mother buy some, too. She was, like, forcing them into her basket." She mimes this, and the girls laugh more, except for Wei, who won't meet my gaze.

I'm burning hot and want to die. My hands squeeze the basket handles so tight, I can feel the edges pressing against the bones of my fingers. I remember Ma coming home with the walnuts a few months back. "They're good for the kidneys," she had insisted after reading some health article in a Chinese newspaper. She bought twenty two-pound bags; most of them are still sitting on the top shelf in our pantry. And out of all people, Connie Zhong's mother saw Ma's walnut frenzy and told her daughter.

It takes everything in me to not break down in tears. I want to say something, smack the eyeliner off her face. Call her a million things in English and Cantonese. But I just stand there, clutching the basket, willing myself not to cry.

Someone's phone goes off. "Yo, that's the boys."

Connie rounds up her troops. "We gotta get out of here. Wei, let's *go*." She delivers her queenly command as her subjects flurry around her.

Wei flashes me a sheepish look and mouths "see ya" before scuttling off after the group. I hear the loud not-so-whispers of their conversations as they drift out of earshot.

I approach the counter, basket in tow. The palms of my hands have sharp red tracks where my nails have dug in. I pull out the items from my basket one by one. The girl behind the counter doesn't look at me as she rings it all up.

"Eight dollars and seventy-two cents," she says in deliberate, practiced English.

I hand over a tenner and take the flimsy blue bag with dumplings and veg. I manage to hold it together all the way down Liverpool Road. It's only when I turn off the main road that I dare to remove my thick frames and dab at my watery eyes. I bring the inner part of my elbow up to my mouth, and I let out a scream. The softness of my own flesh muffles the sound.

Dinner is dumplings and noodles with Campbell's chicken stock as a base. The rice I put in the fridge; Ma might want it tomorrow. There's no time to do things properly. Otherwise I would have loved to make a broth from scratch, boiling a juicy carcass and skimming off the top layer of oil and fat to keep it clear. Like Baba, I love to cook; the methodical processes of chopping, gutting, boiling, and steaming combined with creativity and craft is like a cool salve to the burning soul.

Even if I only have pre-prepped stock, I take the time to slice spring onions into thin slivers to top off the broth and add a generous dollop of sesame oil and a dash of chili for flavor. These are the secrets Baba has handed down to me from the weekends I used to spend in the restaurant kitchen.

Before we moved to Ashfield, our family lived in Gosford. That's where Baba opened his restaurant, a simple Chinese place where locals could go for stir-fry dishes, fried rice, and noodles. We were the only Chinese family in the neighborhood. There was also a Thai family that ran the Thai restaurant, and strangely people got the two of us confused.

The restaurant did pretty well, but Ma couldn't stand living somewhere where there was no one for her to talk to. Ma and Baba used to live in Hong Kong, which was all Cantonese. Not long after getting married, Baba moved to Australia to help his brother-in-law with his new business in Melbourne, leaving Ma by herself in Hong Kong with baby me. He eventually got a visa and permanent residency, and Ma and I moved to Australia when I was two. But instead of Melbourne, Baba decided he was going to open his own restaurant in one of the smaller towns. So they lived in Nowra for a while, where Lily was born, and then moved to Gosford shortly after.

Ma had always been a bit anxious, but things became a lot worse when we were in Gosford. I remember her crying a lot and talking to me at length about how horrible the neighbors were, how racist all the Australians were, and mostly how lonely she felt. I was still little, maybe six or seven, but Ma talked to me like I was her grown-up friend. She criticized Baba and blamed him for her sadness. I remember feeling really bad for her.

Just before Michael was born, Baba moved us to Ashfield, where there were more Chinese people and a community for Ma to take part in. But he had no luck selling the restaurant even though it was always busy—maybe he didn't really try. Instead, he would make the ninety-minute drive up to Gosford every day and run the place as if we still lived down the road. One time, he almost crashed the car coming home. It was two a.m. After that, Baba set up a cot in the restaurant office, so he wouldn't have to make the trip when it was too late. These days, he sleeps most nights at the restaurant.

And we're left at home with Ma.

I lay out our simple meal in chipped crockery with mismatched resin chopsticks that are too worn to use at the restaurant so have been demoted to home use.

"You forgot the toilet paper," Lily grumbles.

Whoops. "I got distracted." I don't bother trying to explain more as I set out an extra bowl of noodles and dumplings.

"Is Ma coming to dinner?" Michael asks when he sees what I'm doing.

Lily fastens her gaze on mine. We speak without words.

She's not coming, says her eyebrow.

She might, say my eyes.

"You eat," I say out loud to my brother. "Don't let your food get cold."

I debate taking the bowl to her room tonight but decide against it. *She's not sick. She can come to the table.* I sound like a mother— not *my* mother, but *a* mother. The thought makes my mouth go dry, and I try to swallow the uneasiness bubbling in my stomach. Connie's cackling voice springs into mind.

I shake my head, walk to my mother's room, and shove open the door.

"Ma, dinner's ready." My voice is brisk and final.

Like I am the mother.

I know she's awake even though she's facing away from me. She doesn't answer, and she doesn't move.

Get up! Why won't you get up?! I want to yell but it's all caught up inside me, like badly knotted cords. I've lost my voice again and there's no point screaming into my arm.

I shut the door and go back to the kitchen. Lily and Michael are slurping their noodles with gusto.

"She's sleeping," I say, ignoring Lily's confounding eyebrow.

"We'll put some in the fridge for her. There might be some for Baba, too."

"Eat, Anna, or it'll get all cold." Michael speaks with his mouth full of noodle. I smile, grateful for the little things like warm, nourishing soup and pork dumplings. And silly little brothers.

Chapter Five

Ng5

THE THIN STRIP OF LIGHT from under the door wakes me. My phone tells me it's two in the morning.

Lily's snoring is breathy and rhythmic in the bed above mine. I fumble for my glasses and pull on a hoodie before padding out of our room.

"Baba, you're home." My father is standing by the sink, holding a small tumbler of beer. I very rarely see him drink, but these days I rarely see him at all, drinking or not.

He smiles sheepishly when he spots me. "Wah! Did I wake you? Go back to bed." He takes another swig from the glass.

I shake my head. "It's okay, I was up anyway." This is a lie, but it's the right thing to say. Baba and I do that a lot. He's not much of a talker, and what he does say is rather stilted and formal. Instead, the emotions he can't express are buried under layers of meaning.

"Did you eat?" His standard greeting for, *How are you doing?*

I shrug. "Yeah. We had dinner." My reply for, *I'm okay.*

We're silent for a while, and he takes another swig of beer. I'm almost tempted to ask for some. Maybe if I'd been a son, he would offer it to me, pour me a glass. But I'm not sure what it says in the Chinese handbook for fathers and daughters drinking together. "How's your ma?" This is a direct question. He always refers to his wife as "our mother."

I shrug again and jam my hands into the pocket of my hoodie. "Same." It's been six weeks that she's been in bed this time.

Baba sighs. "Your mother needs a hobby. A job. Then she won't think so much inside her head. Staying busy is the key."

I press my lips together. Baba's forever trying to get Ma out of the house.

"She didn't really like working before," I remind him. She used to work a little bit at a shop down on Liverpool Road. She kept a diary of all the customers who came in and out of the shop, trying to remember their names. Then she came home and cried when she got them wrong. She said they glared at her and made her feel bad. In the end, she quit after just four weeks, saying her boss put too much pressure on her when she counted out the wrong change.

"Mmm." He considers this. "Idle minds lead to idle thoughts."

I don't know how to reply, so I change the subject. "How's the restaurant?" I ask. It's so nice to see him at home, especially during the week.

He sighs heavily. "Big Wong left. After everything I did to sponsor him here. Bastard. Diu2 keoi1 gaa1." I blush at Baba's coarse Cantonese. Big Wong is a distant cousin and initially came to Australia to learn English and work. Baba took him under his wing, gave him a job at the restaurant, and eventually sponsored him to stay. That was more than seven years ago.

"He got a job at the Chinese restaurant at the local veterans club. What's the point?" Baba laments. "It's not even real Chinese, just sweet and sour pork, short and long soup. Laksa from a jar. Aiyo."

I don't point out that Baba's cuisine is also more "Ocker Chinese" than it is authentic flavors. I want to be the supportive daughter.

"What are you going to do?"

Baba shakes his head. "I have to make Lim head chef, but that boy can't toss a wok if his life depended on it. Ah-Jeff is still there, thank goodness, and Old Yuan said he'll come out of retirement for a bit, but what I really need is someone on the grill."

Suddenly, I have an idea. "Baba, I can help you."

He scoffs. "Don't be ridiculous. What do you know about working in a kitchen?"

I'm hurt. "I used to help you all the time." When we were still living up the coast, Lily and I had spent most of our time after school at the restaurant. We mostly did prep work and took orders, but Ah-Jeff had shown me how to work the grill.

"You have schoolwork. Your mother would be angry."

"Please, Baba, I want to help. Maybe on the weekends?" With Ma in bed, I can't bear to be stuck in the house. "Miss Kennedy at my school said I need more extracurriculars, like an after-school job. To prepare me for the HSC."

He doesn't answer, and we sit in uncomfortable silence for a long while. I can just make out the ticking of our IKEA clock, like my heartbeat loud in my own head. Eventually, my hopes deflate, and I know he's not going to budge on the restaurant front.

But then he surprises me. "I'll think about it."

We smile at each other, and Baba finishes his beer. "It's a little cool; be sure to put on a sweater. You don't want to catch a cold."

I'm already wearing a hoodie, so I know that it's part of his secret code, to tell me, *I care.*

I hang my head. "Okay. I'll take care of myself, I promise." That's how I'm supposed to tell him I love him back.

Chapter Six
Luke

April

IT'S THE FINAL PERIOD of the last day of Term 1, and I have English. Every single person has their eyes fastened on the clock, waiting for the seconds to tick past until we're finally on break.

"My family's going to the Gold Coast. It's going to be so boring, but at least the hotel has Wi-Fi," I overhear Connie boasting to the girls. She's perched on her desk with her back to me, while I try to disappear in the last row.

The past few weeks have been exhausting. Ma has stayed in bed for almost two months now. If she gets up to shower or eat, it's only when the three of us are at school. On weekends we don't see her at all. Lily has been staying at her friend's house most days, saying she needs to study. Ma has never allowed sleepovers, because she doesn't trust the parents. But with her in bed, who's around to stop Lily doing whatever she wants?

I wish Lily and I were closer. We used to be stuck together like glue when we were growing up. In Gosford, people used to mistake us for twins with our home-cut bobs and thick bangs, and likely because the locals had problems telling two Chinese girls apart.

When we moved to Ashfield, we grew apart. With the city at our doorstep, Lily was always trying to push the boundaries of what she could and couldn't do. It started with little things, like eating snacks we weren't allowed. By Year Six, she was putting on jewelry and makeup in school. She hid boxes of tampons in her drawers; Ma was adamant young ladies should only use pads.

Last year, not too long after she started at Montgomery and made new friends, Lily came home one afternoon with pierced ears. Ma had been in bed for a few days at this point.

"What the hell, Lily?" I pinched her inflamed lobes. The rhinestones she chose were sparkly and tiny, a blush pink. "Ma is going to flip when she sees this."

"Leave me alone." She jerked away. "You're not my mother. And she won't even care."

When Ma finally got up, two weeks later, she didn't say a word. The pink rhinestones became dangling tassels and gold hoops. Ma didn't discuss it, not once. Then one night, without warning, she came into our room and yanked open all our drawers. She strewed everything about, socks and bras and undies, until she found the pencil box Lily used to store her illicit jewelry. She upturned it on the floor, stomping and crunching the contents under her feet. The cheap rhinestones and tassels came apart and the thin wire hoops got tangled in the soft soles of Ma's indoor slippers.

Lily and I cried quietly, but we didn't try to stop her. Ma left after a while, and I helped my sister pick up the pieces, putting everything in the bin. Her earring holes eventually closed up, but I know Lily still keeps an assortment of clip-ons alongside her tampon stash. To this day, my ears remain unmarked and bare. I still skip swimming when I have my period. And I stopped babysitting for the checkout lady at Woolworths even after she begged me to reconsider. Lily doesn't agree with me, but it's just not worth it to incite Ma's wrath.

"How about you, Miss Chiu?" I snap back to Standard English and try to focus on Mr. Murray's question. "Who is the speaker in question?"

"Um, Mac-Macduff?" I reach for the most recent literary name I can remember.

"A good guess, Miss Chiu, but we're well past Shakespeare now." He waves the small volume in front of my eyes so I can glimpse the title. *Leaves of Grass.*

The class snickers and it takes every bit of my will not to hide my face behind my hands.

"The character in question, of course, is the speaker himself— Walt Whitman, the focus of the work 'Song of Myself.'"

The class drags on. If Mr. Murray is aware of how antsy everyone is to get out early, he doesn't show it. I think that's a special skill teachers develop, torturing their classes to the very bitter end. Or maybe there's some contractual obligation, like forty-six minutes and fifty-seven seconds of rambling or the school docks their pay.

Forty-six minutes and fifty-eight seconds.

"Now, class, I know you're all excited for the break," Mr. Murray says, and the class emits a single groan. "But before we formally take off, I'm handing back your Term One assignments." More groaning, and I swear Mr. Murray lets out a not-so-subtle chuckle as he traverses up and down the rows, handing back papers.

I'm packing away my stuff so I won't miss the bus. A stack of pages lands on my desk with a heavy thwack, and Mr. Murray hovers over me, tapping on the top sheet before moving to the next desk.

The red mark at the top of the page takes up way more space than it needs to. It's meant to highlight a single line, but instead it lopes across the top paragraph like an elephant onto a stage. Next to it, three angry question marks scream up at me, and then a single word, written in all caps.

???THESIS

Mr. Murray is well-known for his flair for the dramatic, but I think three question marks is overdoing it. Plus, in the top-right corner, where my grade is supposed to be, he's written a demure little *SEE ME*, just a pinkie's-width high. As though he can't bear to write the letters.

I shake my head as the bell rings. Everyone is out the door and I'm late to pick up Michael, but suddenly I can't make myself get out of my chair. The legs of the desk-metal-chair-monstrosity scrape against the floor as I clumsily extract myself. I grab my messenger bag and head toward the front of the room. Mr. Murray has his head down, his fingers tapping on the touchpad to shut down the computer for the next couple of weeks.

"Mr. Murray?" My voice is shaking like an out-of-tune wind chime. I clear my throat. "You wanted to see me?"

He peers up over his rimless glasses, surprise on his face. "Oh, Anna, you're still here. I thought you'd be out of here, ready for the break." He glances at the paper with its red scrawl across the top. "Ah, your essay. Yes, let's talk about that."

My fingers tremble as I set the paper on the desk. Mr. Murray takes off his specs and taps the big red loops with the earpiece. "I'm disappointed, Anna."

"I'm . . . sorry," I say without thinking, which makes me go redder still. Lily says I'm forever apologizing for things that are not my fault. Which just makes me apologize for apologizing.

"'In *Macbeth*, we learn of the physical, and especially of the psychological toll, that occurs in the pursuit of power for its own sake,'" he reads aloud. I cringe. I had three goes at the wording and had arrived at what I thought was a satisfactory result. But hearing them now is like listening to iron bells crashing. And Miss Kennedy said I needed to *challenge* myself; Standard English is clearly kicking my butt.

"Anna," Mr. Murray goes on, "I don't need to remind you how important a skill structuring the essay is. Your overall arguments and summaries are fine—not remarkable or particularly astute, by any means, but fine." My face grows hotter. "However, you're going to need to understand how to craft a thesis and lay out your points. Do you understand?"

"Yes, sir." I can't tear my eyes away from the big red marks on the paper. They are getting larger by the second, like the blood Lady Macbeth was scrubbing. *Is that a thesis? An astute observation?*

He's writing on the paper again, this time in blue pen along the margins, crisscrossing the page. It's like the work of a bad cartographer, my horrible essay and his scrawling.

"I know you have potential, Anna. This is why I'm going to suggest you redo the assessment. You can hand it in after the break."

My jaw drops. This is unbelievable; no teacher has ever reassigned papers. But I can tell Mr. Murray is serious.

"I've marked up the areas that you can start from. Your analysis of Lady Macbeth's madness, for example, and your interesting observation of the brain's ability to manifest olfactory experience into memory—that's powerful stuff."

I can feel my ears burning now, but I just swallow and nod. I don't tell him how back in Gosford, I once found Ma laying our Chinese New Year's Eve dinner out on the table, spooning rice right onto the varnished wood. She then spent a good half hour sniffing the contents. She wouldn't let us near it, and at one point she raised a finger at Lily and asked her to surrender the poison. Baba came home and coaxed Ma into her room. I ordered pizza and we welcomed in the Year of the Dragon with pepperoni, ham, and pineapple.

Mr. Murray tilts his head, gray tufts of hair flopping over like a puppy's ears. "Have you considered acquiring a private tutor, Anna?"

I shake my head no.

"I suggest you do. I think you'll find it helpful." He hands me back my paper with a flourish. "You can do it, Anna. I know you can," he says with a wink. "And enjoy the break."

I mumble some half-hearted thanks. It's not until I'm slamming my locker, trying to swallow my frustration, that I wonder if that last comment from him was sarcastic.

Chapter Seven

Cat1

ON THE FIRST DAY OF BREAK, I wake up early and go to check on Ma. With all of us home, I hope she might be feeling more like getting up. I set her teacup down on the bedside table. The shadows are thin and drawn out, like overstretched bubble gum.

"Ma?"

Not a word. A chilling shroud settles over me as I shut the door. *Is this what my break is going to be like?*

But I find a surprise in the kitchen that makes me instantly feel a million times better. "Baba, you're home."

He looks up briefly from the paper to give me a small smile.

"Ma's still in bed," I say as I put the kettle back on to make more tea. We exchange a look, and he seems resolved about it. Like this is all normal.

"Don't mind your mother." I wait for more wisdom or advice, but that's all he has to offer. He returns to scanning the headlines of today's Chinese newspaper while he's brewing his tea.

"What a pity," he mumbles at the paper. "These people think they can run the country. They're barely out of diapers!"

I glance at the broadsheet he has spread over the counter. I don't recognize the young Chinese people in the picture, but the smaller inset has a bird's-eye view of a sea of yellow umbrellas on a crowded street. I know they are from the Occupy Central protests in Hong Kong that happened a little while back. Local youths took over the streets to protest the increasing Beijing influence over Hong Kong affairs. Hong Kong was "returned" to China from British rule back in 1997, and the locals have historically enjoyed freedoms and liberties that are atypical for the rest of China, which has been under long-term Communist rule. To help ease the transition back to China, the Beijing government had promised a fifty-year period of more autonomous rule. "One China, Two Systems" was the party line pitched to the locals. But the Occupy Central protest had been led by young people who wanted to challenge the Communist Party's increasing authority that took away the autonomy they had been promised. The youths in the picture look knowledgeable and professional. The boy has his mouth open mid-sentence, and the look on his face is passionate and defiant. The girl stands fiercely beside him, her thin fingers clutching a thick compendium, her lips pursed and ready to speak. She reminds me of Lily. I always thought my sister would make a great politician, even if there aren't very many Chinese MPs in Australia.

I know Baba likes to stay up-to-date with the news from Hong Kong, and I do my best to keep up out of some obligation to my roots. I often wonder if he misses it, if he wonders what life would have been like if he had never left.

We never talk about either, of course.

He folds the paper up, and I sip my tea. "How's the restaurant? Did you find a head chef yet?"

Baba sighs. "No. Lim's improving, but he still has a while to go. We have a big party tonight, too. I hope he can keep up."

I'm sparked to try my luck again. "Baba, why don't I come help you?"

Baba shakes his head. "We've been through this, Anna. You have to focus on school."

"We're on *break*, Baba. I'm completely free." *Teeny* white lie because of Mr. Murray's essay that I haven't done yet. But I don't think that really counts.

Baba considers this for a bit. I plead with my eyes, because the last thing I want is to be stuck at home the entire two weeks. It's not a holiday on the Gold Coast, but at least it's something.

Finally, Baba nods. "Okay. Go get your things. I'll meet you in the car."

I rush to my room, thrilled to have a reason to leave the house. Lily is still sleeping, and Ma is in her room. I find Michael playing with LEGOs in his room.

"Anna, come play with me! Look, I made an airship." He shows me an impressive-looking winged contraption.

"Wow, that looks great, Michael! But I have to go. Be good for Lily today, okay?"

He pouts. "You're leaving me. Why?"

"I'm going to help Baba at the restaurant," I tell him. "He has a big party today and needs the extra hands."

"I want to come, too!" He sticks out his lower lip farther.

"You can't come. It's dangerous and you could get hurt." This is a lie, I know. I used to hang out at the restaurant all the time when I was Michael's age. But now the restaurant feels sacred. A special place for me and Baba where I can feel almost normal.

"I'll bring you back some spring rolls. You like those, don't you?" He nods, but I can tell he's disappointed by this consolation prize.

Lily has finally woken up, rubbing the sleep from her eyes as she peers at me blearily from the doorway. "Where are you going?"

"Jade Palace. Look after Michael today, okay?" I don't give her a chance to protest or object.

I hesitate by Ma's door. I should go in again, check that she's okay. I reach for the knob, but at the last second, I let my hand fall away and head outside.

Baba has already started the car and is waiting for me. I climb into the front seat and fling my bag on the floor.

"Did your ma say anything?"

I wince. "She's fine." We both know this is a lie and we both know it's as good as it'll be. My heart is dancing with excitement. I thought I'd spend the entire break trapped in that gloomy apartment and Ma's wrapped-up-blanket sadness. An early morning kookaburra chortles from a branch above.

KOUHAHAHAHAH.

I take it as a good sign.

*　　*　　*

The streets are nearly empty at this time on a Saturday morning, barring a few taxis heading toward the airport. We drive in silence until we hit the freeway, then Baba switches on talk radio.

The host is fired up about a new immigration policy that's been proposed by the Senate. He talks about boat people taking advantage of the system and immigrant business owners abusing the working visa system.

"These migrants come with the sole purpose of getting permanent residency. They get married to a resident, like a business transaction, so they can then get all the benefits and their resident status," the host says. "Then they start businesses right next to each other—you have two brothers both running a restaurant on the same street, for crying out loud. And why do they do it? For the sole purpose of bringing their own extended family over to work and marry. It's a bloody cheat, I tell ya."

I fume silently at the comment. It all sounds racist to me, even though a small voice in the back of my head knows that what the broadcaster says is at least partly true. The problem is, people use these types of arguments to justify their racist behavior against Chinese people and foreigners when they treat us all like criminals because of something they heard on morning talk radio.

Baba's face is stony. I don't know what he's thinking, so I change the station to some boring market report. Baba smiles and nods, so I leave it.

Here, they're talking housing and real estate and something about Sydney's property market. It seems like the only thing adults ever talk about these days. Baba is nodding and murmuring along, repeating words like *economic downturn* and *variable interest rates*.

I've been waiting to talk to him for a while, but now that he's in the car with me, my questions and thoughts are all clunky and muddled.

Baba doesn't look in my direction when he asks, "How's school?"

I shrug. "It's okay." I don't tell him about the report Mr. Murray handed back. Baba cares about Lily's grades because of the scholarship and Michael's because he's so much younger. But me he seems to trust—or maybe he's given up.

He nods, accepting my noncommittal reply. He keeps repeating the host as I mull over the words I want to say next. "Equity management and diversified assets."

"Baba, I think Ma's getting worse," I blurt out finally. "She hasn't gotten out of bed, and it's been more than eight weeks this time."

"Mmm." It's not a reply, but at least he's stopped parroting the radio. He doesn't say anything for a while. "Your mother has moods," he says eventually. "It's difficult, you know. Having two teenage daughters and a young son. You have to be kind to her. Not make her upset."

I'm heavy with guilt. "But we didn't *do* anything."

"Personal equity." He's back to the radio again. "Your mother gets lonely sometimes. You girls should spend more time with her."

I have nothing to say to this. We try, but what can we do when she locks herself in her room?

"Your mother thinks too much. She needs a hobby to take her mind off things. Then she will be better. She just has to keep busy. Maybe a job will do her good," he suggests again.

Baba says this a lot. That Ma is bored and has too much time to think. That's why he's always at the restaurant, he says—so that he can stay busy. That's all he thinks is wrong with Ma, that if she was busy enough, she wouldn't have time to be sad and afraid.

I've tried so many times to talk to him about her feelings, how I can tell she's nervous or upset or feels so bad about herself. But Baba doesn't want to hear it. There's a saying in Cantonese about impossible tasks: laai4 ngau4 soeng5 syu6. *Dragging a cow up a tree.* Neither party wants to be in that situation. That's how I feel when I try to talk to Baba.

As if reading my thoughts, Baba reaches over and pats me awkwardly on the shoulder. "I know. You're a good sister, Anna. You have to look after your brother and sister, too. It's a lot of responsibility. You're daai6 gaa1 ze2." *Big older sister.*

I sigh heavily. What can I say? I have to be responsible and look after my brother and sister. I'm the eldest.

I cross my arms and glare out the window, conversation over.

Baba's team used to be Big Chef Wong, Sous Chef Lim, and Ah-Jeff, an all-rounder and kitchen helper. There's also Minh, a quiet Vietnamese boy on dish duty, and Old Yuan, who comes on the weekends. That's the kitchen staff, or at least it was before Big Wong left. Out front, Baba has Miss Chen as hostess alongside two Caucasian waitresses Baba hired from the local area.

I used to think it was strange that Baba still kept the restaurant after we moved. There's no shortage of Chinese restaurants just down the road from where we live, so why didn't he open one close by? I've come to realize, though, that Jade Palace isn't just a restaurant to Baba, it's his second home, maybe even his first, and I can't begrudge him that little bit of comfort.

Ma hates the restaurant. She's barely set foot in it since we left Gosford, but she carries around its presence like a cancer. On her bad days, the really bad ones, she hurls accusations at Baba, and the restaurant is usually front and center. "You love that restaurant more than us. You think you're a good businessman? How can you own a restaurant and we still live so poorly?"

Her bursts of rage just make Baba work harder. To be honest, I really miss my time in the restaurant.

I love the organized chaos of the kitchen and how everyone has their established roles and that they all work really hard. There's plenty of swearing and lewd comments thrown around, which is probably another reason why Ma doesn't approve. My everyday Cantonese might be crap, but thanks to Big Wong, Lim, and Ah-Jeff, I know more Canto expressions for breasts and penises than a sixteen-year-old girl from Sydney would ever need.

Baba parks out front. The outer restaurant décor is over the top, a bright green pagoda supported by thick red columns and JADE

PALACE in that tacky brushstroke font. The sign still says CLOSED in the glass above the door, with our opening times stenciled in peeling gold.

MONDAY TO SUNDAY: 11 a.m.–10 p.m.

As Baba unlocks the door, I spot the new addition to the storefront. "What's that?" I point to the piece of paper scrawled with black marker. *HELP WANTED. Weekend only. Local. Must own car. Good English. No Chinese is okay.*

"We need delivery," he says. "Ah-Jeff has to be in the kitchen more now."

"But, Baba, you won't recruit people that way. Why don't you join Uber Eats or something?" I try to explain the food app, but Baba just stares at me blankly.

"No, no app. App is tax. This way, I pay *cash*."

I sigh. There's no arguing, because in Baba's world, cash is king. I try not to think about what kind of dodgy math is involved with those declarations.

Miss Chen is folding oversized red napkins into bright fans for the place settings. "Good morning, lou5 baan2," she greets him in Cantonese. *Boss.* "Wah, Anna, it's been so long! What luxury. Wait, don't tell me your father is taking the day off?!"

"No. I'm here to help. I'm on break from school," I explain.

"Trial. You're here on trial. We'll see," Baba warns.

"Wah. How wonderful to see her!" Her clapping is too enthusiastic. "And she's so pretty, too, must take after your wife!"

She addresses me in accented English. "Hey, girl, you have boyfriend yet?"

Sucking up to the boss is a common part of the Chinese restaurant code, and I know it extends to the boss's family. But I still squirm with embarrassment, especially when Baba replies.

"No boys," he says gruffly. "She's too young." I want to throw one of those giant cloth napkins over my head.

"Of course. Good idea. Study hard. Go to good university and you meet rich husband." She waves a napkin fan in the air enthusiastically, her heavy glasses sliding down her nose.

I smile and nod awkwardly. I have never figured out how to speak to older Chinese adults, especially when they all think they have the right to proxy-parent you. Miss Chen is a bit younger than Baba and Ma, but she's never been married. "Leftover woman," Ma always says.

Baba goes to his office to make calls to suppliers and leaves me to find my way to the kitchen to help with prep. I find Ah-Jeff standing at the workbench holding two bottles, about to empty the contents of one into another.

"Wait! Ah-Jeff, be careful," I call out. "That's chili oil, not vinegar."

"What?" He holds the label up to his nose and squints. Ah-Jeff is shortsighted, despite his thick glasses. "Zan1 hai6 wo3!" *That's really true.*

"Here." I pick up the black vinegar bottle. "I can do it." He scoots down the bench to give me room. Out of all of Baba's staff, Ah-Jeff is my favorite. He's super kind and much older, about retirement age. He doesn't have kids at home, so every year he gives me, Lily, and Michael New Year's money. And his English is near perfect.

Without a question, Ah-Jeff is Baba's most loyal employee. Ten years ago, he moved his young family to Australia and had started working at a Chinese building company in Tuggerah. But after suffering a shoulder injury on the job, he was dismissed. He wasn't a citizen at the time and couldn't make claims for workers' comp or insurance, so his wife went to work instead. And then six months later, she left him and took their young daughter with her. She married the dentist who she had been a receptionist for.

Poor Ah-Jeff was miserable and alone when Baba took him on as a kitchenhand. He was limited in what he could do around the kitchen—the heavy wok work was out of the question. But he worked incredibly hard and was a fantastic charmer. Baba used to have him at front of house to greet customers the way Miss Chen does, but he was too nice and kept giving extra things for free. Now he helps with odds and ends in the kitchen and delivery. He eventually remarried but didn't have more kids. A couple of years ago, when he celebrated his sixtyish birthday, I asked him if he would ever retire and he said, "Never. Jade Palace is my life."

"Ginping, what are you doing back in your father's kitchen?" he asks me now.

I grimace. "Ah-Jeff, no one calls me that except po4 po4-2 on Skype." *Grandmother.*

He looks surprised. "But it's such an important part of who you are. Did your mother and father tell you what it means?"

I make a face. "Feminine algae or something." I'd looked it up in the past, using my bad knowledge of Chinese radicals, and I figured out *water* and *plant*. For a while, I thought I was a water lily, until some freshie Chinese expat in Year Eight told me otherwise. I didn't much care for the name after that.

"It's a beautiful waterweed, delicate and strong. Just like you." I make another face and Ah-Jeff laughs. That's another thing I like about him—he's always in good spirits. I often wonder what he's like outside the restaurant. But Baba has strict rules about us socializing with the staff, so I've never met anyone's families.

"Okay, Anna, what are you doing back in your father's kitchen? I thought you wanted to go to uni and become the first Chinese-Australian in space."

"Wow, that was when I was nine." I can't believe he remembers that. "Besides, they don't have those kinds of astronauts anymore. The Americans stopped the program."

"Doesn't mean you can't do it." He pushes his glasses to the top of his head. "Study hard, you can do anything. You do all right in school?"

I shrug. "School's okay. But I'm not a genius like my sister is."

He waves this aside. "Doesn't matter. It's not about the brains, it's about the mind." He points to his head to demonstrate. "Look at me. Dumb as a knob of wood, but my mind is strong and I'm stubborn as an ox to push through anything. You remember that for your school, okay?"

I nod. Unlike Miss Chen, I don't mind his style of proxy-parenting. It actually makes sense.

"You study what? Math? Computer?"

"I have a big assignment in English coming up." My insides lurch just thinking about it.

"English? But your English is perfect," Ah-Jeff exclaims. "You're a regular Aussie girl." The way he says *Aussie* sounds like *o1 si2*, which means *to take a dump* in Cantonese. I used to correct him, but now it's kind of an inside joke between us.

"They don't think of it that way, Ah-Jeff. It's more than speaking and writing. You have to talk about *meaning* and analyze other people's work."

"Just tell them meaning is no meaning. And other people's work is their own business, not yours. Done. A-plus." He smiles with satisfaction.

I smirk. "I don't think that's how it works."

"My daughter says that a lot. 'That's not how things work in business.' She thinks all I know is restaurant. But she doesn't realize, her old man has seen a thing or two."

Before I can exhort him for a story, Lim storms in from the back entrance. As much as Ah-Jeff is kind and gentle, Lim is all fire and energy. Even with the no-socializing policy, I know Lim spends most of his days off—not to mention evenings—drinking and gambling. He's married, but his wife is older than he is, and they have no children. When Ma used to come to the restaurant, she whispered awful things about Miss Chen and Lim in the storeroom together. I can't judge if they were true or not, but no one besides Ma ever talked about it.

"It's still so hot out there," Lim complains as he flings his coat onto one of the countertops. His eyes bug out when he spots me. "Aiyo! Is that Chiu Ginping?"

"She doesn't like to be called that," Ah-Jeff reprimands. "You know those modern girls—they prefer English." My face is on fire, and I really regret saying anything about my given Chinese name.

"Ohhh." Lim nods knowingly and then turns away from me. "Hey, so Wong called me. He says the restaurant is very busy. They've got the Chinese tour buses stopping by the veterans club every day and can't keep up with demand! They want more chefs and the money is good. What do you think? Worth thinking about, yeah?"

Ah-Jeff doesn't answer. I'm shocked. I can't believe my dad's head chef is planning a mutiny right in front of my face. I should say something. But the words and courage don't come to me.

The other workers are filing in, so the topic is quickly dropped. The staff that recognize me greet me with a nod and kind words. Some ask after my mother and siblings. No one seems to question what I'm doing there. It feels so natural, like home.

Before lunch service, I take my spot at the spring roll and grill station. Unlike a lot of other local Chinese restaurants, we hand-make all of our spring rolls and wontons rather than getting frozen ones from the supplier. That means rolling and stuffing literally hundreds of parcels and rolls every week.

I go to the fridge for heads of cabbage, then grab a giant knife and a mandolin and begin shredding. When I first started in the kitchen, I was terrified of julienning the tips of my fingers, but now

I'm hardly even looking as I pass the quarters of cabbage through the sharp blade.

"You are working fast, Anna." Ah-Jeff watches me.

"Not too fast, or there will be hardly anything left for the rest of us," I hear Lim grumble under his breath.

The venom in his voice is unmistakable.

As we get fully into prep, I watch Lim work out of the corner of my eye. He looks uneasy churning the wok. His grip is weak and his wrist lacks the power that Big Wong or even Baba once had. I question Baba's decision to make him head chef. Surely he could have found someone better?

"Anna, how's the school going? Are you getting good marks?" It's Lim's turn to step in as concerned pseudo parent, and I'm pretty sure it's for my dad's benefit, as he's standing within earshot.

"Of course she's getting good marks," Ah-Jeff chimes in. "Lou5 baan2 always says his daughters are top-notch."

Lim ignores this. "Are you on holiday? Break? No assignments, right?"

"I have an English essay. I have to tell them what Shakespeare wrote," I say.

Baba looks alarmed. "You didn't tell me this, Anna. Are you sure you should be here? You know grades come first," he scolds.

"It's okay, Baba. I brought it with me." He doesn't look convinced.

Lim is still sucking up to Baba. "English is so important. Big Wong, his English isn't so good, so he can only communicate with the wok. Not like me!" I can't believe he's trying to prove he's better than his predecessor, even though he's thinking of leaving.

"Some of us know not to communicate with fools who waste their time."

That's Old Yuan, putting Lim in his place.

Lim huffs a little and turns back to his wok. Old Yuan gives me a wink and returns to dicing veggies. He wields the knife with strong, wide strokes, like a feverish painter. He's so fast, I never even see the blade hit the board and only hear the *tuk-tuk-tuk-tuk* as it falls, faster than my heartbeat. Yuan is a man of few words, but he knows how to make them count.

Diners start to trickle in for lunch, mostly after our eight-dollar specials. Miss Chen lines the orders up on the board. "Two egg drop soup. One spring roll."

As service kicks off, we focus on the tasks at hand. I work deliberately, methodically, barely stopping to mop the sweat from my brow.

"You work hard, Anna," Ah-Jeff says hours later, after service is finished. "You have your father's diligence."

I beam with pride. It's nice to feel like part of the team. To be treated like an actual adult.

My father interrupts my moment. "Anna! I have to go to a meeting. You stay out of trouble," Baba barks. "Do your schoolwork. You can use my office computer."

So much for being an adult.

Chapter Eight
Baat3

"ANNA, WHERE'S YOUR FATHER?" Miss Chen pops
her head into Baba's office. She is holding one of her cloth napkins,
this one in the shape of a swan—a fancier fold for dinner service.

I look around. Baba's desk is littered with papers and account-
ing books. There's no space, so I'm cradling my copy of *Macbeth*
against my knees, making notes in the margins.

"I don't know. I think he went to meet with a supplier?"

She shakes her head. "There's a boy here, for the delivery job.
You should talk to him."

"Me?" I squeak.

She raises an eyebrow. "You're the boss's eldest daughter. Aren't
you going to take over the business someday?"

I shiver a bit at the thought. Baba and I haven't ever discussed
anything like this. I often wonder whether, if I had been a boy,
Baba would have worked harder to train me as an heir apparent,
teaching me the business and taking me along to meetings and

things. Maybe he's waiting for Michael to get older, or maybe he doesn't care and is happy to sell the restaurant off to the highest bidder when he's finally ready to give it up. I never know what Baba thinks or feels, whether he's happy or sad, excited or disappointed. Mostly, I think it's the latter.

"I don't know what to do," I tell her.

"Go talk. What, you never interview a boy before?" Miss Chen scrutinizes me from behind thick metal specs. Her hair is neatly permed, although I can see that the curls hang limply. It's like she's stepped out of a 1930s Shanghai gangster movie. I can't interpret the expression in her heavily done-up eyes, but it's something between nosiness, maternal care, and bemusement.

Our huge dining room is eerily dark and empty; Baba prefers to switch off the lights and fans between services to save energy. I shuffle to the counter.

The boy is off to the side, staring at our aquarium, so I don't see him at first. He's tall and super thin, his white legs poking out like matchsticks from his cargo shorts. I think he's only a bit older than me.

"Um, hi," I call from behind the counter. He doesn't hear me, and I try again. "Hello!"

The boy turns, and I get a look at his face. Pale skin, nose a bit too big. His brown hair flops buoyantly when he moves, some of it falling over his eyes.

"Hi." He looks taken aback for a moment, but then catches himself and strides forward, offering his hand. "I'm Rory." He uses his other hand to push the hair out of his face and jerks his head toward the sign out front. "I'm here for the delivery job. Are you the owner?" His hand is so big, it feels like putting on a boxing glove when I shake it.

"I'm Anna. I'm the owner's daughter." *Ugh, what nepotism.*

If it bothers him, he doesn't show it. "Oh, right." He's nodding and shaking my hand too long. "Nice to meet you, Anna. I'm Rory," he says again.

He's nervous, I conclude, which strangely makes me nervous, too. I rescue my hand from his giant grip, and I must have had a disgusted look on my face, because he suddenly wipes his palm against his pocket. "Sorry."

"Oh, no. Not at all. I mean, don't be. You didn't do anything." *Get a grip, Anna.*

"Uh, interesting fish you have there." He gestures to the tank. "They have bubbles under their eyes."

"Yeah, they're really great, aren't they?" I roll my eyes and the boy smirks. I hate those fish and cried the first time Baba bought some to put in the tank. The wobbly eye sacs under their pupils look like giant zits waiting to be popped. I deliberately overfed them when I was little, and they died pretty quickly, but Baba has kept replacing them with the same kind of fish for eleven-odd years.

"So, uh, do you live nearby?" I'm trying to think of things to ask that would be useful in a job interview. If he's close by, he'll know the best routes, I reason.

"Yep, Gosford born and bred. But I lived in the city for a while. Went to high school there."

"Oh, okay." I'm curious about him moving *back* to Gosford

after living in Sydney, but it's probably none of my business. "You have a car?"

"Of course. She's about ten years old but runs well. Um, I'd like to fix her up a bit, so a job thing would be great." His hair is falling over his eyes again, soft and floating, a bit like cotton candy. And his eyes, I notice, are a sensual hazel, like light golden almonds.

Get a grip, Anna.

"Right." *Car—tick. Local—tick. English-speaking—tick.* Baba will be pleased. "Well, um, you should probably meet my dad, since it's his restaurant and all. Maybe write down your details and he can call you or something?"

Rory looks surprised and relieved. "Sweet." I look for a pen.

"You into Shakespeare?"

I've carried my *Macbeth* edition out for some reason, and it's now sitting on the counter. This time, I *definitely* make a face. "Ugh. Hardly. I have to redo an assignment or fail English."

But Rory's gone somewhere else. He pushes the pads of his fingers together Mr. Burns style and starts to recite in a cackling voice:

> *"Double, double, toil and trouble;*
> *Fire burn and cauldron bubble."*

I think that's the end of it, but he keeps going.

> *"Fillet of a fenny snake,*
> *In the cauldron boil and bake;*
> *Eye of newt and toe of frog,*

Wool of bat and tongue of dog,

Adder's fork and blindworm's sting,

Lizard's leg and howlet's wing,

For a charm and powerful trouble,

Like a hellbroth boil and bubble.

Double, double, toil and trouble;

Fire burn and cauldron bubble.

Cool it with a baboon's blood,

Then the charm is firm and good."

He's really into it, throwing ingredients into an imaginary cauldron, even rhyming that last *good* with *blood*. I'm captivated. I can see the witches now, more sinister than I had first considered.

"Wow." I'm genuinely impressed. "You're really into Shakespeare, huh?"

Rory shrugs, like it's no big deal, but I can tell he's pleased with his performance. "Yeah. I'm a bit of a theater geek."

"You'd love my sister. She's so into drama." Maybe I'll reconsider my mocking her for it.

"That's cool. If you want help or anything, with the *Macbeth*, I can do that."

"Really? That would be great. I mean, you actually made Shakespeare interesting!"

"Thanks." He smiles shyly. "I mean, if I get the job, and you know, after work or something, not on the clock."

The job. "Oh, right. That's what I meant, of course." I feel something deflate inside me. "Um, if you leave your details, I'll get my dad to call you." I push forward a pen and the order pad that Miss Chen uses.

"Cool," he says again as he writes down his info, not meeting my eye. We stand there awkwardly for a beat as I wonder if I'm supposed to shake his hand again. Would that be professional?

Rory saves me the trouble by delivering another line.

"God's benison go with you and with those that would make good of bad and friends of foes."

I can't place this one, not even sure if it's from *Macbeth*, but I don't think it matters. Rory gives me a wink before he turns and exits restaurant left.

Dinner service is busier than lunch was, as there's a booking for a fiftieth wedding anniversary. The kitchen is in a shambles, and we're all desperately trying to keep up with the pace.

"Lim! Chicken cashew, they said the chicken's not cooked!" Miss Chen throws a dish onto the service area.

"Do they have taste buds?" Lim fumes, picking up a piece of the offending meat and shoving it in his mouth. "It's cooked through. Any more and it dries out. What the hell is the matter with these British gwai2 lou5?" *Foreigners.* "They all want to char their food to a crisp."

"Just remake the order, Lim!" Baba shouts over the roar of hot flames leaping toward him, kissing the lip of his churning wok.

I don't have time to stop and think. I'm tossing rolls and wontons into the fryer, batches upon batches of them. The second fryer is a bit temperamental and I've burned a few dozen, along with my fingers, but there's no time to stop and cool them or even feel the pain. I'm a little puddle of perspiration and sensation, but I keep going. Around ten p.m., the last stragglers of the party leave. I can finally go out to the dining area and stand under the AC vent. The cool air is weak, but I'm grateful for the teeny bit of relief.

There's still a lot to clean up and prep work for tomorrow to start. My whole body is aching, and I can barely stay on my feet as I'm stacking dishes with Minh. "Anna," Baba calls, and I gratefully step away. I'm secretly hoping he's ready to go home soon, but I don't want to be seen as complaining or too precious. I have to be part of the team.

Baba is in his office, bent over a pile of papers and receipts. He does the books himself, and the only help he allows is for Miss Chen to count the money at the end of the night. Even then, I've seen him recounting the bills before he puts them in the safe.

He waves me over. "Look at this." He points to the figures and shakes his head. "Last year, we were making double this. But no one goes out to dinner anymore."

I don't really know how to read the figures, but I feel like I should say something positive. "Oh, Baba, it'll be okay. Your food is the best."

Baba sighs. "Meanwhile, we pay the rent and utilities for the place, not to mention staff."

It's Baba's dream to buy a house in Sydney. And not just any house—he doesn't want to live in Ashfield or Hurstville or where any of the new immigrant Chinese families live. "If I wanted to live in a village, I would have stayed in China!" he always says. Instead,

Baba has very specific suburbs marked up on a map of Sydney. Roseville on the North Shore, Kellyville Ridge in the northwest, and Dulwich Hill in the Inner West are some of the places that have made the cut. "Good schools, nice neighborhoods," he comments. I also know they're some of the pricier suburbs, especially lately with all of the foreign investment in Sydney property. I don't point out to him that if he had stayed in the village he might already own that dream house he's after.

So Baba is furiously saving his dollars as we live in the run-down unit in Ashfield, even though Ma is always on his case about how poor we look and how useless he is spending all this time in the restaurant with nothing to show for it. I feel bad for Baba. I don't know how far we are from achieving his dream, but in our household, money has always felt tight.

I want to stay upbeat right now. "You just need a new market. What about the delivery service?" I ask.

Baba shakes his head. "No applicants. That sign has been in the window for weeks."

"There was a boy," I say. "He wanted to apply today. I interviewed him for the job. Rory."

Baba looks surprised. "You interviewed him?"

"I did. He's a local boy, experienced. And he has a car." I have no idea if Rory is experienced or not, but I figure it's not too much of a white lie to claim he is.

My father looks skeptical. "How old is he?"

"Oh, he's a bit older than me. And he's really smart, too. He actually offered to help me with my schoolwork, so you'd get a tutor, too! Two for the price of one—bargain, eh?" For some reason, I'm trying really hard to sell Rory to Baba.

"I don't know." But I can tell he's considering it, so I push harder.

"What about just a trial?" I say. "I can call him now and he can come in tomorrow and we can just see."

Baba arches an eyebrow. "Call him now? It's after ten; it's very late to offer a trial."

"He won't mind. He said call anytime." The lies are coming thick and fast. I wave the slip of paper with Rory's number. "I'll call."

"Mmm." Baba shakes his head. "Let me think about it. It's all hazy fog. I'm so tired and my brain has to finish the books." He smiles weakly and turns back to the paperwork. "I have a lot of work to finish up, so I'm going to stay here tonight. Ah-Jeff can give you a ride back to Hornsby and you can take the train from there."

"Oh." I'm stunned and a little hurt. A part of me thought that if I offered to help, Baba would start coming home every night. But I guess he has other ideas. I'm screwing my face away, trying not to look disappointed. "What about tomorrow? Will you drive me in?"

Baba sighs and shakes his head. "Anna, I don't think you should come back," he says softly. "You have schoolwork. And your mother needs you!"

"No!" I'm on the brink of tears. "*You* need me! Did you not like my spring rolls?"

"You did a good job, Anna. Tomorrow, Minh can step in—"

"No!" I sound like I'm six. "That's not fair." Even though my whole body feels like it's been ripped apart and my bones hurt from all the backbreaking work, I don't want to be left at home.

"Anna, you stay home. That's final."

I'm crestfallen, but Baba is done with our conversation. He doesn't even say goodbye when I go.

Ah-Jeff is waiting in his car, an old Volvo from the 1990s. "Why so glum, Anna?" he asks as I climb into the oversized front seat.

"Baba. He needs me, but he won't let me help." I cross my arms and slink down like Michael in full pout mode.

"Seat belt," Ah-Jeff reminds me. "Your father has a big responsibility. He just wants to make sure he fulfills it."

"He just wants me to stay home with my ma," I huff. "I'm no good at school—my sister is the smart one. The least he could do is train me to run the restaurant."

"Hmmm." Ah-Jeff furrows his brow as he squints at the signs in front of him. "I can never tell if it's right or left to get on the freeway. Anna, can you see?"

I groan because I know he's trying to change the conversation. I know he hates speaking ill of his boss, even if it's just listening to the boss's whining daughter.

"Right." I chew the inside of my cheek as he pulls into the lane. Adults seem to have so many obvious ways to get out of situations they don't want to be in. Why don't I get that luxury?

I'm still fuming more than half an hour later, so I don't notice at first that we're still speeding down the freeway. "Ah-Jeff, you missed the exit to Hornsby," I finally tell him.

"Did I?" He doesn't turn around but instead picks up speed. "Your father is a very independent and stubborn man with his ideas," he says with a wink. "He likes to have his way, otherwise he worries."

By the time we get to Ashfield, it's become impossible to stay awake. My whole body is shot. Ah-Jeff pulls up in front of the bland-looking concrete box of our apartment.

"I'm sorry you had to come all the way out here, Ah-Jeff." I bow my head. "Thank you for the ride home."

"Nonsense, it's no trouble at all. Your father with his stubbornness thinks I'm going to leave his daughter alone on some train platform." He shakes his head. "Now, are you good for nine tomorrow? I think we'll miss the traffic."

"What?" I think my tiredness is affecting my hearing.

"You were good today, Anna. Real good. Your father doesn't want to worry about you, but the restaurant could use the extra help." He gives me a solemn nod.

I want to throw my arms around him, but I don't think that's considered proper. So I smile and nod my head like a bobblehead doll. "Yes. Nine is perfect! Thank you."

"He doesn't realize it, but part of my job is to look after your father. Make sure he doesn't run himself ragged as he tends to do."

I'm grateful that someone understands.

I bid Ah-Jeff good night. It's close to one in the morning, and it feels like I could sleep for a century. But a part of me also feels incredibly alive, like I could run a marathon.

Chapter Nine
Gau2

THE NEXT DAY, Baba is furious. "I told you not to come. Why are you here?" He glares accusingly at Ah-Jeff.

"Lou5 baan2, she's good. She helped a lot yesterday and we need the extra hands. You're working yourself to the bone. You need to hire someone to help you . . ."

"Bah! Don't start with me." Baba looks extra cross. "I don't need you yapping in my ear. I get enough of that from my wife. And I already hired someone, didn't I? The delivery boy?" He nods toward me.

"Rory?" I say his name with an almost-squeal that draws curious looks from both the men. *What the hell is wrong with me?* "I mean, he seemed really good. I'm glad you hired him."

Baba shrugs. "He had a car and he was cheap. But he didn't have any experience."

"Oh, really?" My face is starting to feel a little warm. "I must have misheard him." The way Baba's looking at me, I know he suspects an ulterior motive, but if I've got one, it's *not* the one he's thinking.

"Well, we can try him out for a bit. It'll be good to have the help," he relents. Ah-Jeff and I exchange conspiratorial glances. "But that doesn't excuse the two of you going behind my back." That's his final warning before ducking back into his office.

Lunch service is busier today, and the dining room is about half full. Our kitchen runs like clockwork, a well-oiled machine. I've gotten used to handling the fryer and grill, and after just a day, I don't feel the stinging on the pads of my fingers from the hot oil. Lim seems better on the wok, too—he churns with nimbleness and power, tossing and scooping his ingredients swiftly as the metal skirts over the flames. By two, the last of the diners have finally left. Lim doles out a few hearty and homey dishes for the staff lunch and we all sit around the giant lazy Susan and dig in. It feels like family, everyone's chopsticks poised, cradling their small bowl of rice to their chests. I watch as Ah-Jeff goes for a thick mushroom only to have Baba snatch it out from under him. My father laughs and winks at me as he slurps up the slimy mess from his bowl. I can't remember the last time he did that with us at home. I'm happy to have this moment with just us, but I can't help but feel a teeny bit guilty that Ma, Lily, and Michael aren't here.

After lunch, Baba goes to another meeting and I stay in the dining room with *Macbeth* and copious notes. I'm still trying to work out how to restructure my thesis in the way Mr. Murray had explained. But there are too many characters to remember, I keep getting Duncan confused with Malcolm, and I'm starting to doubt everyone's motives.

"They're all pompous twats," I mutter under my breath.

"Nice to see you, too."

I'm startled by the voice behind me.

"Whoa, sorry. Didn't realize you were a jumpy one." It's Rory.

I can't help but smile. "Hey, you're back. I guess Dad gave you the job." Like I didn't already know.

"He sure did. I am now the proud earner of ten dollars an hour."

I wince when I hear the number. I don't think it's much, but Rory doesn't seem bothered by my father's stingy offering. Instead, he looks genuinely proud of himself. I make a mental note to ask my dad about the current minimum wage.

Rory eyes my stack of notes. "Still on the Shakespeare, huh?" He picks up my returned assignment, the one with the big red scribbles of disappointment. I'm pretty sure my cheeks are just as red now.

"Don't worry about it." I push my glasses up.

Rory is reading, a deep look of concentration on his face. It suits him. The thought makes my face flush more and I reach over to grab the essay back.

He waves my hand away as he continues to read. "No, okay, I see what you did." He points at my first paragraph. "See, this is where you can make it work harder."

"Thanks, professor." I leap up and snatch my assignment from him. "But I don't need help from my dad's delivery boy. That's not why he pays you," I snap.

"Whoa, okay. Firstly, my shift doesn't start until dinner." He put his hands up defensively and backs away. "Secondly, you looked like you were struggling. I just wanted to help. But I should have asked first."

I feel like a real heel. I slump back in my chair, defeated.

"I just can't make sense of any of it," I grumble, handing the paper back to him.

"It can be like that if you're trying to think too literally." He nods in an annoying sage way that Mr. Murray would recognize. He points to the first paragraph again. "Act One, Scene Two. The mind of our dear Lady Macbeth. That was the focus of your thesis, right? You should just focus on that rather than trying to summarize all the other characters and subplots. It's an essay, not a movie review."

"How do you know all this?" I muse. "I don't think a teenage English professor needs to be working for ten dollars an hour for my dad."

"Uh, with our state education system?" he scoffs. "Yeah, I would."

I laugh, but my scalp is tingling. *Get a grip, Anna. He's just trying to help and you're questioning his motives.*

We spend a good part of the next hour breaking down the scene and revisiting my claims in the essay. Rory pushes me to take my thoughts further. We reread passages, and he points out the contradictions in the quotes I've pulled. It's maddening, and I'm frustrated because he's always two steps ahead of me. His hazel eyes sparkle, and his eyebrows dance as he counters my passages. *He's enjoying this. He thinks he's so much smarter than me.*

"Okay, Dead Poets' Society, I need a break. I can't keep up." I toss my pen onto the table and massage my temples. "So where do they find English geniuses like you? Where do you go to school?"

"Ah, I—I don't." Rory rubs the back of his neck sheepishly. "Well, not right now."

"What? Oh, you've finished school?"

"I, ah, took some time off." He looks uncomfortable and takes my pen from the table and starts to twirl it between his fingers.

"Where were you before?"

"Montgomery High."

"Oh! I know that. My sister goes there!" I'm super impressed.

The pen spins off his knuckle onto the floor. He looks at me like I've caught him breaking in somewhere. "Really?"

"Yeah. She's really smart. She's in Year Eight this year."

The muscles on his face relax a little. "I was supposed to graduate from Year Twelve a couple of years ago." I'm a little surprised. Not finishing high school has never been an option to consider. In our school, only a tiny handful of students left at Year Ten.

"Right. So you've done all this high school English stuff already." I slump in my chair. "Everyone keeps telling me Year Eleven is easy, wait until next year, blah blah. You have to realize your full potential. But I already feel like I'm drowning and if Year Twelve is supposed to be worse, I might as well just tie weights to my ankles and be done with it now."

Rory chuckles. "I see you have a flair for melodrama?"

"That's my sister. *I* have a flair for doom." I throw my hand over my eyes in a histrionic fashion, and Rory laughs again. I never thought of myself as funny, but it's a nice feeling, making someone laugh.

"Have you ever seen Shakespeare performed?"

"Does the *Romeo + Juliet* movie count?" He arches an eyebrow, so I shake my head. "Then no." I'm uncomfortable saying this, like I've revealed myself as completely uncouth and uncultured. It's not that I haven't wanted to, but when would I find the time to go see a play?

"Well, there you go! To see *Macbeth*—you have to *see Macbeth*."

"Great. How am I going to do that?"

Before Rory has a chance to respond, Miss Chen pokes her head into the dining room.

"Hey, layabouts, it's almost time for dinner service. Time to get to work." She frowns and crosses her arms when she sees it's just the two of us alone. "Anna, you bring boyfriend here?"

I know there's no hiding my crimson cheeks. "Miss Chen, this is Rory. Dad hired him for delivery. He's just . . . helping with homework before his shift." I grab my books and pages from the table, but I can feel Miss Chen's eyes boring into me. "Um, thanks for your help."

Rory smiles. "Anytime."

Sunday dinner service is quiet, but the kitchen is alive. Ah-Jeff had been right about the kitchen needing my help and Baba had been right about hiring Rory. The delivery orders are flying in thick and fast and I'm turning out batch after batch of fried foods, stashing them in foil pouches so they stay warm on the ride over. "That boy is taking too much time. He should know where the streets are, but he has to use the app," I hear Baba grumble.

"Give him some time. He was a student, he's never done this before." I can't help coming to his defense.

"If he's a student, why he apply for job?"

I've been wondering the same thing since this afternoon, but right now there's no time to ask about origin stories.

The last of the diners eventually file out and Miss Chen stops answering the phone. Calluses that formed today sit atop calluses from yesterday and my muscles are stiff and immobile like they've been wrapped in plaster. I can't move, I can't think, but I'm strangely euphoric.

Rory staggers into the kitchen, totally wiped. "Oh my god, I'm starving. My whole car smells like food." I laugh and offer up some leftover spring rolls. "Here, have one of these. The blackened edges are a staff specialty."

"Awesome." Rory dunks an end into some of my homemade sweet chili sauce and takes a huge bite. "Oh wow, these are amazing, Anna. You really have the touch."

I blush. "It's just a family recipe. Here." I hand him another roll and a napkin for where he's dribbled sauce on his shirt. "How'd your first day go?"

He groans. "I went down the wrong end of a one-way street and got told off by an old lady. Also no one tips."

"It *is* Australia," I point out.

"That's true. These are so, so good." He goes for a third helping. "How'd your day go?"

"Good, but I'm exhausted." I yawn. "I just need a giant sleep. Speaking of—Ah-Jeff, are you ready to go?"

"Oh, I'm sorry, Anna." Ah-Jeff looks embarrassed. "My wife was quite upset I was so late last night, so I don't think I can go out all that way again."

"I can drive you. No problem." Rory finishes the last spring roll and dusts his hands.

"Oh, that's nice, but I'm, like, *way* out of your way." Ma's frequent words about getting in cars with random men are echoing in my mind. Rory's still a *boy*, not a man, but I don't know if that makes it better or worse.

"Whereabouts are you?" He's got his keys in his hands.

"Ashfield. Really, it's too far, it's like three hours there and back." I shake my head. "I'll just wait for my dad."

"It's no problem, really. I like driving."

I'm stuck on what to do. Ah-Jeff just nods apologetically. "Well, um, let me just ask my dad." I sound like a child, but I can't help it.

"Sure."

Baba doesn't look up when I poke my head into his office. "Um, Baba. Ah-Jeff can't drive me home, so I was going to get a ride from Rory." My heart is thundering in my chest, like I'm about to dive off the high board.

He doesn't turn around. "Who's Rory?"

I bristle. "Rory, the delivery boy you hired? Ten dollars an hour," I add pointedly.

"Oh, right. That's a good idea, Anna. Go with your friend. I need to stay and do some numbers." He shifts some papers around in front of him and struggles with the stiff buttons on his jumbo calculator. I can't see his face, but just from the way he's slouched over, I know something is up.

"Baba . . ." I step into the room. "What's wrong?"

He spins in his chair and looks up. I see the giant bags under his eyes, and I feel frosty fingers squeezing inside my chest. As usual, he doesn't say anything, but I can read it in his eyes.

"Baba. Is it the restaurant? Is business bad?"

"It's okay, Anna." He gives me a toothy smile, but it doesn't hide the weariness in his expression. "The supplier prices are going up again. And they want to open a Red Rooster restaurant next to the Gosford train station. More competition, that's all." He tries to wave me off.

"But the delivery is good! It was Rory's first night and there were so many orders."

"It's good, Anna, but it's not enough. We need more business or we'll have to raise the prices, which will make the customers unhappy. We need new ideas."

"Tour buses," I remember suddenly. "Lim said Wong is working at the local veterans club and it has Chinese tour buses. Their business is booming. We should get some tour buses to come here."

Baba shakes his head. "Anna, it's not so simple . . ."

"Well, we can try," I insist. "There's a tour business on Liverpool Road, right near home. We could ask them if they want a partnership, offer a cut or a discount."

Baba isn't even listening. "Anna, you don't know anything about running a restaurant."

"Well, why won't you teach me?!" I demand in English.

There's a long pause, and I can see the vein bulging on Baba's shiny head. He sighs heavily and his lips turn down. "You're a good girl, Anna. Haau3 seon6. *Filial pious.* Your ma and I are very lucky to have you as our eldest daughter." He switches between Cantonese and English. "You have school. And next year, you have the HSC. You get good job. Become doctor, lawyer, teacher, m4 sai2 zou6 ngau4 gong1." *Not do an ox's job.*

"Baba, I don't have the grades for those courses. And what's wrong with running a restaurant like you?"

"Every parent want the children better than them," he finishes in English.

It's my turn to twist my mouth into a frown. I want to say something more, but my father swivels his chair again. "Go home. Your friend is waiting for you." The angle of his slump means he's done with our little chat.

Rory's already in the car when I come out. I feel guilty and a little grumpy now, and suddenly I'm not sure that being trapped in a car with a boy I barely know is such a great idea. I just want to collapse in a corner and hide.

But I put on a semi-decent smile and climb in the front seat. Leather interior, I notice. The car is pretty old, but still way nicer than anything I've ever sat in. "Sorry about the wait," I say. "Dad needed some help and I couldn't get away."

"No worries." He puts the car into drive and we pull out of the alleyway. "It's cool that you help him out with the business."

"Hardly," I scoff. "He pretty much treats me like a child. I'm just supposed to be the good Chinese daughter and respect my elders." Baba's words echo in my mind. *Haau3 seon6. Filial pious.* I make a face and Rory laughs, deep and rumbling. It's a nice sound. The freeway back to Sydney is pretty much empty.

I try to think of something to talk about, but my brain is as exhausted as the rest of me.

"You can just drop me off at Hornsby or something, I can take the train." I still feel bad about making him drive so far out of his way.

But he insists. "It's no problem at all. I've always wanted to check out Ashfield."

"You've never been?"

He shakes his head. "It's kind of a bit . . . I don't know . . . ethnic?"

It's like I've been smashed in the face with a bowling ball. "Wow. Okay, I wasn't expecting *that*." I cross my arms and will this ride to be over.

Rory is bright red. "No, that's not what I meant. I didn't mean for it to sound racist."

"Well, it did." I stare at him. "What about all that *ethnic* food you deliver at the restaurant? Should we be making meat and three veg?"

"I—Uuugh." He growls and grips the steering wheel. "You're right, I'm sorry. That was a microaggression and I'm sorry."

I'm taken aback. "A micro-what?"

"A microaggression," Rory repeats. "My friend Louis told me about them. Everyday Aussie society is full of microaggressions toward nonwhite people. Things like asking someone where they're from or saying 'Nihao' to an Asian person. It might seem small or not important, but it's still racist. It reminds people of their 'otherness'—makes them feel that they don't belong."

"Hunh." I consider this. I didn't know there was a word for it, but I know exactly what Rory's talking about. It's that semi-cringing awkward feeling I get whenever someone randomly tells me they know how to make kimchi (which is Korean) or tries to speak to me in Mandarin (I speak Cantonese). It's exactly why I was so pissed at Rory for calling Ashfield "ethnic," like it was a reason not to go there. I'm wary about where this conversation is headed, but I want to test it out.

"Most of the time, I have to pretend it's no big deal," I say, "so I don't come off as some angry Asian, you know."

Rory nods. "It's how 'minorities' are expected to act, polite and understanding and forever explaining their otherness, because it's not the so-called norm."

"Exactly!" I exclaim. "I took a first-aid class where we learned about RICE, you know, rest, ice, compression, and elevation to treat a sprain. My teacher thought she was so clever when she put 'Uncle Ben's' as a question on the test. I had never heard of Uncle Ben's in my entire life. She didn't believe me when I said Chinese people don't buy Uncle Ben's. I felt really weird and angry about the whole thing."

"That sucks." Rory is sympathetic as he listens. "I'm sorry for what I said before and for all the other stuff you have to deal with."

"Apology accepted." It feels good to talk openly with someone who's not a minority and feel like they "get it." I'm relieved, pleased, and a little intrigued by him. I watch him out of the corner of my eye and say, "You've thought a lot about this stuff, huh?"

"Yep." He pops the *p* as he says it. He's silent for a while, then adds, "I've had a lot of time on my own to think."

"Oh." I wonder what that means, but Rory's not offering more, so I drop it and reach for the radio. He cracks a smile when a Taylor Swift song comes on.

"You like her?"

"She's a legend." I can't help picturing Lily's appalled face as we belt out the lyrics and bop along to the catchy chorus.

It's not long before I'm giving him directions through Ashfield to my apartment. The shops are all closed on a Sunday night, even on Liverpool Road. Rory looks around with interest anyway, and seeing them through his eyes, I feel a little embarrassed by how dilapidated the stores look at night. But it's home. "Thanks for the lift," I say. "You really didn't have to come all this way."

"It's all right. I got to see a bit of Ashfield." He grins. "It looks cool. I like it."

I swell with pride. "I'd love to show you around when things are more lively. If you like spring rolls, there's this place with spring rolls and dumplings that are to *die* for."

"That'd be great. I'd like that." He smiles, and his teeth are like stars.

It's well past midnight, but Lily and I are both up. Lily's in the shower, and I'm still trying to wrangle Shakespeare. It's an uphill battle to make sense of it. Rory's words echo in my head. I wonder if I could call him and ask him to recite a passage for me. He could probably do it from memory.

My phone pings in my pocket.

Rory Smalls has requested to be your friend.

I smile as I click on "Accept." There's another notification almost straightaway.

Rory Smalls sent you a video.

The quality is low and the image is dark, so I have to squint hard to realize I'm looking at a bedsheet strung up like a curtain. I frown but then Rory steps into frame. "What are you smiling at?" Lily pokes her towel-clad head over my elbow, craning to see.

"Nothing." I pause the video and jam my phone back in my pocket. Lily goes to get dressed and I climb into bed where I can get some privacy, away from her prying eyes. I pull up the video on my laptop to play it full-screen. Rory steps into the frame, all smiles. I can't help smiling back. He looks younger, so I think it's an old video.

Rory does a jerky stop and lock but then comes back into view. He has on tights and an old ruffled collar, and he clutches a real-looking dagger in his hand. He moves awkwardly, keeping his profile in view and only one eye on the camera. When he's positioned himself in the middle of the curtain, he begins to speak.

"I have done the deed. Didst thou not hear a noise?" He does an abrupt 180 and I see what he's been trying to hide. The other

half of his face is totally made up—drag-queen levels of bright peacock blues with gold highlights and magenta rouge. He has a blond wig covering half of his head and the tights on this side give way to a full-length ball gown. It's Lady Macbeth.

My jaw drops as Rory winks at the screen and delivers the next lines. *"I heard the owl scream and the crickets cry. Did not you speak?"*

He pivots again for Macbeth's turn. *"When?"*

The pivots make the lines more dramatic—it's supposed to be a quick exchange, but the jerky, staggered delivery add to the suspense and tragedy of the script.

"Now."

"As I descended?"

"Ay."

"Hark! Who lies i' the second chamber?"

"Donalbain."

"This is a sorry sight."

The scene goes on and Rory doesn't falter. I'm impressed—he knows the lines perfectly and delivers them with the bravado and commitment of someone with a longstanding theater background.

He finishes the scene with a dramatic bow, this time looking fully into the camera. The half makeup, tight tights, and gown are on full display. He's split perfectly down the middle—two sides of the one boy.

I laugh and applaud out loud. I wonder what the proper response is to his stellar performance. I pull up the Messenger app to reply.

> You were right! Shakespeare is much better performed.

> Thanks again for your help. See you soon.

I wonder about adding an *x* at the end, but decide that's a bit much.

He replies straightaway.

> Glad you liked it.

There are pulsing gray dots as he types.

"What are you so giddy about?" Lily is dressed in cozy pajamas with freshly washed hair.

"Here. Check this out." I show her the video of Rory's *Macbeth*. She squints as she watches the screen. "Is that a Montgomery jacket?" She frowns at the garment in the background. "I've never seen him at school before."

I forgot he used to go to her school. "His name's Rory. He left two years ago. He just started working at Baba's restaurant as the delivery boy. He seems okay." Suddenly, I'm uncomfortable talking about him to her.

"Hmmm." Lily plonks herself down at our shared desk and pulls out her laptop, the keys clicking like she's firing a machine gun. "Here he is." She pulls up his profile on her school website.

I can't help scrutinizing the picture. School Rory is dressed in his navy-blue uniform and has braces. I snort and have to cover my mouth to hold in a laugh.

Lily takes back the laptop and peers at the screen. "It doesn't have the year he graduated. Is he a dropout or something?"

"He just took some time off. I'm sure he'll finish soon." I don't know why I'm so eager to defend him. "You know work experience is looked upon favorably by university programs." I think of my own conversations with Miss Kennedy.

"Work experience in a *Chinese restaurant*?" Lily's eyebrow quirks up. "Seriously, Anna, I don't know why you're wasting your time there."

I recognize the elitist, mocking tone in her voice. It's the same when Chinese parents compare their kids or when Connie talks about her dad's booming import-export business.

"Baba needs the help," I insist.

She shakes her head. "No, he doesn't. The restaurant is fine."

"Of course you'd say that. You never care about anyone but yourself." I'm picking a fight now. Calling someone selfish and a bad child is the ultimate diss in a Chinese family.

But Lily doesn't take the bait. "Anna, I helped Baba do his restaurant taxes last year. The business is fine. Baba just keeps the money to himself so he can teach us about working hard and so we don't get too comfortable. That's what immigrant parents do."

"Then why are we so poor? Why are we still living in this dump in Ashfield?"

Lily says nothing as she heads to bed. But then she looks at me and says, "You sound just like Ma," before switching off the lights and plunging us into darkness.

I'm left frozen by her words. I was wrong. Because as it turns out, *that's* the ultimate diss in our family.

Chapter Ten
Sap6

I SPEND THE REST of school holidays at the restaurant. Gradually, my muscles start to harden and the aches begin to fade. I form tough calluses where I grip the knife handle, and I'm almost keeping pace with Ah-Jeff and Old Yuan. Baba still doesn't come home at night. I know he's thinking of ideas for the restaurant, but I would rather he think at home than alone on the tiny cot in his windowless office.

On the kind-of bright side, Rory drives me home from the restaurant every night. We've worked through every single TayTay album on my phone. We're now on Dionne Warwick, his suggestion. I had never really listened to the "older" stuff, but Rory's really into it. He seems to love female power ballads, which I can really get behind.

And if I'm a hundred percent honest, it's not the only thing about him that I'm into.

"So are you looking forward to the new term?" Rory asks me

as we sit in the giant dining room, trimming snow peas after the lunch service. A steady rain beats down, so service has been quiet. Miss Chen, as our self-appointed mom, has put Rory and me to work cleaning the restaurant and tidying odds and ends (even though Rory is underpaid and I work for free). We scrubbed the bathrooms and cleaned the windows outside. Afterward, she dug out a gargantuan bag of snow peas, which now sits on the lazy Susan in front of us next to an ever-growing pile of stems. Rory keeps chucking the stripped ones in with the unstripped ones and I have to fish them back out, but he doesn't seem to notice.

I make a face at his question. "Yeah, because I need more Mr. Murray like I need a hole in the head."

"He's going to love your new essay. It's got the Rory Smalls guarantee."

I finished the rewrite a few days back and showed it to him. Rory had some good suggestions to tighten my arguments and cut some of my run-on sentences. It's been great to have him as my unofficial tutor.

"Can I get that in writing? I'm sure I can use it in one of the million and one citations I already have."

"Only if you present it to me in the form of this thesis: 'Rory Smalls is the most badass English professor I've ever had.'"

"All right, Mr. Badass. What do you know about Whitman?" That dreaded text has been sitting at the bottom of my bag since the last day of term.

"Aside from the fact he's the world's biggest pervert?" He

waggles his eyebrows. I chuck a snow pea at him, and he fires back a handful of ends. It's about to be an all-out snow pea war.

"Ahem." Miss Chen is hypervigilant when it comes to watching us from her perch on the counter. She offers us a warning glare.

Rory leans over conspiratorially. "Seriously, though. '*Welcome is every organ and attribute of me, and of any man hearty and clean, Not an inch nor a particle of an inch is vile, and none shall be less familiar than the rest.*'" He sits back, arms folded and looking smug. "Perv central."

I blush and snort at the same time. I feel a tingling in my stomach, which I've noticed more and more whenever I'm around Rory. It's not butterflies, exactly, but it's something.

Maybe I should be looking forward to Whitman!

Miss Chen clears her throat again and we go back to stripping peas. A couple of times, my fingers brush against Rory's and the contact lingers like static electricity. Rory's so easygoing and quick to laugh, I haven't been able to figure out if he's flirting with me or not. And I realize, I don't mind if he is.

At closing time, Baba calls me into his office. "I have something to show you." He lays some papers down in front of me, a contract of some kind. I read the top line. *Agreement between Roger Chiu, owner of Jade Palace, and Bob Lau, owner of Golden Unicorn Tours.* "Baba!" I'm bursting with excitement. "Is this what I think it is? We're doing tour buses?"

"I think about your idea, Anna. I call some places and found Bob. Uncle Bob has his tour group for seventeen years. He's good

man. Honest. And he like us being partners so we signed a deal."
He taps the paper proudly.

I squeal and jump up and down. "Oh my gosh, that's awesome!
I knew it was a good idea. Baba, this is wonderful."

Baba, of course, is ever cautious. "It's only trial," he says. "He'll
bring his Brisbane tours here on the weekend. I am thinking we
should try some new dishes for the customers. Any ideas?" he asks
in Cantonese.

"What about a lunch buffet?" I suggest. "We make some of the
easy and cheap dishes, charge twenty dollars a head, all-you-can-
eat. Dumplings, spring rolls, fried rice, and stir-fries. The buses
are on a schedule, so it's not like people will be hanging around."

"Lunch buffet." He considers this for a bit. "I like it," he says
in English.

I'm bursting with pride. Baba is actually taking my ideas seriously. "I can help you make the menu."

"It's late. You should go home now." But he smiles. "Next weekend, we can work on the menu together."

I can't help myself and give my father a giant hug. He returns
it only briefly and then pats me on the shoulder. "Go home, rest."

Rory's waiting for me as I bound into the dining room. "Ready
to go?" he asks.

"You bet!" I'm overly excited and I don't bother trying to hide it.

"Good night, Mr. Chiu," he calls out toward Baba's office. I
notice Rory is still extra polite around my dad. I also notice that
there are teeny caterpillars crawling in my stomach waiting to
burst into butterflies as he says this.

"So, why the fangirl enthusiasm?" he asks when we're in the car. I tell him about Baba's plan for the tour buses.

"Wow, that's going to be great for business. That was your idea?"

"Well, I kind of overheard Lim talking about it," I confess. "But I figured, why not?"

"That's going to be awesome. Well done, Anna. I'm super impressed."

I can't help feeling pleased with Rory's compliment. I steal a glance at him driving. His hair is matted with sweat, and I think the stench of Chinese food has burrowed itself into every crevice of the worn leather seats of the car. And still there are pirouetting caterpillars in my gut.

"We should celebrate!" I say suddenly.

Rory raises an eyebrow. "It's kind of late, isn't it? It's half past ten."

"Come on. It's the last day of school break." He makes a face, and I remember too late that he's not in school. "Don't you want to do something fun?" I ask anyway.

His eyebrows go higher. "What did you have in mind?"

That caterpillar in my stomach morphs into full butterfly. *Gulp.*

I'm quiet for a moment, considering our options. It's been a while since I've considered *something fun.* Back in the day, when my friend Emily still lived in Sydney, we'd go have bubble tea or maybe watch a movie on the weekends. We never went to each other's houses or to parties like most normal teens do. But Emily's gone now so my weekends are pretty fun-free. At home, we just do family stuff when Ma's not in bed.

"I know what I want," I decide.

"Yeah?" Rory's voice has an edge of curiosity and I'm sure he thinks I'm going to say something cool and normal, like find a party, buy some beers, or go to a concert. I'm not sure he's ready for it, but I say it anyway.

"Dumplings, my absolute favorite. Xiao long bao, especially." I can see them now, heavy parcels of soupy, tasty elegant goodness in a paper-thin wrap.

Rory bursts out laughing, big belly guffaws. I cringe and try to hide any obvious signs of salivating. It doesn't help when he adds, "Wait, you're serious?"

"Um. Yeah." I cross my arms protectively. "Why wouldn't I be?"

His chuckles die down, but I can see the spark of amusement in his eyes.

"Forget it. I didn't say anything." I lean against the window, half wondering if I can throw myself out of the car. "Just take me home."

"No, I think it's great! Anna Banana, fan of the dumplings!"

I frown. "Don't call me that."

"Call you what?"

"'Anna Banana.'" I stare out the side-view mirror, watching the lights disappearing behind us. "It's a terrible name."

"It's rhythmic." He starts up a bad beatbox. "Anna. Banana. Bofana. Mimymomama." I frown more. His smile fades. "Okay, okay. I'm sorry. I was just having some fun." He reaches out to pat my knee, and I jerk it away.

"I'm sorry, seriously," he says softly.

"It's an annoying nickname. When we first moved to Ashfield, kids at school used to call me that, because I never went to Chinese school," I explain. "Banana is yellow on the outside, white on the inside. Like 'Twinkie' in America. It's like saying I'm a bad Chinese."

He cocks his head. "Wait, what do you mean a *bad* Chinese?"

"My Mandarin is pitiful. Even my Cantonese is worse than a child's in Hong Kong. I can't read or write it. Hence, bad Chinese," I say.

"That's bizarre. Like saying I'm a bad white person."

"You could be!" I exclaim. "You could be an egg."

"I thought eggs were good. A good egg."

I shake my head. "To us, it means someone who's white on the outside but yellow on the inside. An Asian wannabe."

Rory pauses to consider this. "Isn't that all a bit—I don't know—racist?"

I wince. "Kind of. Maybe."

I had thought this once or twice, but everyone just throws the terms around. Baba's generation whines about ABCs, Australian-Born Chinese, and their zuk1 sing1 kids—born overseas—while kids at school talk about fobs, freshies, weebs, and Western eggs.

"It's all kind of silly," I mumble. It *is* silly, I know. It's racist to the core to think that there's some *right* way to be Chinese and not Chinese. But I can't help how much I hate the nickname.

When I went to school in Gosford, my classmates and even my teachers would turn to me as though I should have an explanation for everything remotely Asian. Like why Chinese people spit on the street (they shouldn't, it's gross) or if I can understand what the chatty tour groups are saying (I can't). To be honest, I'd often wondered the same things. But when I asked Ma, she explained them easily; that it was the Mainlanders who were all uncouth and had no manners and they were the ones who do the spitting. Which just left me more unsettled and confused because now she was being racist within our own race.

Thankfully, Rory doesn't ask any more questions.

For now.

"So where am I headed for these dumplings?" he asks.

The mention of dumplings instantly puts me in a better mood. Dumplings are the great social equalizer, and so many cultures and communities have some version of meat wrapped in dough, with recipes handed down through generations. It's one of the reasons I love them so much. Plus they taste so good!

"There's Shanghai Knights on Liverpool Road. They have the best xiao long bao in the city, I swear."

Rory chuckles. "Liverpool Road it is." He pauses a beat and then adds, "Anna Grapefruit."

I give him a half smile.

On weekend nights, Ashfield is usually alive and bustling. It's pretty quiet now, but I know a couple of places will be open until two in the morning. I love the ambience of the main strip on a typical evening. There's bubble tea, dumplings, and a seedy karaoke joint where a whole group can pay twenty dollars an hour and croon their little hearts out. I know most people from school go to Burwood these days, since it's more modern and the restaurants are hipper, but I personally love the old-school local feel of Liverpool Road.

Shanghai Knights is one of many similar restaurants within a hundred yards of one another, but I love it because it was the first place we went to as a family (minus Baba) when we first moved to Ashfield. Ma was delighted to finally speak Chinese to a waiter, even if it was in her butchered, cockeyed Mandarin. We ordered all the dumplings, steamed and pan-fried, fish and veggies, and Ma let us get a fried rice even though it's a "white person dish."

We find a place to park and walk to the restaurant, past a number of tiny shopfronts with FOR LEASE signs out front. I keep thinking that Rory is going to turn around and say he has somewhere else to be.

"It's okay if you want to go. I don't need you to keep me company, you know." There's a cruel undertone in my voice that I can't help. It's like picking at a scab. I don't want to be disappointed when I find out he's just taking pity on me. Or maybe Baba paid him to do it.

He shrugs. "This will be fun. Who doesn't love dumplings?"

Thankfully, the kitchen is still open. That's the other thing I love about this place—it's always welcoming in the way a homey place should be.

A middle-aged waitress with a low ponytail points to a plastic-covered table and goes to fetch hot tea. The cups are chipped, the napkins flimsy, and they use the same melamine chopsticks we have at home.

Rory tries to pour the tea and ends up sloshing beige liquid all over the cups. "These things are ridiculous," he grumbles. He sets the too-full pot back down and turns to the menu.

"So what's good, Anna Cherry?"

I groan. "Are you just going to keep adding random fruits to my name?"

"You got it, Anna Plum."

I groan again, but this time, I do it behind the menu so he can't see that I'm smiling. *Caterpillars*. I focus on the words in front of me, Chinese text next to Roman ones, and get down to business.

"Everyone gets the xiao long bao. And wo tie, which are pan-fried dumplings. Maybe some noodles?" I frown. "How hungry are you?"

"Ravenous."

"Okay, then let's get the stir-fry as well. You okay with beef?"

"Sure."

I wave the waitress over and give her the order. I'm thankful that she responds to me in English so I don't have to try to stumble over bad dialects. Some places do that, especially if they're trying to sell you something—they see a Chinese face and they assume they can build better rapport by approaching me in my so-called native tongue.

The waitress leaves and Rory does a slow 360, surveying his surrounds. "Retro. Cool. No pretense. I like it." He holds up his cup of tea, and I clink cups with him.

"So how do you like working for my dad?" I ask.

"Great! I like everyone. Ah-Jeff's really awesome. Did you know he almost became a race-car driver when he was in China?"

This is news to me. "What happened?"

Rory shrugged. "Who knows? It's Ah-Jeff, so he was probably just pulling my leg."

I nod. "I wouldn't be surprised."

The food arrives, piping hot and fresh. I show Rory how to eat the soup dumpling without burning the inside of his mouth. "You bite a hole in the skin and slurp out the soup first," I explain, holding up the dumpling with its splash of vinegar in my ceramic spoon. The steam rising from the inside fogs up the bottom of my glasses.

Rory tries his best to mimic me, but he takes too big of a bite and ends up with soup flowing down his chin and splashing onto his shirt. I try not to laugh too much as I hand him a napkin.

"Rookie mistake, huh?" He flashes a sloppy grin. "Which is a shame, because that dumpling's out of this world."

"I told you." I shovel in a mouthful of noodle.

"Seriously, why don't we make this at Jade Palace?"

I've wondered the same thing. "It's Shanghainese, so my dad has no idea how to make it. And I don't know if Gosford is the right place for it. Our most popular dish is lemon chicken."

"The Chinese KFC?"

"Pretty much." I coax another dumpling onto my spoon, careful not to puncture the skin.

"Real shame. They don't know what they're missing." We eat in hearty silence, our mouths too busy to chat, our stomachs too happy to wonder what the other could be thinking.

When there's nothing but brown oil and sauce left in our dishes, I lean back and sigh happily.

"So, Anna Kumquat, how come your dad owns a restaurant all the way out in Gosford?"

I'm not really comfortable with probing questions. My fingers grip the table and I try to relax. "We used to live there, but my mom wanted to move to the city." I keep my tone light and breezy. "Dad didn't want to sell the business, so he kept it."

"I can see that," he muses. "But it's such a long way. He has that bed in his office, doesn't he?"

"Yeah. We don't see him much." Rory nods sympathetically. His pity and care make me squirm, so I change the subject. "What about you? Have you always lived in Gosford?"

"Mostly. We lived in the city for a while. I went to school there for a bit, but it didn't really work out, so we went back." It's his turn to avoid my gaze.

I remember Lily showing me his photo on the school website. "Why did you go back?" I ask.

He sighs heavily. "I had some . . . problems with school . . . and had to leave." I think about Lily's comments about being a dropout but keep them to myself. *There's something more.* Rory is biting down on his lip, and I can see him mulling his next words over.

"I was in the hospital for a while," he says quietly.

My heart is beating deafeningly loud, like a jackhammer. "How come?"

He takes a deep breath. "I . . . tried to kill myself and was hospitalized with depression."

A long silence hangs between us. My head is spinning as I try to process this new information.

"W-wow. What?" is all I manage to get out.

"Yep." He pops the *p* and picks up his chopsticks, one in each hand like he's about to snare a drum.

"What? What made you— I mean . . ." There's no sensitive or eloquent language for this. "What—what happened?"

He shrugs. "Stress. A lot of stress, apparently. It was Year Twelve, and I was on the swim team and soccer. Lots of school shit. There was a girl. Then there wasn't a girl. I really don't know what it was." He stops for a moment.

"When Dad moved us to the city, I hated it so much. They told me I was smart, but I felt weird in school and I didn't have many friends and I was stressed out about everything, but you know, that's normal teen stuff, right?"

I nod. *Normal teen stuff.* "But it wasn't?"

He shakes his head. "I just remember feeling like . . . I couldn't take it anymore. It's not like . . . I thought my problems were bigger than anyone else's but just . . . I was just . . . miserable. All the time."

He looks like that right now. I'm struck by the sudden urge to take his hand, cradle it in mine.

"What happened?" I ask again.

"I didn't sleep for weeks. I thought I was failing and the coach was yelling at me and I started missing practice. And then one day I just couldn't, didn't want to do it anymore. It just . . . all was kind of numb inside. I stopped going to class, stopped swimming. Stopped caring. I didn't have the energy to do anything anymore. I stayed in bed or I'd go driving. I drove ridiculous places. Everywhere. Driving was like nothing."

He stops for a long breath. He doesn't need me to ask.

How?

"I read about this spot. Above a train tunnel. There's a fence you have to climb to get to the ledge overlooking the tunnel. A girl did it a few years back. You just have to time it.

"I knew the schedule. I went up there and waited for it, watching it pass under me for about a week. Same time, every day. I could feel the earth vibrating through my legs, rattling my body. It was the most I'd felt in a long time.

"Then one day I went up there; I knew I was going to do it. I went to the top and leaned over the side. I could feel gravity pulling down on me, just that little tip of weight hovering, like right before the drop of a roller coaster."

My lip is hurting. I'm biting down too hard, but my jaw is locked and I can't release it.

"But the train didn't come. It was delayed or canceled or whatever. I never found out. I didn't know what to do. I felt betrayed, because I couldn't do it. And then finally, some part of me realized this was *pretty* messed up." He laughs a little here, like he still can't believe it.

"So I went home and I told my sister what I had thought about doing, that I thought something might be wrong with me. She told my parents and we talked about it and we decided I needed to go to the hospital."

I don't move. Don't breathe, really. I don't know what to say. I don't think I was ready for that amount of candor. *Honesty.* I hadn't expected him to be honest.

I feel something shaking inside me, like a rupture through my guts.

"What happened then?" I whisper.

"I went to the hospital. It was shit and it made me feel a lot worse. But they tried out a bunch of meds and then I started to feel slightly less worse. I stayed there for maybe about three weeks and then went home. And there were more meds, and I got a therapist. And I still felt shit, but there was less shit. And now, it's been two years. I'm still on some meds and I'm still talking to a therapist, but I think I can say I feel almost normal, whatever that means." He pauses and looks at me, and I know he's trying to gauge my reaction.

"Whoa." That's my reaction. We sit in silence for a bit, and I gaze at him, still holding his chopsticks. Rory always seems so easygoing and peaceful, at ease. I never would have guessed.

But things aren't always as they seem, are they? "I—I'm glad you told me," I say softly. It's the truest thing I can say.

"Me too." He gives me an awkward not-smile, looks around, and rubs the back of his neck. "My therapist, Cindy, says it helps to be open and talk about it. So long as it's with people I trust."

He trusts me. I can feel the thin dumpling skins in my stomach pulling tight. Would I ever trust him with *my* secrets?

"She also said it'd be good to get into a routine, nothing too stressful," he goes on.

"Is that why you took Dad's job?" I ask.

He nods. "Yeah. At first, Mom and Dad thought I should try to go back to school, but that was out of the question for me, and Cindy agreed. So last year, we decided we should move back to Gosford, and I could look to get a job or something to keep a routine. It was a huge thing, meeting new people, interviewing, all kinds of anxiety triggers. Mom saw the ad in the window and thought it'd be a good change. No questions about . . . you know, before. Easy interview process." He gives me a coy smile.

I gulp. "I guess I should have been tougher on you."

"I'm glad you were a soft touch." And he closes the gap between us so just the tips of our fingers touch.

I'm blushing and I know the dumpling skins have been eaten by the caterpillars.

Rory leans forward and whispers, "Do you want to get out of here?"

We pay the bill. Well, Rory pays, even though I offer. It's late, but I don't want to go home. I can tell Rory feels the same. As we head back to his car, he reaches out and takes my hand. His fingers are long, his palm a nice padded roughness. The feeling from our joined fingers lights a fire in my warm, full belly. It feels much better than caterpillars and butterflies.

"Anna?" The familiar voice yanks me from my happy cocoon of thoughts. I spin around.

Lily's gaping at me from the middle of the road. She's all dressed up, wearing short shorts and a crop top with patent leather sandals. I don't recognize the two girls she's with.

I drop Rory's hand like a stick of dynamite as my sister comes toward me. "What are you doing?" I hiss. "You're supposed to be at home watching Michael!"

"He's asleep. I decided to go out with my friends for once." Lily crosses her arms and arches that confounding eyebrow. Up close, I can see she's wearing makeup, the dusting of glitter on her cheeks shimmering in the dim streetlights.

I'm seeing spots of red. "You can't just leave him alone like that. How can you be so selfish?"

"He's not *alone*; Ma's still there." Her eyes shoot daggers. I know we're making a scene in the middle of road, but I'm too angry to care.

"You know she's in no condition to look after him. Lily, I can't believe you would be so irresponsible."

"Irresponsible?" She waves her arms and stamps her foot. "You're the one who left us with her the entire break!"

"I went to help Baba at the restaurant. So we can have food on our table and the clothes on your back." I sound like a haughty parent, but *someone* has to be the adult here.

But Lily's not letting me have it. "Oh, really?" she snaps back. "Because to me, it looks like you're on a *date*." She spins on her heel and storms off.

Her words are a slap in the face. I still have Rory's heat burning against my fingers, and my body is shaking as I clench my fists tight against my side. I take mighty heaving breaths. I'm about to break down crying in the middle of the road.

I'm vaguely aware of Lily's friends whispering to each other as they follow her, and Rory coming to my side. I feel a large hand gently grasping my shoulder. "You okay, Anna?"

I give him a wry smile, still trying to keep the tears at bay. "I'm so sorry about that." I take off my glasses and wipe my eyes. "I'm—"

"Hey." Rory spins me around fully so I'm forced to look at him. "It's okay. I get it. Things aren't what they seem. It's okay."

The way he looks at me, his eyes dark and full like new moons, I believe him.

"Come on." He takes my hand in both of his so that it's all wrapped up like in a nest. "I'll take you home."

Rory and I say goodbye with an awkward hug. I want to explain, to apologize, to tell him everything about what's going on upstairs. He's told me so much, the least I can do is return the favor, right?

"I'll see you next weekend," I blurt out before running up the stairs. I try to ignore the clear disappointment on his face.

The apartment is heavy with sleep. First, I check on Michael. Out like a light. His tattered stuffed penguin has fallen to the floor, and I pick it up. That penguin used to be mine, and then it was Lily's. One of his eyes is missing now, and his tag is illegible. I used to call him Tux, though I know Michael prefers Herbie, so he's been rechristened.

I tuck Tux/Herbie back into Michael's arms, and my brother curls around him, like a prawn. There's that dull, aching tug in my heart again, and I kiss his temple and let him sleep.

Ma's room is still. I don't bother to go in but press my ear against the door. Her breathing is steady. *Rory said he couldn't get out of bed, too.* I wonder, for just a moment, if Ma would try the same thing he did, but I don't—I can't—think about it right now. I just hope she gets up soon.

My footsteps slow as I approach my room. I can hear soft

sobbing coming through the door. *Lily's home.* A flood of relief washes through me.

She's in her bed, facing away from the door. The crying stops the moment I step inside.

"Lily." She doesn't answer. I put down my stuff and carefully climb up to her bunk. Her body stiffens, and she doesn't move as I lie down beside her and whisper her name. "Lily. I'm sorry."

No answer. I lean my head on my arm, propping myself on her narrow pillow. When we were little, every time Lily got scared, she was too proud to come sleep in my bed. Instead, she demanded that I come to hers for a visit, and we'd lie huddled together in her tiny toddler cot that I had long outgrown. Always feisty and headstrong. I reach over and stroke her smooth hair.

"Lily, I'm so sorry. You were right. I haven't been fair to you. It wasn't fair you had to watch Michael by yourself the entire time. I should have been here."

I feel the tension in her body slacken. She doesn't turn to me still, but she doesn't pull away either. We lie in silence for a long while and I start to think she's fallen asleep, but finally she shifts her weight toward me. I scooch over to give her some room.

"I hate this," she says at last, leaning her head on my arm. This is the closest we've physically been in a long time. The thought saddens me, and I lean into her.

"I know. I do, too."

"When do you think she's going to get up?"

"I don't know. Soon, I hope." That niggling thought returns. *What if she doesn't?*

We lie in silence again. I'm about to drift off, so I almost miss it when she sleepily says my name.

"Anna?"

"What?"

"Be careful."

"What do you mean?"

She snores in answer.

Chapter Eleven
Sap6 jat1

MY HEAD FEELS THICK AND SODDEN. A stress dream, just in time for the new school term. In this dream, the whole class was taunting me with Shakespeare. It feels too real and I have Mr. Murray's voice echoing inside me. I try to push it out of my mind as I stumble sleepily out of my room, Lily still snoring softly.

And then all thoughts of Shakespeare, school, and dreams leave me.

Because Ma is standing in the kitchen. *Ma is out of bed.*

My heart bounds with joy. She is still in her sleep clothes, an old worn shirt of Baba's and faded pajama bottoms, but she is up and out of bed. Her hands shake as she fills up the kettle to make tea.

"Ma." I smile and have to restrain myself from propelling full force into her arms. "So early?"

She peers at me through half-closed eyelids, still heavy with sleep. "I thought I'd get up and have some tea." She clears her throat, her voice rasping from lack of use.

My insides slosh around. I'm so glad she's up and about. She looks frail and small, like she might splinter right in front of me. But still, she's up. *This is a good sign. A good day.*

"Ma, I'll make tea. Do you want some breakfast? We have cereal."

Ma shakes her head. "Cereal, too jit6 hei3, *hot air*. I'll have Chinese tea." She watches as I measure out the bou2 nei5-2 leaves with a little scoop. "Not too strong."

"It's okay, Ma. I know just how you like it." I can't help but feel smug as I pour the boiling water from the kettle into the teapot. Tea is my specialty, and I'd rather make it for her when she's up and can enjoy it. I inhale deeply as the sweet, earthy aroma wafts through the room.

"Here you go." I keep my hands as steady as I can when I pass her the porcelain cup. She takes a small sip.

"Mmm. So fragrant." She reaches up and pushes my hair out of my eyes. Taking after my father, I've been taller than her since I turned eleven. Lily is petite like Ma is, and for now just barely grazes my shoulders.

"You're a good girl, looking after your ma. Haau3 seon6." *Filial pious.* "I'm sorry I've been so tired lately." She yawns to demonstrate. "I just can't move. I have no energy at all."

"It's okay, Ma. You can rest if you want to." I say the words, but inside I can't help but feel crestfallen. I don't want Ma to go back to bed.

"This weekend, maybe," she says in Cantonese, "we can do something as a family. Go yum cha, eat rice crepes. They're your favorite, right?"

I can already taste the slippery rice noodles. But then I remember.

"I don't know. I might have to help Baba at the restaurant. It's been busy."

Ma's whole spirit crumples, and I feel like I've shot a baby bunny. "You can go with Lily and Michael, though?" I suggest. "They like yum cha, too."

Ma looks uncertain, but before we can say anything else a tiny form launches into the room.

"Ma! Ma!" Michael catapults himself into Ma's arms.

"Shh. Not so loud." She cuddles him tight and kisses the top of his head. I'm all fuzzy just watching them. Michael looks like he's just found out it's Christmas and Chinese New Year in one.

"Are you going to take me to school today?" Michael asks. "I want to show you my drawing from last term. It won first prize."

I smile. There's no bashfulness when it comes to a son showing off for his mother.

"Wow. That's so wonderful." Ma looks overjoyed but weary.

I see her hesitate, so I step in. "Michael, Ma's probably still really tired. She should rest more. But Lily and I can take you like usual." Ma looks grateful.

"Go wake your sister," I tell him, and he's off like a rocket. Ma quietly sips her tea.

Later, when I pass by Ma's door, the shadows have gone. Instead, there's a sliver of color, a literal rainbow streaming into our hallway.

I smile. *Good sign.*

Ma sees us off to school, saying she'll take a shower, maybe do a bit of cleaning. I'm worried that she'll exhaust herself too quickly and tell her to take it easy. Michael is in good spirits as we head to the bus stop, but I can see Lily's face is all glum.

"What's up with you?" I ask out of earshot of Michael. "Ma's out of bed. She'll be fine in no time. It's going to be okay."

"Is it, though?" My sister crosses her arms and feet simultaneously. She is the only person I've ever seen scowl with her whole body. "You know just 'cause she's out of bed, she's not *better*."

Lily can be such a negative Nancy. Her worrywart perfectionism can often turn into a real downer.

"She's getting better," I say. "If she's out of bed, it means she's not sad anymore. And that's a good thing."

There's no changing her frown. "You know, her being sad isn't always the worst thing."

A tiny part of my chest twinges, but I shove it aside. I don't want anything to ruin this beautifully good day.

Chapter Twelve
Sap6 ji6

May

THINGS ARE DEFINITELY LOOKING UP. Ma's been out of bed for more than a month now. She's cooking and cleaning, dropping off and picking Michael up from school. She goes to the markets to get cheap and fresh groceries, venturing out as far as Cabramatta and Hurstville on her journeys.

And best of all, *best of all*, Baba has been coming home, sometimes even early enough for us to have a very late supper. We work together on the buffet menu at the dining table while Lily studies in our room.

I'm still at Jade Palace on the weekends. Baba's hired a new sous chef to make the tour bus lunches. He even hired Rory to help in the front of the restaurant and to bus tables during the week. The only downside to Baba being home is that he's the one driving me to and from the restaurant now, not Rory.

The thought of Rory still brings butterflies out from hiding. Despite the weird way we ended that night in Ashfield, something's different now. I catch him watching me out of the corner of my eye, and he doesn't look away. It makes my insides all slippery, warm, and fizzy at the same time.

Once, Rory winked and touched the small of my back as he passed me in the kitchen and Miss Chen promptly threw a proxy-parent fit. She dragged me aside and lectured me on unwanted pregnancy and irresponsible teenagers.

"Teenager is crazy. You see all the time, single girl with baby. So young. No life. No future! You want to throw it all away?"

"No, no. Of course not." The shame had lit my face on fire, and I wished I wasn't so polite or so Chinese so I could tell her to mind her own business. She's always asking if I have a boyfriend, and now she's going to panic if I do?

The other problem is, I can't tell what Rory's thinking. We message each other almost every night, but it's just dorky stuff. But it has to mean *something*, right? He hasn't asked for nudes, which my once-best-friend Emily said was how you knew a boy liked you. I know that's not the *only* way, but I can't really read these signs.

When it comes to boys, I'm still a gazillion kinds of hopeless.

And then, a few weeks into Term 2, the signs begin to change.

Before, Ma was too tired to get out of bed, and now it's like she has too much energy. Most nights, I can hear her in the kitchen, cleaning or stacking dishes. She tries to be quiet. At first, the clinking of crockery sounded more like tiny wind chimes, but after about a week, they became crashing cymbals. And above all that, I can sometimes hear her talking to herself.

"Good for nothing. It's all no good. No good. Get rid of it all."

Lily doesn't hear any of it, or she pretends not to. She snores above me like an old diesel engine. When I tell her about it in the morning, she shrugs and says, "Just use earplugs."

The night before a major chemistry test, I can't fall asleep. Ma's low voice and venomous words spiral through me, mingling with formulas and equations. I get out of bed to check on her.

"Ma, is everything okay? It's late." I'm grumpy and nervous from studying.

She looks surprised to find me standing there. "I was trying to be so quiet. You shouldn't have woken up."

"What were you saying, Ma?" I ask.

"I wasn't saying anything. I'm just cleaning up here. It's so dirty. Can't you see? Ugh, filthy." She grabs a rag and starts to wipe non-existent crumbs from the counter. "Here, don't be a layabout. Help your mother clean all this up."

"Ma. That can wait until morning," I plead. "Why don't you go to bed? I have a test tomorrow."

"Wah, don't be so selfish. You think your mother is useless because I don't have a fancy education like you and your sister?" The accusation comes out of the blue. I've pushed a button that I didn't know existed. "Is that why you treat me like the garbage?"

"Ma, please. It's late. We'll both help you tomorrow."

She ignores me. "Your mother has to fix this up. Or I won't have any respect around here." She goes back to muttering and cleaning with fervor.

I leave her then and go back to bed, but I can't fall asleep. I just hear clanking crockery and Ma's muttering. I wish she wouldn't do this. *Why now?*

I try to block it all out. I know I need to sleep before my exam. I try deep breathing and meditation, but my heart is racing too fast. My brain is counting the waking minutes ticking past like a bomb.

How does anyone live like this?

On a whim, I get my phone and text Rory.

> Are you up?? I can't sleep. 😟

The reply comes straightaway.

> Anna Strawberry does booty calls. 😦

I can't help smiling as I type.

> Ew. You wish.

> I do. #sorrynotsorry

A beat, then:

> What's up?

I think about what's really wrong. I hear the water running from the sink and Ma mutters louder to hear herself over it.

> Can I ask you something?

> Anything.

>> If you were so . . . sad . . . before, how did you . . . like . . . snap out of it??

There's a long beat and then the three dots. It takes a long while before I get his reply.

> I didn't. I was in the hospital and therapy and took a lot of drugs and things before I started to feel remotely better.

>> But you're okay now.

Another long beat. I see bubbles and then they disappear. More bubbles. And then nothing.

>> Rory?

The bubbles come back and then he replies.

> It's not like I was suddenly better. I'm just taking it day by day.

I frown at that. Ma cusses in Cantonese. I pull the blanket over my head, so I'm wrapped in a gentle cocoon of blue-white light from my phone.

>> But you SEEM okay.

I squeeze my eyes shut as I hear more crashing outside.

> Some days I'm okay. And some days I'm less okay.

> I know my triggers. I have my strategies on how to cope when things get too bad.

It's just kind of . . . getting used to that being the normal.

That sounds tough.

It's not easy.

There are footsteps approaching and the door to our room suddenly opens. I switch off the phone and squeeze my eyes shut. The only sound is Ma's angry breathing and Lily's gentle snoring coming from above.

It stays that way forever.

Finally, Ma closes the door and I hear her shuffle back to her room. I exhale slowly and listen to my heartbeat thumping like a pack of wildebeests in the dark.

In the morning, the kitchen is spotless, but Ma's not in it. I'm shattered—a part of me thinks she's started another stay-in-bed episode. But maybe she's just worn out. I don't know. I want to go back to bed myself. I can barely keep my eyes open, and my head feels like soggy newspaper. It doesn't help that Michael and Lily are both having bad starts today.

"Anna! The bread is frozen."

"Anna! I can't find my socks."

"Anna!"

There's no time to check on Ma or make her tea. I can't miss the bus. "Gotta go!" I yell. "Lily, get Michael to school."

"What?!" Lily sticks her head out of the bathroom, her hair standing on end with static from brushing. "That's not fair."

"Anna, I still can't find my sock," Michael wails from behind his door. I clench my fists. I just need ten more bloody minutes in life.

Something in me snaps. "Just go without. It's a goddamn sock. Deal with it!" I yell through the thin wooden door.

There's silence on the other side. A sudden calm descends on me, like mist falling. I let the clamor and chaos wash over me, blending the noisy din into something I can roll up like a ball of lint and flick away. *Deep breath.*

I feel a bit better. My stomach's not churning anymore, though my head is still fuzzy. *Good enough.* As I turn to go, I hear my brother's weak voice call out once more: "Who's going to pick me up from school?"

I let the door fall shut behind me.

The test is a disaster. I can't tell numbers from symbols and balancing equations is like working with Egyptian hieroglyphics.

I can hear Miss Kennedy's disappointment. *You're not reaching your potential.* I wonder how much sleep one needs for potential-reaching.

I have to stay behind at the end of the day, so there's no time to take the bus to Michael's school. I peel away a few precious bills to take a taxi so I can make it in time.

I hate taxis. The idea of being locked in a little metal box with a stranger deciding if I need to make small talk is all sorts of awkward.

Ma's filled me with scary stories about pervert drivers whisking young girls away and doing the unthinkable. I hate being in my school uniform, because I can't even pretend I'm a proper adult taking a cab to work or an important meeting. But with only minutes to spare and Michael depending on me, what choice do I have?

Fortunately, I get a driver who spends the entire ride jabbering away into his headset in another language. I will myself to relax and slump against the door, trying not to seem too obvious as I watch the meter ticking up behind the gearshift. If we're caught in traffic or have to take a detour, I might not have enough to make the fare.

But we arrive without delay or drama. I hand over the money and leap out of the taxi, my bag slung low against my behind. I hurry across the street as fast as I can, unsure whether I've made it in time or already missed the bell.

But I don't have to worry. Just as I'm getting to the entrance, I see a small familiar figure stalking toward the school gate. My heart soars and I pick up my pace to try to catch up.

"Ma!" I call out.

The figure turns and the look on her face makes me freeze mid-step. The expression, it's more than a glower or a glare—it's the look I've seen on Lily when I wake her up before dawn or that time she found out I'd broken her phone charger.

Ma is *hella* pissed.

"Anna, where did you come from?" Her tone is suspicious, but her voice is even.

I fall into careful step beside my mother, trying to find the right words to speak, what to tell her, what to check, like I'm following a sequence to defuse a bomb. "I took the bus," I lie. "You're out of bed. Are you feeling better?"

"Of course, I feel fine. What are you on about?" Her voice is scratchy and her eyes dart about anxiously. There's a nervous edge to her.

The other parents and guardians are gathered in front of the office, most of them thumbing idly through their phones as they wait for the kids to emerge from their classrooms. Ma is eyeing the other mothers like a rabbit in a lion's den.

I want to distract her, keep her calm. "I had my test today, but I don't think it went well. I didn't get much sleep," I say.

She ignores my comment, her eyes flicking this way and that. "Wah, Anna. You're so dark. Too dark! No good. You are Chinese. Chinese should be light skin," she says loudly in English.

I feel my face go red-hot and I look around, but fortunately there's no one within earshot or they're all pretending not to have heard.

"Ma, you can't say things like that," I whisper in Cantonese. I'm annoyed and deeply embarrassed. My complexion has always been darker than hers and Lily's. Michael's pretty tanned, too, but he's a boy, so Ma never comments. Me, she constantly shoves whitening cream at.

She stays with her broken English. "It's the true thing. What wrong with say the true thing? Too much lies and greedy, it's no good. You should always speak true. Honest good."

Honesty. I hate that word so much. Because how do I ever tell her what I really feel if I want to be her daughter?

The bell rings, and I'm spared further commentary. The parents put away their phones and peer eagerly. Slowly, a few classroom doors open, and small bodies tumble out, worksheets and papers flying out of notebooks as they make the dash across the schoolyard, transforming from pupils to kids.

Pickup is quick—most parents don't dawdle the moment they spot their child, little Annie or Timmy hanging on to their arm and jabbering away as they head to their cars or to the crossing.

Michael's class hasn't come out yet, and I can tell Ma's anxious, her lips pulled tight, her eyes darting from parent to parent. I can't tell what she's thinking. She doesn't like crowds and strangers. I see a dark-haired woman squinting in our direction, but she doesn't seem familiar.

"Hello, Kate Mom." Ma waves, but the woman doesn't respond. Ma waves again just as a pigtailed girl bounds up to the woman and throws her small arms around her neck.

Ma's face crumples as she watches the scene. My heart sinks. Ma's unhappy—she hates to be slighted, and I know this encounter won't be easily forgotten.

"Mommy!" Michael rockets toward us, his hat flopping behind him. The smile on his face is so big and so bright, it could be the bat signal. Ma still keeps her eye on the brunette woman and her daughter, but her scowl is gone. She squats down and motions her son over. I feel a part of my insides goo up as the two embrace, hard, fast, and tight. I'm worried Michael's arms might snap in two.

"I didn't think you were coming to get me. Lily said Anna would come."

Ma eyes me but says nothing. "Your mother was just feeling tired, that's all. Who doesn't take naps when they're tired, right?"

Michael makes a face. "I don't like naps."

"Well, I'm not as young as I used to be, and I must have exerted myself cleaning the house. That's why you should be a good son and help Mommy clean, so she won't be so tired next time, okay?"

"I'm sorry, Ma! I'll help you more next time, I promise," Michael says earnestly.

I clench my fists at my sides, gnashing my teeth together. She's tired because she cleaned the house top to bottom in the middle of the night, all at once.

But guilt trips are a part of my mother's parenting, filial piety and duty being supreme. My own daughterly duty is slipping right now, and it's taking every bit of restraint to not retort or say something that I might regret later.

"Come here, bou2 bou2, *precious one*." Ma pulls out a thin tissue from one of the packs Baba uses to advertise the restaurant and wipes Michael's face. He makes a show of squirming, but I can tell he enjoys the attention. She holds him out at arm's length, her adoring gaze traveling down to stop at his feet. "Wah! No socks?!"

Uh-oh. I'd forgotten about our rushed dash out the door this morning. My stomach sinks.

Michael doesn't help. "Anna said I didn't need them." He sticks out his lower lip, but I can tell the cute pout isn't going to save my ass. And sure enough, Ma turns to glare at me.

"Anna!"

"We couldn't find them and we were already late . . ." I suppress

the urge to add *because you wouldn't come out of your room.*
This is why I can never be fully honest no matter how much my
mother asks.

Ma tsks loudly, looks at Michael, and shakes her head, muttering
under her breath in Cantonese. "Jau5 mou4 gaau2 co3. *Are you
kidding me?* Not wearing socks, what is she thinking? So dirty,
huh?" She wipes Michael's face again and says to him, "Your sister
is a bit silly, huh?"

I'm trying my best. The words are on the tip of my tongue,
and that's where they stay. The rage is bubbling up, but I clamp it
down. *It's not her fault*, I have to remind myself. She's not thinking
straight, she doesn't know what she's saying.

But I can't help feeling cast aside, broken.

"Mrs. Chiu. Anna." Miss Holloway appears in a bright peacock-
blue scarf adorned with desert rose swirls. "I'm so glad you
could come by, Mrs. Chiu. You must be very proud of Michael's
accomplishments."

"He win prize." Ma's English is choppy, short words and angry
scowling. I can never tell if it's because of her mood or the frustration that she can't manage more than a six-year-old's vocabulary.

Miss Holloway smiles. "That's right, he did. He's a very talented artist. Anna must have told you about the art program?"

Ma swivels to me. "Program? I know no program."

I squirm under the women's scrutinizing looks. "I didn't get a
chance to mention it," I mutter.

"Oh, of course." Miss Holloway goes on to talk about the
young artist scholarship, the diversity program. Ma nods along

like she knows exactly what she's being told, and I listen discreetly beside them. Michael has slipped away to play, and I wish with all my might that I could join him rather than stand here and seem pathetically diplomatic.

"Mrs. Chiu, I would like to recommend Michael for the program, if you're okay with that." Miss Holloway eyes my mother carefully, like she's seeking her approval.

"You library teacher? Yes? Not Michael teacher teacher?"

Miss Holloway tightens her scarf defensively. "Well, I teach all the students at the school, but no, I'm not Michael's classroom teacher," she replies.

"My son good school? Good grade?"

"Yes, his teacher says he's doing very well. Very bright."

"Math homework, he said he didn't understand how to do subtraction. He show me his paper, very red."

"Oh, subtraction is hard for many of the kids to grasp. I'm sure Michael is doing just fine."

Ma frowns. "Michael is a good boy. He try very hard. My Anna, she try to, but she forget sometimes. Can you believe, she tell Michael no socks!"

I can feel their eyes on me. My face is on fire, and I pretend to be absorbed in studying the pattern of the concrete at my feet.

Miss Holloway laughs nervously. "Oh, I'm sure she's a great big sister. Michael always talks about her."

My heart explodes with love.

"Yes, Michael love his sister very much," Ma says evenly. Is that *jealousy* I hear in her voice? "I don't think Michael should go program. His math not good. He can't do subtraction. Art make him lose mind."

I snap my head up and gasp. Miss Holloway looks taken aback, obviously not expecting such an answer. "Oh, but, Mrs. Chiu, s-surely—" she stammers.

"No art. School first. Art for when he old man, retired." She turns to her son. "Michael, come. Pick your things. Go home now."

"Mrs. Chiu, please." Miss Holloway is trying so hard. "I don't think I've explained what a wonderful honor this program is, and did I mention that it's free?" Miss Holloway nods earnestly like she's hit on the magic word.

It has no effect on my mother. "Michael, come, come."

"Mommy, look!" He points at the ground where he's been busy sketching on the concrete with a cast-off bit of street chalk. I'm expecting stick figures of the family, but no—my little brother has managed in the span of a few minutes to start a detailed sketch of a chick in an egg.

"Wow!" I exclaim, my voice steady and boisterous as I go to his side. "That's so cool. So realistic."

I spot Miss Holloway nodding furiously, but she keeps quiet. Ma doesn't seem to notice, extending an arm out toward Michael. "Let's go."

I stop to take a photo of Michael's drawing with my phone. The two of them are almost out the gate, and I catch Miss Holloway's eye. She looks stunned, hurt even. Most of her pink lipstick has flaked off and the rest bunches together into a tight-lipped frown.

What can I do? I give her a small shrug and mouth "sorry" and follow.

We're waiting at the bus stop to go home. The bus is running late, and Ma clutches her purse in her lap like it might grow legs and run off.

"Wang tiu bao dong goo geung hee sui lew."

The vaguely Cantonese sounds and tones catch my ear, but it's not Cantonese. I turn to their source, an older woman hobbling toward us. Her hair is done up in a flawlessly tidy bun. She's wearing rouge and her eyes are perfectly rimmed in kohl.

"Lin moong meet tong hee yiu jik. Mee tiu shuon tiu hee sip jung." I *think* she's babbling about Chinese herbal remedies for the heart, that much I can tell.

Ma shakes her head. "So4 po4-2, *crazy woman*, talking to herself. Pay her no mind," she says for our benefit.

We watch as she takes a seat at the end of our bench, still cawing on about remedies like she's hawking wares at the markets. "Pin gwua diu sim jonng hau." She pulls a tissue out of her tiny purse and blows.

"How curious. Crazy that she doesn't know what she's doing, but she can do her hair so neat and makeup so nicely," Ma muses. "She won't draw herself like a clown."

I squirm with discomfort and clear my throat to get her attention. "Ma. Do you think—do you think we should ask what Baba thinks? About Michael's art program, I mean?"

I'm trying to save the situation with the only card I still have to play, even if it means dragging cows up trees. Deep down, I know that my dad will just default to my mother. On matters outside the restaurant, he leaves it to her, like when it comes to her own health. But I'm hoping that by suggesting it, Ma will reconsider the decision.

I don't tell her what I really think. That it's a once-in-a-lifetime opportunity. That Michael's talent is astounding, and he'll figure out subtraction eventually.

Ma doesn't say anything. A bus pulls up on the opposite side of the road, and a few people get off. Ours is nowhere to be seen. Ma ignores my comment.

"Michael." Ma leans in to whisper in her son's ear. "I want to tell you something. Okay?" Her voice is low and conspiratorial, and I have to strain to listen.

He nods, his attention on the screen. Ma has surprisingly let him play a game on her phone.

"Michael, I don't want you to be friends with that Kate girl anymore, okay? Her mother is not a nice person, too snobby. Not even a hello. No manners. A rude mother will raise a rude daughter, okay?"

I toy with the zipper on my bag. I know all of Michael's friends in class, and Kate isn't one of them. The only reason Ma has ever heard of the girl is because she and Michael both played owls in preschool. But I can't help feeling bad for Kate all the same. Banned from a friendship she didn't have.

"Michael, are you listening?"

"Sure, Mommy. Shhh. I'm trying to beat this level."

Chapter Thirteen
Sap6 saam1

June

MISS CHEN STICKS HER HEAD into the kitchen. "First bus is in seventy-five minutes. Ah-Jeff, where's the sauce?"

"It's coming. It's done." He caps the bottles and puts them on a tray. "I'm scared of you blowing up like a firecracker."

It's our first Saturday with the tour buses and the kitchen is running on spitfire and energy. Baba and I were up before the crack of dawn, chopping and churning to get things ready for prep. I've got a huge pot of soup bubbling away by the time Lim and Ah-Jeff come in. By ten, everyone's running at full steam with bucket loads of stir-fry and cascading mounds of soy sauce noodles with ginger and shallots. Miss Chen takes the tray of sauces without a word and the kitchen falls quiet, save for the rhythmic chopping, slicing, and sizzling. I can't feel my fingers anymore, but it doesn't stop me from rolling tight little cigars of spring rolls. Before long, I have giant trays of them, all lined up like tiny beige soldiers heading into battle, and I deposit them in the bubbling fryer.

Seventy-five minutes goes in no time, and before long, we can see the tables filling up through the kitchen cutaway. Rory is out there filling water glasses and I can see he's putting on the charm. The table he's serving laughs heartily, and it makes my stomach tighten.

"They're here!" Baba shouts over the din of sizzling woks and fire. "First servings go out." He mops his brow and catches my eye. I give him a small nod. It's showtime.

I take out my tray of spring rolls; Ah-Jeff follows with a bin of fried egg noodles with oyster sauce.

Everything comes out at a specific time like clockwork. The idea is we get the patrons to fill up on noodles and spring rolls—the cheaper carbs and veggies—before we bring out the protein dishes. We don't do snow crab legs or seafood dishes, but we have Mongolian style lamb and beef with black beans. Lim has whipped up a salty pineapple fried rice with chicken that everyone loves and keeps going for seconds. Miss Chen, Rory, and our two waitresses flit from table to table, filling up water glasses and bringing out cans of cola and lemonade.

And exactly forty-five minutes later, with barely a second to spare, the dining room is empty and the last of the stragglers in the restroom are ordered back on the bus. "How'd we do?" Baba asks nervously, watching Miss Chen punching buttons on the till.

"Forty-five diners, twenty dollars a head. In just forty-five minutes!" she exclaims. "And it's not even noon."

Baba and I whoop and holler, and he offers a surprise high five.

"It's working," he says, and I can see my own glee reflected in his eyes. "It's really working!"

But there's no time to revel in our awesomeness. We throw ourselves straight back into prep. The next bus pulls in about an hour later, and we go through the whole service again. This one's a smaller van, only sixteen passengers, but some of them decide to order off our dinner menu rather than go for the buffet, so I'm grilling up barbecue pork alongside my spring rolls. Service takes a bit longer this wave, but an hour later, the last table has paid and the oversized van pulls out of our near-empty parking lot.

I barely have time to wipe the sweat from my brow, let alone sit down. But I feel the energy buzzing through me—a sense of liveliness and belonging that I've come to love.

The restaurant is a part of me. And I thrive in it. "And that's it." Miss Chen flips the OPEN sign around to CLOSED, signaling the end of service.

"Woohoo, we did it!" Ah-Jeff fist-pumps the air, and Baba offers another high five. My cheeks hurt because I can't stop smiling. My eyes seek out Rory. He gives me a grin and a wink that sets the caterpillars alive.

Baba claps his hands together. "Okay, enough. Lots to do before the dinner service. Back to work!"

After dinner, Baba wants to stay behind to crunch the day's numbers. I see the twinkle of excitement in his eyes. He looks younger: reinvigorated and . . . happy, I realize. He's happy and I don't ever want to take that away from him.

And there's the part of me that *really* doesn't mind Rory driving me home.

I'm babbling away with too much energy the moment I get in the car. "That was unreal! Did you see how many people we had for lunch? Baba must be so happy."

Rory laughs. "*You're* so happy." Before I realize what's going on, he's grazing a bony knuckle against my cheek. "It's cute."

I turn all shades of crimson, and those caterpillars are doing gymnastics in my gut. The inside of his car feels electric with energy and my whole right arm can sense his presence in the other seat. I lean over a little and our elbows bump together and neither of us pulls away.

I'm melting faster than butter on a hot plate. Gone. *This is it.* All my nervous shyness and hopelessness is suddenly suspended. Because out of nowhere, like an alien being taking over my body, I lean over.

And *I* kiss him.

He's not expecting it. His lips are stiff at first, but then they soften and part. I have no idea what I'm doing, but I keep the pressure up to what I hope is the right amount. He presses back just a bit; he tastes like salty, savory dumplings.

The caterpillars turn to butterflies.

I pull back after a few seconds. His grin is wide; his irises stand out against the white of his eyes, like beautiful shiny amber. I'm a bit dizzy, excited, and weirded out.

My first kiss.

It takes just a nanosecond to burn it into my memory. But it's not over. Rory moves to tangle his fingers into my thick hair to pull me toward him. I smile and lean forward, letting my eyes flutter shut, ready to do this again. *Holy crap! I'm making out in a car. Like a normal teenager.*

The *thunk!* against the windshield is followed by peals of male laughter. I open my eyes to see the insides of one of my spring rolls splattered across the glass, like a ballistics crime scene. I look outside; a blinding yellow Jeep is angled beside us. A blond head pokes out of the driver's window and calls out.

"Hey! Hey, Smalls!"

Rory is stone stiff beside me, his eyes fixed on the car. The boy gestures for me to open my window. I look at Rory again, but he doesn't say anything. I'm stuck on what to do, so I slowly roll it down. The hooting and hollering gets louder, and I feel the heat against my face.

"Can . . . we help you?" I try to channel Lily's defiant sarcasm to mask the pounding fear in my chest.

"Yo yo, ni hao there." He smirks and I ignore the veil of disgust creeping over my body. "I just want to talk to your boy."

Still nothing from Rory. I clench my fists against the seat. "He doesn't want to talk. And this is my dad's restaurant, so I think you should get out of here before I tell him to call the cops."

The boys in the car laugh. "Feisty one there. Aren't the Asian ones supposed to be submissive?"

"Leave her alone!" Rory is suddenly jumping out of the car, nearly tripping over his seat belt. I barely have time to unlatch the door handle.

"Hey, hey, easy there, Smalls." The boy holds up his hands in mock surrender before Rory is out of the car. "Back up there, didn't mean to set you off." He glances knowingly at the boys in the back, who snicker. "How you been, Rory? You got some feelings you want to talk about? Do a little sharey-share?"

"Get the hell out of here, Gary."

"Rory." I'm out of the car and can see two other boys in the back. Rory is standing, glaring, the veins bulging from his forearms. I've never seen him this way before.

"Oh, watch out, I don't want to set you off, Smalls. Who knows what you might do, am I right?" Gary looks at me, then back at Rory. "Come on, guys. We're headed to a party anyway." He catches my eye again and licks his lips and that icky, disgusting feeling coats my whole being. "You want to come along, Rory?"

I watch Rory's fingers piston back into fists, and he doesn't reply.

"Loser," Gary sneers. "Hey, next time you try to off yourself, do us all a favor and finish the job." The laughter from his buddies is drowned out as he revs the engine. The Jeep slowly pulls out of the parking lot, and Gary gives a little wave as they peel off.

"Love you long time, Smalls."

"Rory." My blood is raging under my skin, and my thoughts are swimming against ginormous waves. But I stave off my anger because beside me, Rory looks like he's been hit by a truck.

No, wait, he looks like his dog's been hit by a truck and then he's been hit by the body of the dog.

"Rory?" No answer. "Are you okay?" I lay a hand on his shoulder.

He suddenly snaps to attention. "*I'm* okay, are *you* okay?" His voice is a little too loud.

"I'm—I'm fine." I withdraw my hand, not sure of what to do. Rory paces a couple of steps, left and right, clutching at his hair.

"Great. Great, then." He's still shouting. "We're fine, then, let's go."

"Wait . . ." But Rory is already in the car.

I try to talk Rory out of driving, saying that he should head home and I can wait for Baba, but he insists again. "We're fine." He seems extra twitchy and I keep getting nervous, my angry thoughts taking me to all sorts of weird places.

"Do you want to talk about what happened?" I ask. Rory's still as stone. "Were they your old schoolmates?"

Finally, he nods. "Before Sydney. Local kids from primary." I wonder if Rory was bullied at school.

"Ugh, what a bunch of turds," I jibe, trying to lighten the mood.

Rory looks sullen. "We used to hang out a bit. Even after we moved and I changed schools, our moms were in the same online book club or something."

"Oh. Did they bully you?"

He gives a small shrug. "When I came back to Gosford, I tried to talk to them about the depression and hospital. They treated it like one giant joke. And after I told them about what I went through they were . . . like that." He winces.

"I'm sorry." I frown. "But they're real assholes, and you're nothing like them."

Rory's eyes are kind, but their hollowness makes me shiver. "I know." And he turns back to the road.

We're quiet for the rest of the drive home.

As I'm getting out of the car, I try to think of something reassuring. Or something. I mean, assholes aside, there was the buffet day and then *the kissing*.

It wasn't supposed to be this way.

But the moment I close the door, Rory's pulling out of the driveway and back onto the road. And I'm left standing alone in the night.

Chapter Fourteen
Sap6 sei3

"RIDICULOUS. THESE AUSSIE BOYS, they're all lazy and complain too much. Don't know how to work." Baba storms into the kitchen, phone in hand. He glares at me. "Anna, pay attention. Put up new sign. New delivery boy. Say Chinese only."

"What? What happened to Rory?" I cry in dismay.

"Boy call, says he not coming in today." Baba's face is bright red. "He need mental health day. Ridiculous. What mental health day? New holiday? Ridiculous."

My insides turn stone cold. After he dropped me off, I texted Rory a few times, but he hasn't texted back. Today I sent a few silly GIFs (one I found involved a flying burrito) but nothing. All that stuff with Gary and the boys left me shaken and I can only imagine how Rory must feel.

And now he's not coming to work.

I feel upset, angry even, and almost a little betrayed. But I remember that harrowed look on his face as he left me at the door last night. Mostly, I'm just really worried.

"Mental health days are important," I stammer. "They talk about it all the time at school. And I know a few kids who have taken them." I think back to the assemblies we've had with advocacy groups like Beyond Blue and Headspace. "In fact, I think it's the law now that employers have to give this to their workers." I make a note to fact-check this later, but I'm relying on Baba not being well-versed on these types of details.

Baba shakes his head and grumbles. "Mental health day. Maternity leave. No wonder nothing gets done in this country. Look at the Parliament House. Like a bunch of zoo monkeys."

Behind me, I hear Ah-Jeff chortle. As much as Baba complains about Hong Kong affairs, nothing gets him more fired up than Parliament Question Time.

"Lou5 baan2, let the boy have his day," Ah-Jeff says. "I can cover the delivery, and Anna's more than capable of running my station."

My heart skips. On Sundays, Ah-Jeff looks after the dumpling steamers and soups, pretty much any dishes that don't require wok work. It's a big step and Baba has never let me off the fryer before.

Sure enough, Baba seems skeptical. "Who look after fryer, then?"

"I can do both," I say quickly. I really, really, *really* don't want Rory to be fired.

Baba looks from me to Ah-Jeff and back to me and heaves a sigh. "You all will be the end of *my* mental health."

I mouth a silent "thank you" to Ah-Jeff, who returns a smile and motions me toward his bench. There's so much to do, and I have to rush to prep. But I pause quickly to check my phone.

Still no messages from Rory.

I want to text him again, ask about his mental health day. See if he needs to talk. Anything. And not just because those kisses are seared into my memory.

I want to tell him I miss him, but that seems like too much.

My fingers hover over the keyboard but I'm at a loss for words. Finally, I write:

> Are you okay? x

And I go back to prep.

The gentle ping from my phone wakes me.

> Hey. Today was a bit rough, thanks for asking.

Rory's reply. The caterpillars awaken and I'm flooded with all sorts of happiness and relief.

> I'm sorry. 😔

> Those guys were such dickheads. You shouldn't let them get to you.

> I don't think it was that.

A long pause. I wait for him to elaborate, but instead he says:

> I saw my therapist today.

> That's good! Are you feeling better?

I'm working on it. I told her about running into Gary and the guys.

They were always dickheads but I used to kind of go along with it. And then after the whole hospital thing, I realized they weren't my friends.

They were jerks.

But it still gets to me. I just wish I hadn't said anything to them.

> They're complete jerks!

> You're so open and honest and that's incredible!

> Don't be so hard on yourself.

I'm just so pissed I let them get to me. 😞

> Forget about them.

> You're awesome!

I'm being super lighthearted and optimistic, desperately trying to get a smile or positive emoji from him. I'm so glad he's talking to me. But I can sense the gloomy seriousness on his end, and it makes me want to reach through the phone and hug him. Tug him against me and snuggle into his chest.

Was your dad pissed I didn't come in?

A bit. But Ah-Jeff and I worked it out, so I think he's okay.

I worked the steamer. 😌

Sorry I couldn't make it in.

It's okay! I just hope you're feeling better?

Getting there.

I frown and wonder if I should say what I really want to say. Before I can reconsider it, my fingers are typing.

I missed you.

I missed you, too.

I feel the showers of relief. The honesty engine is on, and I don't try to filter my whole emotional self.

I thought after everything, you might not like me anymore. 😟

Impossible.

You're amazing, Anna Strawberry. 😊 x

There it is. A smiling emoji. Finally, a good sign.

Chapter Fifteen
Sap6 Ng5

July

IT'S SCHOOL BREAK AGAIN and I'm back at the restaurant almost every day. Which means I get to see Rory all the time. Which means there's nowhere else I'd rather be.

"Anna!" Ah-Jeff snaps. "Stop daydreaming. Can you get some cabbage from the fridge?"

I compose myself and put down the knife I'm holding and head to our huge walk-in. I open the door and am suddenly yanked inside. I almost scream.

"Hey, you."

His smile is wide and his tousled hair perfect. He has his arm around my waist, and his big hands make me feel thin and petite, girly.

"Hey, yourself," I say.

We've been sending memes and funny messages every day and

talking on the phone until all hours of the night. All through service, I noticed him giving me secret winks and cute smiles.

Now we're squished into a cramped walk-in fridge.

"How you doing today?"

"Peachy." I giggle. The space in the fridge is narrow and the chilled air heightens the sensations of his body pressing against my skin.

"Anna Peachy, then."

He closes the space between us, taking the lead. I feel his lips slacken, and I do the same. We press our mouths harder against each other. Kissing still feels a bit strange and weird, but exhilarating at the same time. I think we're getting better at it. He tastes like the bitter herbs that Ma makes when we're sick, but not unpleasant.

Rory's fingers tangle against the nape of my neck, and I feel a deep pull from inside me. I lean into the kiss, and the pulling grows a little stronger, reeling me in as I fall forward, fall faster, fall farther in. His lips move softly against mine, like a kitten kneading.

The door to the fridge suddenly swings wide open. We break apart quickly, but it's too late. Ah-Jeff is gaping at us, his reading glasses dangling around his neck.

No one moves for the longest time.

Finally, Ah-Jeff shakes his head and sighs. "Just bring the cabbage, will you?"

Rory and I grin.

The next morning, Michael and Lily are taking turns grossing each other out by opening their mouths and showing off their chewed-up bits of food. I'm so tempted to snap a photo of my sister, mouth wide open so it takes up more than half her face. I'm sure it'll come in useful.

It's Saturday morning and Ma is out buying groceries. Baba is reading the Chinese newspaper, a dollop of custard cream at the corner of his mouth. I check the clock on the wall. "We should go soon if we want to beat the traffic."

"I think you should stay at home today," Baba says quietly. "I'm worried about your schoolwork, Anna. You go back to classes soon."

A shroud of dread drapes over me. "School's fine. I want to help," I insist. It's been more than a month since our grand buffet debut. Weekend business is booming and Baba's had to hire more help, but most days we're still run off our feet.

"I'm worried about you. You're spending too much time at the restaurant. Not focusing on your studies. Too many distractions." He presses his lips together and gives me his knowing look that says things without him saying anything.

I gulp. And I understand.

Ah-Jeff must have told him about me and Rory.

I want to plead my case to Baba now, to tell him how good Rory is, that he's helping me with school. But one look at him and I decide against it. *There's no way I will ever convince him.* Poor Baba. His eyes bug out like a puffer fish. There's no hiding how exhausted he is. Despite the initial delight in the buffet's success, it's taking a toll on his health.

"Okay, Baba." I hang my head, deflated and defeated.

Baba nods approvingly and I wonder if he'll ever let me back to the restaurant again. I feel sick inside. I think about Romeo and Juliet never being able to see each other again. Is that the fate awaiting me and Rory?

"Anna, look at this," Michael says. I turn, grateful for the distraction even if it's to see gooey, gloppy bits of half-chewed egg tart. He giggles and swallows.

"Oh yeah?" I take a huge bite of my pineapple bun, too big to fit in my mouth, and chew until it's a wet, warm, sticky mess, bits of it caught along my gums, then show it off.

"Eew. Anna, that's disgusting." Lily is doubled over in hysterics. Out of the corner of my eye, I see that Baba's cracked a sorrowful smile.

"Okay." He downs the rest of his cup of tea. "I'm off to the restaurant." He doesn't hug or kiss us goodbye, but he does stop to ruffle Michael's hair. "Be good."

The air feels thick and heavy with his departure. I start to gather up the dishes, wondering what I should text Rory. If I can't go to the restaurant, there's almost no way we'll see each other regularly. The butterflies have all drowned in the churning acid of my stomach.

I'm moping in the kitchen, cleaning up the breakfast dishes, when Ma comes home, her arms laden down with shopping. "Anna. Did your father leave already? Why aren't you at the restaurant?"

"He said he, uh, doesn't need me today," I say breezily. But I'm almost crying.

"Oh, Anna, that's good. You stay home. Restaurants are not a good place for a proper young lady." Even though I'm trying not to look upset, she comes over and hugs me from the side. I lean against her sturdy form, soaking in her warmth.

"You stay home with Ma today, okay?"

I nod as she pulls away.

Lily comes out of our room, study notes in hand. "Did you get toilet paper?" she asks as she rifles through the bags on the counter.

"I know. Let's all go somewhere," Ma says out of the blue. "All of us together."

Lily and I exchange a *look*. "I have lots of study to catch up on. Term Three starts soon," Lily says.

"Me too," I add quickly.

"Nonsense, when was the last time we did things together? Family time together is most important."

Neither of us replies. *Do something*, Lily's face screams at me.

"How about the aquarium?" Ma says.

And before either of us can say anything else, Michael leaps out of his chair. "Aquarium! They have a new penguin exhibit. I have a brochure!"

"Oh, that sounds fun!" Ma says. "Lily, remember you had the toy penguin when you were little? You named it Tux."

Lily rolls her eyes. "That was Anna, Ma."

I frown. It's true that I owned the penguin first, but Lily had adored it much more than I had. "But you tied a scrap of black cloth around his neck to give him a real bow tie."

She rolls her eyes again. "You never took care of your toys, even though you got them first." There's no way to win with her.

"I have it!" Michael comes out of his room, brochure in hand and something tucked under his arm. "Look who else I found." He holds up the matted gray-and-black lump.

Lily and I shout in unison. "TUX!"

Darling Harbour is teeming with stroller-pushing families and tourists, dressed in everything from T-shirts, shorts, and flip-flops to light sweaters and flowing saris. Even though it's pretty much the middle of winter, the Sydney sun is relentless. The heat gets trapped in the netting of my thick black hair so that the top of my head is hot to the touch.

Ma, of course, carries a dark purple umbrella to shield herself from the sun. She used to make Lily and me carry them as well, saying the harsh Australian sun is poisonous to the body, but neither of us could tolerate the embarrassment. She relented eventually, but she doesn't shy away from making comments on the melanin levels of our skin.

We join the masses queueing in the sliver of shade near the aquarium's entrance. Michael stands quietly, Ma's iPhone in hand and a rather beat-up-looking Tux clutched in his arms. Lily has study notes in her hand, drilling herself on formulas and theorems. I wish I had her level of diligence when it came to studying. I shield my eyes, trying to gauge the wait. It's strange to think that thousands of other people woke up this morning and thought the aquarium was a good idea.

My phone pings.

Hey, are you coming in??

Rory. There's a sharp tug in my chest.

Not today. We're having a family day 🐬

What are you doing?

We're at the aquarium.

I resist adding a dolphin emoji for fear of being too childish.

Fun.

Unless we get eaten.

That escalated quickly.

"Anna, don't hold the phone so close. You'll go blind from the radiation." Ma still comes from the world where televisions emit gamma rays. We've tried to explain that new technology is safe, but I can't tell if Ma forgets or doesn't believe us.

Lily and Michael are on their screens, their noses practically touching the glass. There's no use pointing this out, so I just tuck the phone back into my pocket and stare ahead.

We finally get to the front of the queue and order tickets.

"That'll be $115.72," says the young girl behind the counter. My heart sinks when I hear the figure, Baba's pained face comes to mind. It's a lot of money for a single afternoon.

"Don't worry. Mommy's treat for you. Study hard and be good, okay." Ma pulls out two crisp one-hundred-dollar bills from the fanny pack strapped to her waist.

I can see Michael's eyes shining. I give Ma what I hope is a grateful smile, but there's a deep-seated uneasiness in me.

"It wasn't even our choice to come," Lily murmurs under her breath, but Ma doesn't hear. She's right, though, and that edgy sensation tingles stronger. *But we're out and about like a family.*

A NORMAL family.

"Smile." The photographer at the entrance catches us by surprise, the white flash blinding us. "Gorgeous," he says without looking and ushers us into the aquarium. We're swallowed up by the inky-blue darkness of an imitation sea.

Despite the size of the crowds, we're sucked into the magic of the experience. There's something creepy and surreal about walking through a glass tunnel surrounded by toothy predators. I watch Michael watching the jellyfish. He is absolutely mesmerized, bathed in their neon-pink glow, his brow high, his mouth hanging slightly open. What's going on in his mind? Is he imagining the colors and tracing the lines to draw? I don't think that's how kids approach art; I don't think that's how anyone worth their salt approaches art.

I sidle up beside him in the semi-darkness. "They're pretty cool, aren't they?"

He nods. "They're like plastic bags but not as sad."

"I'm going to find a way to get you into the art program," I tell him suddenly. "I promise."

He shrugs. "It's no big deal. Miss Holloway is doing a music class with us now. We're making flutes from bamboo."

I have to laugh. Miss Holloway is definitely not shy about inviting trouble into her students' lives.

"Come on!" Lily materializes beside us, tugging on my sleeve. "The penguin show is about to start."

We take our seats in the amphitheater-style exhibit. This is meant to be the showstopper. The lights dim and out trot the little tuxedoed stars in a shimmer of pastel lights and camera clicks. One by one, they plunge into the sparkling waters, like Olympic swimmers leaping off their blocks. Lily has tucked her study notes away to watch the penguins in their underwater acrobatic show. Ma is humming along and smiling, her eyes as bright and shining as Michael's. She claps the loudest when the stars take their bow. She turns and smiles again, and I see the creases and crow's-feet around her eyes and the strands of silver in her hair. But behind it, I can't help but think of her as a giggling schoolgirl.

I often wonder what Ma was like as a child. Was she up and down, like she gets now? Was she angry or happy? There are two sides to everything. Every thought, every gesture, has a good and a bad. Most of the pictures I've seen of her in Hong Kong, she's all serious and scowling. But there are one or two where she's all brightness and sunshine.

I'm glad that today she is the latter.

"So cute!" she squeals. "Who knew that penguins were so graceful?"

After the show, the lights come back on and the keepers go about feeding their charges some bits of fish, rewards for a job well done. We all crowd around the tank, murmuring and holding up our phones like paparazzi.

"Take a photo. Come, come, Anna." Ma poses by the tank, an awkward half smile plastered on her face.

"Smile, Ma. Like with teeth," I tell her. She flashes the pearly whites for a microsecond, but it's just long enough. *Perfect.* She looks radiant and happy, pointing to the tank like a billboard ad.

"Oh wow. I think there's a baby over there. Look." Lily jabs her finger toward a far corner of the exhibit.

"What? Where?" Ma leans forward suddenly, before I can warn her. *Thunk.* "Aiyo!" She clutches her forehead, her eyes squinty and mouth pursed like she's just sucked on a lemon.

I clasp my hand over my mouth. "Ma! Be careful. There's glass there." I rush to her side, half laughing, half crying. I rap gently against the barrier. In the dimly lit exhibit, with the pristine whiteness of the penguins' ice kingdom and magic of the show, it's not hard to forget that it's all an illusion.

"Aiyo. I was too keen to see the baby." Ma pouts like a child, and I can't stifle my teasing smile as I stroke her arm in sympathy.

A good day. This is a good day. My mother, all smiles and light. I need to remember this moment, so I can replay it later in slow-motion memory when I need to.

On the way out, we stop by the gift shop. I spot a large emperor penguin with a snow-white belly and yellow chin.

"I think Tux needs a girlfriend," I say. I take the old battered

Tux from Michael and hold the two penguins side by side, making them dance like water acrobats.

Lily makes a face. "He's old and dirty. What girl is going to want him?"

"A beautiful and sensitive darling, looking for someone smart and wise." I cradle our old beloved soft toy against my chest, protecting him from my sister's harsh judgment. "Love's not just about youth and good looks, you know."

"Is that why you're into Rory?" Lily lets the comment slip casually, with just a sly twitch of her upper lip.

"I am *not*!" The denial is overly loud and forceful, and Lily smirks knowingly. The heat in my face is unbearable, and I quickly set down the now-offending penguin girl and stomp outside, Tux in tow.

I can hear my sister chuckling behind me. And even if she's laughing at me, that's okay. Because at least we're all together.

Chapter Sixteen
Sap6 Luk6

August

"WHAT ARE WE DOING HERE?" I ask.

In another earth-shattering record attempt at being normal, Rory and I have managed an "official date." Since Baba has stopped letting me come to the restaurant, we haven't seen each other much. We text and chat a lot, but it doesn't feel like we're a real couple. For starters, we're not a couple in front of a group of friends—you know, the type that sit in each other's laps and drink out of the same soda can, while everyone gossips or talks about their weekend plans.

So I was kind of stunned when Rory asked if I'd go somewhere with him on a Saturday night. The Jade Palace has a function on, so Baba canceled delivery and actually gave Rory the night off.

We're in the Eastern Suburbs, at the Entertainment Quarter in Moore Park. I've only been in this area once before when I went to

Bondi Beach as a kid. Ma screeched about the topless sunbathers and Australian values. We haven't been back since.

Rory looks nervous as he hands me a paper printout. I read the ticket. *Roller derby.*

"Really?" I'm totally confused. I've seen *Whip It*, girls pushing and bruising each other on skates, but I didn't think it was an actual thing here.

"I thought it'd be a bit of fun." I know there's much more to it, but I don't press.

Rory takes my hand and leads me to the queue. I haven't been "out" in a long time, what with school, Ma, and the restaurant stuff dominating my life. I feel a long-forgotten tingle of excitement and anticipation.

"Oh my gosh, you made it! I thought you had to work!" A cute blond girl in short pigtails rushes over and hugs Rory. I seethe a little and watch him hug her back, his arms wrapping familiarly around her curvy body in its short black tank top.

"I got the day off." Rory turns to me. "This is my girlfriend, Anna. Anna, this is my sister, Stacey."

Two words I was so not expecting. *Girlfriend. Sister.* And now, Rory's nervousness makes sense. *This is his sister, oh my!* He'd never really mentioned her except that she was the one he talked to first before going to the hospital. I pull myself up and try to make my face look friendly, presentable, like a nice girlfriend. "Nice to meet you." I smile, conscious of how many teeth I'm showing.

"Oh my god, Anna! Finally! It's so good to meet you. I've heard so much about you." Stacey is friendly and sweet, and I like her straightaway.

I immediately calm down and lose some of my self-consciousness. "Nice to meet you, too." I offer my hand awkwardly.

"Oh my god. Come here, you," Stacey gushes, and steps forward and hugs me. I like her smell, soap and salt. She pulls away and then scrutinizes her brother.

"Are you *sure* you're okay to be here?" Her bubbliness has switched to earnest concern.

"I'm fine, I promise. A hundred percent."

"Okay, give me another hug." They embrace quickly but fiercely. "Daria's here with some friends, go find them. I'll see you in there. It's so awesome to meet you." She waves with both hands as she runs off. Only then do I notice the rest of her outfit, shorts and thick kneepads.

"Is she . . . is she part of the team?" I ask.

Rory grins proudly. "Yep. She's been competing three years now. Last year they toured the state. Gives Mom a heart attack when she comes home with the bruises, but she loves it."

"Wow." This is a side of Rory I haven't seen. Happy and excited. I really like what I see. "She seems awesome."

"To be honest, I was a bit nervous. I haven't really had a girl-friend since . . ." He trails off and I nod. I'm honored, actually. And that word *girlfriend* sends electric shock waves all through my system.

I grab his hand and we link fingers. The queue moves forward, and we're finally inside. The Hordern Pavilion is a giant hall with a slick polished concrete floor. There are stadium seats set up, but no one's really in them; instead they're milling around along the sides of the ring, which is a circle marked out with white tape. The track is flat with a few orange cones scattered about. It doesn't look nearly as intimidating or hard core as what I'd seen in the movies.

We find Daria, who turns out to be Stacey's girlfriend. She's with a few guys who are drinking beer out of clear plastic cups.

Rory gestures. "You want one?" I give a tiny nod. I've never had a drink in my life. But this is what I wanted, *normal teenager*, right?

The lights dim and some people finally head up into the bleachers. We find a spot on the floor close to the track. I take a sip of my beer—it's flat and a tiny bit warm, I think, but it's not too bad. I take a bigger gulp and people-watch. Most of the crowd looks about college-aged, a few slightly older, but all in all it's a pretty mixed group. I guess I expected goths and emos or some kind of deep alternative vibe, but it's more hipster casual cool. No one's all into themselves or super drunk, and while I spot more than a few selfie snaps, it all seems to be in good fun.

"Having a good time?" Rory cuts into my thoughts. He lays his hands on my shoulders, and I have to crane my head up to look at him. He gives me a wink and a smile. I lean against him and sip my beer.

"Ladies and gentlemen, let's get ready to rumble." The crowd roars as the poppy tunes start to play. Two lines of skaters come out, and everyone goes wild as the spotlights trail after them. The visitors are from Canberra and the locals clap them enthusiastically.

The Sydney team is introduced, and they skate in relatively straight formations, making a couple of turns and twists around the cones, nothing super fancy, but the crowd cheer them on like it's the Olympics. Stacey catches my eye and winks under her glittery skull helmet. I smile back. She really is awesome.

The announcer introduces the teams and explains the rules (sort of). A whistle blows, and they're off. I try to keep up, watching the girls push and roll along the track. There's some shoving and a couple of girls roll out of the lines and are penalized. It's fast, but not blinding, no one loses any teeth or gets a black eye, but the energy is fierce and strong. I'm shouting and clamoring with the group, jumping up and down and screaming my head off when I think we've scored a point.

Stacey is small and fast and really good. I recognize the intense look of concentration on her face—I've seen it in Rory.

At the end of the first period, the score is tied. Stacey skates over to our group and throws herself into her girlfriend's arms.

"You're incredible, babe," Daria says.

"Nice work, sis," Rory says, and they exchange a high five.

"You're really, really good," I add enthusiastically. Stacey beams and takes a sip from Daria's beer before she grabs me by the wrist and pulls me away. I'm too stunned to protest.

"Bathroom. Back in a bit," she cries over her shoulder, and leads me out to the hall.

Stacey threads expertly through the crowds. "That's Sheryl and that's Rachel. She's our captain, been on the team for fifteen years." She points to a brawny, tattooed girl still in her helmet. "She's got more battle scars than all of us put together." She still has a firm hold of my wrist and I can feel my pulse throbbing against the pads of her fingers. I'm not sure where she's leading me until she pushes open a door that says GIRLS' LOCKER ROOM.

"I gotta piss," she announces, and finally lets go of my arm to go into a stall.

"So my brother says you used to live in Gosford?" she calls out from behind the door.

"Um, yeah. About six years ago." I turn to the mirrors, feeling awkward as I hear the stream of urine hitting the bowl.

"Uh-huh." Stacey, on the other hand, is clearly not fazed by this situation at all. The girls we passed were in various states of undress, bits, boobs, and bobs all hanging freely as they gab away, nothing like the girls at school hunched into their towels after PE.

I will myself to relax. "We live in Ashfield now," I say.

"That's so cool! I love it there." I can hear her enthusiasm above the roar of the flush. She yanks open the door and catches my eye in our reflection. "Daria took me to the best dumpling restaurant there. Gosh, what was it called?"

It's my turn to be excited. "Shanghai Knights?"

"Yes! That was it!" Her eyes light up with delight. "They were so juicy and plump. Like nothing I had ever tasted."

"I took Rory there. He loved it." I'm kind of proud, like I want to prove to her that I'm a good girlfriend.

"No way, that's awesome. Rory's always been so damn fussy. Like, needs to be in control, you know?"

I'm surprised by this. "He always seems really chilled out to me," I say honestly.

"Yeah, well, he's come a long way." She's quiet for a bit as she suds her hands, and we watch the soap go down the drain. "Can I be honest with you?"

I nod.

"You're so different from anyone he used to hang out with. That's a good thing!" she insists when we both see my crestfallen expression. "No, that's what I mean. He's more talkative than he's been in a while. Relaxed and happy. He never hangs out with people his own age. You're good for him."

"He's good for me," I say. "He—he's helped me a lot."

Stacey nods. "He's a sweet boy. Big heart. I always worry he'll get hurt again. I didn't realize how much he was holding in . . . he never said anything about what he was feeling inside."

She drops her gaze, abruptly shy. "I should have done more. I always thought it was my fault."

"It's not your fault," I say quickly. "You didn't know."

Out of nowhere, she pulls me into a tight hug. "I just want what's best for him. I care about him so much."

I find myself wrapping my arms around her. She's sticky with sweat, but it makes me feel closer to her somehow. "I care about him, too."

She pulls away and her smile could light up a football stadium. "Let's get back," she says, and takes me by the hand again.

Rory looks a bit relieved when we return to the group. "There you are."

"Hey." I'm happy to see him and fold into his embrace.

"I like her," Stacey tells her brother, and gives me a wink. "Don't mess it up."

"I won't." Rory pulls me up against his side as she heads off. "You okay?" He looks worried. "Was she tough on you?"

"She's great," I say. The encounter had been strange but reassuring. I know where Rory gets that raw honesty from. It's so nice and refreshing to hear people say what they mean and talk about their worries, anxieties, and feelings.

Maybe one day, I'll do the same.

I feel myself blushing and push against the bridge of my glasses. I've got all sorts of warm fuzzies inside me; maybe that's the beer.

The whistle blows for the second period. Things are more subdued this time around, including the crowd. My cup is empty. I'm not wobbly or anything, but my whole body feels like a toasty marshmallow and I'm smiling a lot more than I can remember doing in a long time. Rory hugs me from behind, resting his chin on the top of my head.

The other team pulls ahead at the final minute. Stacey tries to make a last-ditch break for it, but she's horribly boxed out. The whistle blows and the match is over. The Canberra team hoot and holler and high-five their victory. It's disappointing, and the fever of the crowd has died a little bit, but everyone seems to have had a good time.

Stacey huffs over, and Daria hugs her, sweat and all.

"We should have won," she pouts.

"Next time, babe. You did good out there."

"Really good," Rory adds.

Stacey's eyes shift a little. "How are you doing, little bro? You good?" She looks worried again. I recognize the undying love of a big sister.

"Ace good heart, I promise," Rory says. And they exchange a look that I know has some sort of coded meaning. Stacey relaxes a bit, but I can tell there's still a bit of an edge. Rory nods toward her arm. "How's the bruising?"

Her eyes light up again. "Oh, so awesome. Mom's gonna dig this one." She twists her right arm around so we can see where a giant red welt has formed on her tricep.

"So where are we headed? Newtown? The Bank?" one of the guys asks. "You guys coming?" He raises an eyebrow at us.

I crane my neck up to look at Rory. His gaze is heavy-lidded and adoring, his hair kind of sticking to his forehead. He shrugs to say, *Up to you.* Stacey gnaws on her lower lip, and I can't tell how she wants me to reply.

I feel the weight of my body. Maybe it's the beer, or maybe it's just the weariness of the entire day.

"I think we'll go home," I say.

Chapter Seventeen

Sap6 cat1

Hey, beautiful.

I smile at my phone. It's Rory. It's been like this since roller derby, all lovey-dovey like some Hollywood rom-com. Nothing *happened* afterward; he dropped me off after the event and gave me a reasonably chaste kiss. But something was different. I don't see him lots, but I feel him with me, all the time. It leaves me warm and sated inside. I feel really . . . safe.

I get it now. All the cheesiness of the love songs. The absurdity of sonnets and poetry. They all mean something. Because I have Rory.

Ma's still been erratic at home. She's cleaning again and not sleeping much. But maybe that's okay. I mean, a little bit of insomnia never really hurt anyone, right?

I look at his message again. What do I write back? *Hey, handsome?* Is that too corny?

"Can you flirt quietly, please? I'm trying to study," Lily scolds from behind me.

I roll my eyes, but she can't see. "Sorry, Your Highness. And I'm not *flirting*."

"Whatever." She waits a beat before saying, "Tell Rory I said hi."

I turn around this time to stick my tongue out at her, but she doesn't look up.

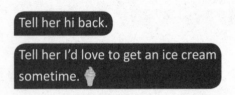

My sister says hi.

Tell her hi back.

Tell her I'd love to get an ice cream sometime. 🍦

"I'm going to bed," Lily proclaims too loudly. She makes overly exaggerated movements of turning off the main light and pulling the covers over her head.

I sigh. I could keep my lamp on, but I know I won't get anywhere with my problem sets.

I should go. Lily has a test tomorrow.

Aww.

And then.

I really missed you this week.

His words melt me and I'm a puddly mess. They're not butterflies anymore; they're gooey, squishy gummy worms. I'm writing back but it's really hard—my fingers are shaking as I type.

I missed you, too.

Good night, Anna Apple.

The bright light slices through the darkness and sleep. I could have been dreaming, I don't know, or maybe I was just out to the world. But the light is on now, and I have to be awake.

"Get up! Both of you! How dare you both be asleep when your poor mother is up? What ingrates you are! Get up and show some respect."

I suppress a groan as I try to yank myself out of slumber. *What time is it?* The windows are still pitch-black, so I know it's not yet morning. I resist the urge to peek at my phone, because I know that's inviting trouble.

"Get up, both of you."

"I'm up." My voice is scratchy and hoarse, but I don't try to clear it. I know I was heard.

"Get up! Now!" Ma is reaching over my bunk, and I know she's shaking Lily awake. My heart pounds, but I don't protest. I don't stop her. I just make myself sit up, shoving my head in my hands. *It had been such a good day yesterday.*

Lily moans and the mattress squeaks above me as Ma shakes harder. Poor Lily is a deeper sleeper and slow to rise, which incites Ma's rage.

"Get up now. You sleep easy in your bed, not a care in the world, and make your mother suffer. You ungrateful, spoiled brat. Get up and answer your mother, now."

This is not the first time Ma has stormed into our room in the middle of the night. And it likely won't be the last.

"Ma, she has a test tomorrow." I sound so weak, like cornered prey pleading for its life. *There's no point.*

"Test? She doesn't need to study. Forget school. Don't go. Lily, you think you're so much better than me and Anna? Because you go to a fancy scholarship school and you know so much more than your poor uneducated mother, huh?"

Lily bursts into tears.

But crying means she's awake, so Ma draws away. I hear the bed squeaking, and I know my sister is struggling to sit up through her tears. I want to reach a hand out, to let her know I'm here, but I know better than to show any outward solidarity with my sister.

It will just enrage Ma more.

"How come you two only talk to each other in English, huh? You think your teachers are better than your ma? Tai2 m4 hei2 ngo5." *You don't rate me.*

I bow and shake my head. "No, Ma."

"Ma, it's three twenty in the morning." Lily has looked at her phone. "I have a test tomorrow. Please."

"So? You have a test and that makes you queen? I am your mother, and I deserve some respect around here." She raises a palm again and moves forward. The springs squeak, and I know Lily

180

is trying to move out of the way. There are a few muffled thuds and a sharp cry, so I know Ma's blows have landed but probably across a blanket.

"Ma, mou5 daa2 keoi5 la1." *Don't hit her.* There's little I can do to protect my sister, but I still try. I pull at Ma's nightshirt to steer her away.

"You're both always together. Ganging up on me. What rotten, spoiled children." She flails her arms at me, but she doesn't try to attack. She knows I'm stronger, but she also knows I never fight back. "What did I do in a past life to deserve such horrible children? Which gods did I anger? What wrongs have I done?" Her voice stays low, despite her fury, and I know why: Even with this amount of rage, she doesn't want to wake Michael.

And now Ma is crying and sobbing, her arm thrown over her face to muffle the cries. I approach her carefully, like I would a wounded tiger, hands in front of me. Ma screams and picks up the nearest object on my desk and hurls it against the far wall.

Crash. I wince and watch my beloved Bluetooth headphones crack, bits of plastic flying as they hit the ground. Part of me cracks with them, but I choke down the hurt and rage. *I can use normal headphones*, I tell myself. *No big deal.*

But I do a quick mental check that my laptop and phone are out of reach before I go back to my mother.

"Ma, deoi3 m4 zyu6." *I'm sorry.* "Ngo5 co3." *I'm wrong.* "Ngo5 m4 jing1 goi1 gam3 mou4 jung6." *I shouldn't be so worthless.* "I shouldn't make my mother so angry," I finish.

The words come easily to me, soft and soothing, melodic almost.

It's taken my whole sixteen years to perfect the sincerity and trust I need for them to work. It's not foolproof; she'll sometimes push me away even more, accuse me of lying. But I know it appeals to her best self, the knowns in her life where filial piety and respect are paramount.

Lily hates that I appease her in this way. She used to scoff or even yell at me, tell me to stop, that it isn't right. But slowly, over time, she saw the tactic worked. And as much as she can never bring herself to do it, she lets me cower. Offer myself as the sacrifice to my mother's rage.

This time, my humbleness works. Ma is sobbing and sinks into the chair. I take her worn hand in mine and stroke the back of it, and she doesn't pull away. I don't hug her, not yet. "It's okay," I tell her. "It's okay. I'm sorry. It's okay."

Now she reaches for me and she cries. And I know it's over. I feel her strong arms wrap around me and the tears roll freely down my cheeks. We both cry and sob, like orphaned cubs clinging to each other.

She pulls away and looks into my eyes. "Anna. You're a good daughter. Ma is sorry, too." I purse my lips and nod, the tears blurring my vision, but there's no mistaking her sad smile. She reaches up and brushes my eyes with her thumb. The fury is gone, but I can see her real misery.

She is always the worst victim of her own rage.

Ma gets up and goes to Lily. She reaches for my sister's arm. "Do well on your test tomorrow, okay? You're a smart girl." She gives it a quick squeeze and leaves the room. I wait until I hear her footsteps disappear into her room before I go to switch off the light and shut the door.

"Lily, you okay?" I ask in the dark.

Lily is still crying, loud sniffling and snotty wails. I hoist myself up onto the top bunk and cradle her bony body. Her hair falls like a fluffy black cloud in my lap.

"Shhh. It's okay," I whisper. She sobs quietly and I hold her, rocking her softly and stroking her back.

"Why is she like this?" Lily whispers. "She ruins everything."

"She's not herself. What she becomes, that's not her." I rub her shoulders in small circles, inhaling her scent. It's coconut.

"This was worse than before. She's never broken stuff before," Lily says.

This isn't entirely true. Ma, in her previous fits of rage, might throw a mug or plate. But she's frugal at heart and has never broken anything of value. Like not waking Michael—it's how I know there's still a leash on her rage.

Lily is right. This was worse, but then she seemed better. *Maybe it will be okay?*

"She's just upset. You know how she gets." I try not to worry.

"We can't keep doing this. It's not fair."

There's a gentle knock on our door. Lily and I stiffen as the door opens slowly.

Baba's large silhouette takes up most of the doorway.

"Ba." I lean forward, squinting at the light. Lily stays wrapped up in her blanket cocoon. My father stands, half in and half out of the room, uncertain of his place.

I chew my lip. I want *him* to tell us it'll be okay. That he'll talk to Ma and make her see sense. I want him to promise that this won't happen again. I want him to tell us that he'll protect us, show us how to avoid the bad signs that lead to Ma's fits. Because he has to be the adult. He's our dad. He has to know the answer.

Instead he sighs heavily and says, "We can all go back to sleep now." And he pulls the door shut behind him.

I cower in the dark, pressed against my sister's form. We don't say a word, and eventually I can hear Lily's soft snoring.

Baba is wrong. I can't sleep at all. So I lie wide awake by myself, watching the dark.

The next morning brings scents of sweet sugar and spice.

Ma is humming merrily. She smiles warmly, steaming buns for breakfast like nothing happened. I don't return the smile; my stomach is tangled, but my feet move automatically toward the kitchen counter. I'm wary as I approach her, but my body is screaming, *It's okay, these are all good signs.*

"Sweet lotus-paste buns." She lifts off the giant wok cover and pillows of steam waft toward the ceiling. "Your favorite when you were a little girl. Do you remember we used to queue up outside that shop in Haymarket and the aunty gave it to you fresh in the bag?"

She's reminiscing, her gaze lifted, her thoughts following the steam skyward. I don't say anything as I pull the milk out of the fridge and look for a glass.

Michael comes into the kitchen in his pajamas. His eyes light up when he sees the wok. "Steam bun for breakfast?"

"*Half* of one," I say automatically. "So much sugar in the morning, you'll feel sick." I'm reaching into the wok to grab one, gripping the edges of the paper so I don't get burned. "But hurry up and get ready first. This has to cool."

"Okay." His bare feet slap against the tiled floor as he gallops down the hall, pausing outside our bedroom door. "Lily, hei2 san1!" *Get up.* "There's buns for breakfast."

There's no answer.

Ma replaces the lid on the wok and comes to stand beside me. She's so little, coming just past my shoulders. I remember when I tracked my growth against her body, first coming to her armpits, then her nose, until finally, I could peek past the top of her head. She reaches up and around my neck and pulls me down into a one-armed hug. Her grip is strong. I stiffen my back and limbs, refusing to give in to her proffered blanket of comfort.

"You're a good girl, Anna. A good daughter. Maa1 sek3 faan1." *I kiss you again.* "I'm not angry anymore."

Her words have a cathartic effect on me, like soft feathers stroking my cheek. She's offering peace and love and while my stomach is still in tangles and my lack of sleep hangs heavily from my eyelids, I'm overwhelmed with relief.

Slowly, carefully, I hug her back. She smells like Pond's cold cream.

When I finally pull away, my heart feels lighter, but the gnawing discomfort in my stomach won't go away. Her eyes are wet and shining, but there's no hate in them. I don't know what's happened from last night to this morning, but she's like a whole new person.

Lily comes storming out of our room, a gale blowing through our kitchen. She blusters past without a hello, good morning, or goodbye, heading straight for the door.

"Wait, Lily." I run and reach out to grab her arm. She turns her head and her eyes tell me everything.

Traitor.

It takes no force for her to shake herself free, and she's out of the apartment in an instant, the heavy metal door slamming shut so hard that the walls shake. I'm left stunned and on the verge of tears.

My limbs move, zombielike, and carry me back to the kitchen.

"Eat quickly, or they'll get cold," Ma calls from the kitchen.

I'm on autopilot as I sit down at the table. Michael comes to sit beside me, dressed for school now.

His little brow knits with confusion. "Why is Lily so angry?"

"You know how your sister gets. Gwaai1 zai2, *good boy*, eat your breakfast or it'll get cold." Ma coaxes the bun in front of her youngest, all smiles and sweetness. She doesn't mention Lily's outburst because that would mean admitting she did something to make her daughter upset. Michael eats heartily. I try to follow suit, but it tastes like ash and dust. I choke it down as best I can.

Baba emerges from the bedroom. His eyes are bloodshot from lack of sleep and his features are pulled tight. He doesn't take a bun but pours himself a cup of tea and sifts through yesterday's discarded paper.

"I don't think I can come home tonight." He speaks generally to the table, and his eyes stay glued to the page. "There's too much admin I have to catch up on."

A sodden lump of bun is caught in my throat as I watch them sit in silence, not looking at each other. They won't even talk about what happened. My father won't try to fix anything. He's just running away.

Disappointment tastes like chalky lotus bean.

Chapter Eighteen
Sap6 baat3

Good luck today.

The text I send Lily is pitiful. I want to tell her I'm still on her side. It doesn't help that my head is too foggy and my limbs feel like heavy weights hanging from my body.

> *"Earth, my likeness,*
> *Though you look so impassive, ample and spheric*
>   *there."*

A boy in class is reading from *Leaves of Grass*. Well, trying to anyway. He has none of Rory's dramatic flair and theatrical flourish. He is robotic, stilted, stone.

Mr. Murray is dragging us through more Whitman this term. I'd received just a pass on my rewritten *Macbeth* essay. It had been a bit of a lead balloon. After everything I'd been through, after all Rory's coaching, a pass felt like finding pink mold on good cheese.

I stifle a yawn and try to force myself back to the droning voice that butchers Whitman.

> *"For an athlete is enamor'd of me, and I of him,*
> *But toward him there is something fierce and*
> *terrible in me eligible to burst forth,*
> *I dare not tell it in words, not even in these songs."*

"Excellent, Lincoln, you may sit down." The boy slumps in his chair, relieved of his duties. "So, what is Whitman saying? What is he hinting at?"

"You always hurt the ones you love?" Wei ventures. I can't help being impressed. She's always been smart, even though I can tell she tries to hide it. Connie can't stand the idea of anyone being better than her at anything.

"That Whitman's a loony tune," Connie offers, and a few girls snicker. Wei looks uncomfortable.

Mr. Murray cocks his head. "Interesting take. Care to elaborate, Ms. Zhong?"

"He's talking about something terrible bursting forth. I mean, we all have our dark sides and bad days, but he sounds like there's something not right up there. Like, stalker tendencies much?"

"There are many who hypothesize that Whitman may have suffered bipolar disorder," Mr. Murray adds.

"See? I was right." Connie crosses her arms in smug triumph. Wei is staring at her desk, her hair shrouding her face like a curtain.

"It's not a surprise," Lincoln interjects. "Many modern creators and heroes have mental illnesses. Like Robin Williams. He had depression."

"Or Stephen Fry!" I say. "He's bipolar."

"Kendall Jenner, even," someone else says. "She talked about it on her Insta."

Mr. Murray lets the conversation go as we offer up celebrities from all areas. Connie has her lips turned in a pout, her arms still crossed defiantly.

The bell rings and we all file out. I catch Wei looking at me. I wonder if she wants to ask something and almost go over to her.

"Hey, earth to Wei." Connie's expression is still sour and cross as she tips her head toward the door. "You ready?"

Wei ducks her head and scuttles past while Connie scowls.

I gather my book and belongings and head to my locker. My phone buzzes in my pocket. Lily.

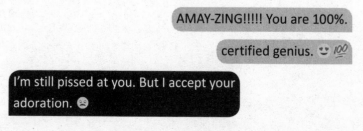

I scored 99% on the exam! 😵

I can't believe it, but of course I can. I'm so proud of her. Even with the worst, she can still be the best.

AMAY-ZING!!!!! You are 100%.

certified genius. 😍 💯

I'm still pissed at you. But I accept your adoration. 😩

Chapter Nineteen
Sap6 gau2

September

Hey, beautiful. 😉

I'm too tired and emotionally wrung out to be charmed by Rory's text. So rather than the perfect witty response, I opt for a direct answer.

Just finished last period. Tons of homework to do. 😫

Go outside.

Outside? What? I slam my locker door and head for the door. It's peak exit hour, and I have to fight my way through the loitering crowds.

When I'm outside, my jaw drops.

Rory is standing outside the school gate, leaning casually against a shiny black convertible. He's donned aviators and is sporting a leather jacket, carrying a single red rose.

He looks hot!

My life right now is a drool emoji.

I'm too surprised to make words or exclamations. My legs are barely moving, and I almost crash into someone hurrying past.

"Where—where did you get the car? I know my dad's not paying you that much."

"Birthday present." He stoops to kiss me but I'm still too stunned to react. This results in him sticking out his lower lip and presenting the rose. "I thought it'd be a nice surprise."

My sensibility returns and I take the rose. "No. It's wonderful— It's, wow. I just can't— Wait, when was your birthday?" I frown.

"Doesn't matter." He pecks me on the forehead and goes to open the passenger door. "Come on, get in."

I clamber in and wrestle with the seat belt as Rory goes to the other side. Just as I feel the satisfying click of metal against plastic, I glimpse something in the rearview mirror.

Connie Zhong is staring, her mouth wide. I catch myself grinning and memorizing the look on her face.

"You good?" Rory's in the driver's seat, hands on the wheel. His hair flops over his sunglasses and his half smile tumbles my heart.

"Peachy."

"All right then, Anna Peachy."

And we're off.

*　　*　　*

The shadows stretch behind us and I put up a hand to shield my eyes from the sun. The wind whips my hair, my ponytail a thick, punishing flail against my neck. And the noise is all-consuming—I don't know how the movies make convertibles seem sexy, but actually sitting in the leather bucket seat is anything but.

I brush my hair aside for the umpteenth time and steal a glance at Rory. His grin is bigger than the Cheshire Cat's, and I can tell he has some ultra-cool soundtrack playing in his head as he drives. I wonder what it would be—a pop tune or some unknown indie number? Or his typical female power ballad?

"You didn't tell me it was your birthday," I try shouting above the wind.

"What?"

"I said, I didn't know it was your birthday." My words are lost by the rumble of a passing motorcycle coming up behind us.

"It's awesome, isn't it?" Rory is all boyish jubilance, and there's no point trying to eke out a conversation. I nod and flash what I hope he thinks is an exhilarated smile.

We join the lanes of cars crossing the Harbour Bridge. I crane my neck skyward to watch the thick iron lattice pass overhead.

"Where are we going?" I try again.

Rory shakes his head. "Hang on, I can't hear you." He hits a button on the dash. The soft top whirs and slides into place and the windows wind their way up until we're sealed inside.

With the top up and the windows in place, the space feels tiny and safe. The roar of the wind and rush of cars is gone, and it's just me in my head and all of my unanswered questions.

"Better?"

I manage a nod. "Yeah, better." And before I can gather my thoughts, Rory suddenly reaches over and brings my hands to his lips. The feel of him kissing my knuckles shorts my logical circuits and I'm speechless again, just noticing the little jolts and sensations of his warm lips, slightly chapped so I can just feel the soft pinpricks against my skin.

"Where are we going?" I finally manage to retrace one of my original lines of thought, while Rory traces one of the lines of my palm.

"It's a secret." He grins playfully and despite the tingling sensations in my stomach, I don't like that he's being so evasive.

"Why didn't you tell me it was your birthday?" I pull my hand away.

He sighs deeply. "You didn't ask?" He says it like someone guessing at the right answer.

I frown. "I knew you *had* one. I just assumed you would have told me if it was going to be . . . this week?"

He sighs again. "I'm telling you now. Why does it matter?"

I cross my arms. "I just feel like I should know these things."

"Okay. Tell you what." He grins wickedly. "Next time I have a birthday, I'll tell you."

I roll my eyes, but I can't suppress my smile. "I'm serious, though."

Rory pulls over and kills the engine. We're in a cul-de-sac in some residential neighborhood north of the bridge. He leans over and takes my hand again.

"Anna." His tone is serious. "The reason I didn't mention my birthday is because the day I was going to jump, that was—that was my birthday."

My heart drops to my stomach. "Oh." I feel like a heel. "I didn't realize."

"Two years ago, I was in the pits around my birthday. So I'm kind of mindful now that it's not a great time for me."

I frown. "It's a big deal, Rory. It's a milestone."

He shrugs. "That's what the parentals said. Hence, the over-compensating present, I guess." He turns away. "I always feel bad. They try so hard and I'm such a shit son."

"But you're not!" I exclaim. "You're a wonderful son, and I'm sure they love you so much."

"I know." He hangs his head. "I feel like I'm letting them down, you know. By not having some big party or something."

"Why *don't* you have a party?" I ask. "What about your friends?"

He gives a sad laugh. "What friends? You mean Gary and that lot?"

"I mean . . ." I struggle for the words. "I just assumed you had other people . . ."

The shake of his head slices into my core. I see the loneliness in his eyes. Rory is always so likable and put-together. Everyone at the restaurant loves him, staff and customers alike. This is a side of him I haven't seen before.

I take his hand, but he doesn't look at me. I bring his fingers to my cheek and finally he looks up.

He closes the distance between us and kisses me. And this time, I kiss him back, and he lets out a guttural moan and deepens the kiss.

I try to shove everything out of my mind and focus on the feel of his lips, his large strong hands cradling my sides, tangling in my hair. I search for my own soundtrack, swelling violins and rocking crescendo.

I kiss harder, press against him more, willing my mind to quiet, to just make out with a hot guy like I'm supposed to.

Somehow we're in the back seat. I feel his tongue on my skin, his breath against my neck, a hot and wet sliding. My whole body is buzzing, emanating from my chest.

"Your boob is buzzing," Rory mumbles against my skin. He's right. My phone is going off in my blazer pocket.

I pull it out, thinking it's just a low battery warning. But it's a missed call from Lily. I go to put it on silent, but then the text message comes through.

Ma is gone. And I think she took Michael.

I get out of the car, my fingers trembling as I punch at the screen to call my sister back. Lily picks up on the first ring.

"What's going on? Where's Ma? Where are you?" I'm rapid-firing thoughts and questions like a machine gun.

"Anna, breathe! Just breathe." Lily sounds like she's on the verge of tears, but she's still issuing orders. And I know she needs me to be the calm, reasonable one, the big sister.

I inhale deeply and try again. "Okay, what happened?" My phone beeps. Low battery. I groan.

"I came home and Ma's phone was on the counter. Michael's school had called."

"Why is his school calling?"

"I was getting to that!" I can sense her eye roll from the clicking of her tongue. "I broke into her phone, listened to the voice message, and it was Ms. Thompson from the office. Apparently Michael didn't show up to school."

"You broke into her phone?" I've tried to do this myself a few times but haven't had any luck.

"Oh my god, Anna!" The eye roll is even more apparent. "The pass code is your birthday; how could you not know this?!"

Lily's shrieking and I can tell she's about to cry again, so I try to stay focused. "Okay, I'm sorry. Good detective work. Okay, so Ma left her phone, Michael didn't go to school. Was he sick, maybe?" I'm racking my brain for some logical explanation. "Maybe they just went to the doctor and Ma forgot her phone?"

"Anna, she's been gone all day. There were six missed calls."

My heart sinks. "Have you called Baba?"

"I tried but it's the start of dinner service and I can't get through."

"My phone's dying. Keep calling. I'm going to try to look for her, okay?" I don't even know where to start.

"Anna." Lily chokes but the sob still escapes. "Can you please come home?"

"I'll be there as soon as I can, okay?"

My phone dies before she answers. My heart is thundering, and I feel a heavy pressure through my chest, like I'm caught in a swathe of bodies. *Breathe, Anna.* I reach up to loosen the strap of my bag, but I'm not even wearing it. I inhale, once, twice. Count to ten.

A single drop splashes onto my phone screen, and I realize I'm crying. My body shakes and it's hard to breathe. I suddenly remember a wedding Ma once took me to. I was tiny and Ma was nowhere to be found. I was caught in the tide of people pushing against the door. The hinges creaked and I was flattened against the heavy timber, knees of strangers against my face.

"Anna." I turn toward the voice behind me. I blink up at the blurry form.

"Is everything okay . . . I . . ." Rory looks down, worry all over his face. "Anna, what's wrong?"

The hinges have come off the door now, and the bodies surge inward. And I scream.

Chapter Twenty
Ji6 Sap6

THE SCREAM TURNS INTO A wail and then sobbing. Strong arms wrap around my shoulders and pull me in.

"Hey, it's okay. Anna, what's wrong?" Rory asks.

But even now, with everything coming apart, I have no words. "I just . . . I can't . . ." There's no shortage of tears, so I give up and just stand and cry.

Rory hugs me and strokes my hair. "Shh . . . shh. It's okay, Anna. It's okay."

I want to believe him. I really do. But I'm just exhausted. Suddenly, my body feels too heavy, my limbs jellylike, and I fall against his chest.

Rory half drags, half carries me to the car, me babbling and crying like a baby. My chest is burning and I'm trying to cry and breathe at the same time, but everything just bubbles back out.

"Deep breaths. You're hyperventilating. Count to three before you breathe." I try to follow his instruction and eventually manage to slow my erratic inhales. Rory pulls out a mangy bottle of water from somewhere. It's tepid and a little slimy, but I drink. Rory holds out a tissue.

"Anna, tell me what's wrong."

And I tell him everything. Ma staying in bed. Her outbursts. Lily's exam. Michael. Everything I can muster, but it's all bits and blurts and incoherent sentences. I start crying in the middle of it again, and the blubbering muddles my words like spilled cream.

"I don't know what to do. I can't control her moods."

Rory's face darkens as he listens, his brow knitting more and more. Finally, he sits back in his seat, pushing his hands through his hair, and lets out a deep guttural noise that sounds a lot like *duck*.

"I'm sorry." I blow again into the tissue and glimpse my reflection in the side mirror. I'm a wreck, my eyes red and puffy, face blown up. The air against my cheeks makes them sting because of the salt from my tears. I want to bury my face in my hands—I look monstrous, but I can't wipe my eyes and hide at the same time.

"Stop apologizing." Rory's voice is tinged with anger, a sharpness I've never heard before. And it scares me.

"I'm sorry. I don't mean to." I sit up and wipe my eyes again in a desperate attempt to dry them. "I shouldn't have said anything. You have your own shit to deal with. It's no big deal, I'm fine."

"Anna!" He grabs me by the wrists, a bit too hard. "This is ridiculous! Stop beating yourself up. This is not your fault."

"I don't have a choice." The tears are brimming again. "I have to look after Lily and Michael. I'm their big sister."

He shakes his head. "All this time. Why didn't you tell me? After everything I told you about what I went through. Why don't you trust me?"

"I *do* trust you." I have to speak through hiccups. "I just haven't been totally honest." The last word lurches through my esophagus.

Rory looks stunned. "Why?"

"I—I just don't know the words to talk about this." I know it sounds pathetic, but it's the deepest truth I can give him.

Rory drops his head as I sob uncontrollably, giving up on coherence. I have to get home, I have to be there for Lily, I have to look for Ma, and I have to find my little brother. I have to stop crying. All of these thoughts go through my head in a crazed loop, but nothing happens except that the rivers of tears and snot keep coming.

At some point, I notice that Rory has started the car. We're on the road again. He looks pissed off.

"I'm sorry, Rory," I manage to choke out. "I didn't mean to ruin your birthday."

His chilling laugh shudders my bones. "Anna, stop being a martyr." He glances at me.

I'm too numb to process what that means, so I stay silent. The sobs have died down now. I peer out the windshield and realize we're headed away from the city.

"Where are we going?" My thoughts turn to Lily, but my phone is dead and Rory is headed in the opposite direction of home. I'm about to protest, but a sudden weariness claims my will and I can't wring myself free.

Rory drives silently, his hands gripping the steering wheel like parachute straps. The last bit of sun winks behind the horizon and the sky is cotton-candy pink.

At some point, the lights, the signs, the speed of it all is familiar again. And then we're pulling up to Jade Palace.

"Why are we at the restaurant?" I whisper.

"Anna, you have to talk to your father. He's the adult; he needs to fix this. Not you."

I shake my head. "I don't want to worry him."

"I was like you, Anna," he goes on. "With all the stuff in my head, I thought I could handle it. I didn't want to burden my parents; my sister had her own thing. So I didn't say anything. I thought I could handle it. But I couldn't." He takes a deep breath. "You need to talk to your father."

I let Rory's words sink in. "I can't bother him. The restaurant—he's worried about his business. This is too much."

"Anna, this is his family!" Rory roars. "This *is* his business."

His hazel eyes fix on me, focused, hard, and fierce. And the last bit of resistance in me cracks. Because I kind of know he's right.

There are a few cars out front, more than I'd expect for a Monday evening. Outside, I see a small silhouette standing on its lonesome, under the neon red-and-blue TAKEOUT light.

"Michael!"

My door is open before Rory can pull the handbrake up, and my seat belt springs back with a heavy snap. My brother doesn't see me at first, but when he does, his whole face is like a summer sparkler.

"Anna!"

He wraps his spindly limbs around me, and I hold on for dear life. My heart skips ahead with relief, joy, and weariness, and I start to cry. Michael cries, too. He smells faintly of fish and salami.

"Thank goodness, you're safe." I close my eyes and thank all the ancestors, gods, and higher beings that I can think of. "How did you get here?"

"We took the train." Michael pulls away to look at me, his lower lip quivering. "Anna, I think something is wrong with Mommy."

Rory is by our side, and we all glance toward the restaurant doors. I hoist my brother onto my hip. My stomach wrings, and I feel a tightening in my gut. We hurry inside.

The restaurant is full for a Monday evening, and more than half of the tables are occupied. But none of the patrons are tucking into their food. Their eyes are riveted to the far wall. At first, all I can see is Miss Chen, Baba, and Ah-Jeff, shouting, holding their empty hands up in front of them. They part slightly, and I see what they're trying to fend off.

"Ma!" someone cries out. It takes me a beat to realize that it's my own voice. Michael buries his face in my neck.

My mother doesn't hear me. She's standing by the restaurant aquarium, pointing at what's inside.

"Fish, you see. They are bad." Ma is gesturing wildly at the tank. "The fish, they are no good."

"Lou5 po4, *wife*," my father pleads in Cantonese. "Please, let's go outside and we can talk. You're scaring the customers."

"Lou5 gung1, *husband*, you have to listen to me. They've been playing tricks on you. They're spies. All of them." She narrows her eyes at Miss Chen. "Her. She tries to take you away from your family. Harlot."

Miss Chen gasps. Ah-Jeff shakes his head and stares at the ground. My father buries his head in his hands.

"Mommy." Michael squirms out of my arms and before I can stop him, he's running toward Ma.

"No!" I push past Ah-Jeff and Baba, but Michael is too fast.

"Bou2 bou2!" She reaches for him and cradles him in her arms. "Don't be scared. Mommy will protect you. They won't harm you. I won't let anything bad happen to you." She looks up and sees me.

"Anna, what are you doing here?" she says with a frown. "Are you with them, too?"

Them? What is she talking about? I look from Ah-Jeff to Baba, but neither of them can meet my eye. I take a hesitant step toward her, but she reels back, shoving Michael behind her tiny body.

"Stay away from us. You can't take us away. You can't take my son." Michael looks more scared now, trying to pull away, but Ma has his arm in a strong grip.

"Lou5 po4, please," my father pleads again. His voice is strained to the verge of breaking. "None of us want to hurt you. We just want to go home."

"Mommy?" I whisper.

Suddenly, I feel a presence at my side. Rory pushes past, hands in his pockets. "Mrs. Chiu, how are you today?" His voice is too loud and too chipper, putting on some bizarre friendly act.

My mother narrows her eyes, scrutinizing the young stranger

before her. "Who are you? You a spy, too?" she accuses him in English.

"Nope." He pops his *p* and rocks onto the heels of his shoes. "I'm a friend of Anna's."

"My daughter, she learn the bad thing. It's so hard to be good parent."

"I understand, Mrs. Chiu. It must be very hard." He nods sympathetically.

"So hard. And I do it by myself, you know. My husband never home. Just me and three children. I protect them. So many bad people. I keep them safe."

Baba buries his head in his hands again and moans in Cantonese. "Please, not here, I beg you." I shush him and jab him in the side with my elbow.

"You're doing a great job, Mrs. Chiu. I can tell. Anna is such a wonderful, warm, and caring person."

"She like me. She have big heart." Ma beams with pride. "Always look after her brother and sister. She help me a lot." Ma shifts her gaze back toward me, and it's no longer wild and accusing. "I know she good daughter. Maybe she learn the wrong thing, sometimes, you know."

Rory nods again. "I'm sure she didn't mean to. You can still teach her. Show her the way."

"Of course." Ma bobs her head enthusiastically. "I'm her mother. She my daughter. I always teach her."

I don't know where Rory is going with this, but he's keeping

Ma's attention and she's talking, not shouting. The entire dining room is quiet.

Michael suddenly yanks his arm away and comes barreling toward me. Ma looks on in shock as he tumbles into my embrace. "Anna! Anna! I want to go home!" my brother cries. He wraps his arms around me like a vine, his eyes squeezed shut. "I want to go home. Take me home."

"Michael. Gwaai1 zai2, *good boy*. Come here," Ma commands, but my brother won't budge. She stares at us, her eyes wide. She looks from me and Michael and then back to Rory.

"You see, they change his mind. The eyes are bad, you see," she says to him, and gestures at the aquarium. "They watch us with bad eyes, change our thinking and feeling no good."

We all watch in horror as Ma plunges her arm inside the tank. She holds up a slippery orange fish, no bigger than a mackerel, and before I can do anything, she pops its eyes between her fingers.

Customers at their tables scream. I put Michael down and run toward my mother. I stumble. The sounds of sirens cut through the commotion and flashing ambulance lights cast an eerie red glow over the grisly scene before us.

"No good, see." She holds the trembling orange body up in triumph as thin red lines run down her fingertips. "The eyes all cloudy."

Chapter Twenty-One
Ji6 Sap6 Jat1

TWO EMTS TAKE MA AWAY on a gurney, her arms and legs pinned down. She doesn't put up a fight, but they secure the leather straps anyway. She swings her head around, her eyes searching, and finds me and Michael huddled together just past the kitchen gangway. Michael has his eyes screwed shut and his face buried in my shoulder.

"Michael, Anna, it's okay," she says in Chinese. "The fish can't hurt you. I took the eyes out. You're safe now. Don't be scared, okay?" She gives me a big toothy grin and a little wave from the wrist up as they wheel her down into the ambulance.

When she's out of sight, I burst into tears. My whole body shakes as I cry. The restaurant patrons are all getting up, their meals half-finished, their evenings ending on a rather unpalatable note. Miss Chen waves away polite requests for the bill, asking them to please come again. A few of them peer over the counter, eyeing me curiously, full of pity. I feel the shame burning through me, but I'm too numb to care.

One of the EMTs goes over to Baba. "Are you the husband?" she asks.

"Ah—no English," Baba stammers. He gestures to me. "My daughter, you ask her."

I'm stunned. Baba's English is more than capable and he's never asked me to translate before.

She looks at me. "Are you over eighteen?"

I shake my head.

"I'll need you both to come to the hospital so she can be admitted."

I look down at Michael, who's still clinging to me like a barnacle. His whole body is limp, a forty-pound deadweight. "I'm tired," he murmurs, his head heavy against my shoulder. I'm worried about Lily, alone at home.

"I'll take him home," Rory offers, as if he can read my thoughts. I smile gratefully.

Rory and I get Michael's car seat set up in Rory's car while Baba gets in his vehicle like a zombie. I have to remind him to put his seat belt on. We follow the ambulance in stony silence.

We're ushered into the waiting area full of stiff metal chairs. We don't see Ma getting checked in. Baba just stares, his face ashen. He doesn't even glance at the forms the receptionist gives us, so I do my best to fill them out.

Eventually, Ma's name is called: "Siuling Chiu."

Dr. Patel looks young, not long out of med school, but she carries a no-nonsense air of authority. She sits in a chair beside us and leans forward like she's trying to peer into my soul. I can't help ducking under her gaze. "Are you her daughter, Anna?" She has a prim Indian accent.

I nod.

"Okay, Anna. Tell me about your mother. Has she done anything like this before?"

Baba is right beside me, and I know what I'm supposed to say.

"No. Never." This is true—I'd never seen her pull a live fish out of an aquarium and maim it in front of a whole crowd of strangers.

Dr. Patel scribbles and ticks on her clipboard. "Has there been any recent trauma? Or a history of alcohol or substance abuse?"

I shake my head in alarm. "No, of course not. She never drinks, not even at weddings."

"Trouble sleeping or hearing noises? Anything she might have mentioned?"

Ma hasn't been sleeping, she's been cleaning and yelling at us instead. But I can't find the words to explain what happened. Baba's eyes bulge, and I know he wants me to hide the truth. "I, ah, I—I don't know. Maybe?"

Dr. Patel is still scribbling. "Has she been under any particular stress?"

"Ah! The terror shootings in America," Baba pipes up. *So much for not understanding.* "She is watching the news and the terror, the shooting." He mimes looking down the barrel of a rifle and clocks off a few shots. "She always want go to America. Maybe this is the reason she is so upset. I tell her not to watch because it makes her upset."

He nods decisively, like he has just made some miraculous turn to beat the peak hour traffic. Dr. Patel looks less certain.

"I see, Mr. Chiu. Yes, these types of incidents could be a contributing factor to your wife's mental well-being."

"Yes. This is no good. The news, terrible things. I tell her not to watch. I tell her already. She no listen. She come home, she no watch anymore. I tell her. She come home now, no more problem."

Dr. Patel presses her thin lips together. "Well, Mr. Chiu." She's forgotten me now. "We've already gone ahead and admitted her to psychiatric care. You're very lucky as there are very few beds in the adult ward at the moment, and we've had to move all of our adolescents into pediatric care. But your wife's psychosis meant we could move her in straightaway."

"Psy-psy—" I stammer. "Psychosis? What do you mean?"

Dr. Patel leans forward again, but her voice is gentler. "Your mother is experiencing delusions. A psychotic episode."

"Is—is—is she going to be okay?"

"She's fine. At the moment, the orderlies have her under a mild sedative and we'll be administering an antipsychotic, which should help. But she needs to be kept under strict observation for the time being."

"Anna, what is she saying?" Baba addresses me in Cantonese, his tired, baggy eyes pleading.

"She says Ma has to stay in the hospital. They gave her medicine."

"No, no, no," he protests in English, then switches back to

Cantonese. "Tell her, it's fine. I'll stay home from work and look after her. No problem. We'll keep an eye on her." I swallow the tears that are backing up in my throat as I shake my head. Baba ignores this and turns back to the doctor. "She no watch news. I take care. I tell her. She come home. We are family. We take care." He points to both of us.

"I'm sorry, Mr. Chiu." Dr. Patel is a model of practiced sternness. "We must keep her here in the hospital under careful observation and care to assess her state. Once she has been monitored, we can discuss longer-term options."

"How long? How long she stay? One day? Two days?" His eyes widen in fear. "Three days?!"

"I'm sorry, Mr. Chiu. I simply can't tell you at this point."

"She family. She mother. Who take care children if mother is here?" His eyes bug out, the way I've only seen during an exceptionally busy dinner service. He is angry, demanding. But Dr. Patel is having none of it.

"I'm sorry, Mr. Chiu. I really am." She scribbles and dots heavily on her clipboard. "But right now, my job is to make sure your wife is looked after."

Baba says nothing, slumps in the chair. He looks too worn and too stretched, like a burst balloon. My hope sinks with him, but there's no moment for pity, because Dr. Patel is sticking a piece of paper under my nose.

"The ward has strict visiting hours and rules that must be adhered to—no exceptions." I can't help but shiver hearing those words. "Here is a list of things that she'll need. Please stick to these items only. Do you understand?"

I cast a glance at Baba, but he doesn't look up, just stares off in the distance. I give the tiniest nod and Dr. Patel looks encouraging.

"We can supply some basic things for her tonight. Next visiting hours are tomorrow—two p.m. to four p.m. only. I suggest you bring them to her then. Will that be okay?"

"Okay." My voice is hoarse and crackly, like I've swallowed a chirruping cricket. I clear my throat and give Dr. Patel a weak smile.

She looks pleased. "Good. Don't worry, Anna. She's in the best care, I promise." She sounds sincere, reassuring even, and for that I'm grateful. "It's very late. I suggest you try to get some rest for the night." She stands and shakes my hand like a proper adult. Baba doesn't get up, so she gives a polite nod.

"Baba." I shake him gently by the shoulder. "We have to go."

Baba leaves the hospital with me but doesn't say a word the entire trip home, stuck in a catatonic state.

When we get home, Baba is still silent. Lily is standing in the kitchen, wiping down the counter, her brow knitted in concentration. She cleans with the same fury Ma does. "Where are Rory and Michael?" I ask.

"Michael's sleeping." Lily doesn't look up from her cleaning. "Your boyfriend went home."

"Here, I'll do it," I say, taking the sponge from her clenched hands. She turns to me and her red-rimmed eyes glower with menace. And a touch of fear.

I want nothing more than to fold her into my arms, but the moment I reach out, she ducks down and away. "I'm going to check on Michael."

The kitchen is already spotless, but I go through the motions of cleaning as Baba disappears into the living room. The air is heavy all around me, smothering and thick. I clutch the edge of the counter as my tears fall. I let out a single silent sob.

After I squeeze out the sponge and dry my eyes, I check on Lily and Michael. Lily is curled around Michael protectively.

I sometimes forget she has to be the big sister, too.

"Lily," I whisper, and she turns, finger pressed over her lips. Michael is sleeping soundly, worn out. She sits up in the bed, and we listen to his soft snore.

"Was she really bad?" Lily asks finally.

I nod and my eyes are stinging again, and Lily is the one to wrap her arms around me in a tight hug, like she's the big sister.

"Thanks for looking after him," I say. She nods and stays on his bed to watch him sleep.

I go back to the kitchen. Baba has moved to the kitchen bench. He holds his head in his hands, his shoulders shaking. It takes me a moment to realize he's crying.

In my sixteen years of being, I have not once seen my father cry. I didn't think that he could; he's always so stiff and devoid of emotion. He isn't one to laugh much, but when he does, he does it with his whole body, shoulders, limbs, and belly shaking. He's the same now with the tears—his head shakes, his back heaves, and he lets out dark, billowy wails of sorrow.

I go to him, hesitant, and lay a hand on his back. My touch urges him on and his sobs get louder.

"It's okay, Baba. Don't cry. It's okay." His past words of comfort come out of my mouth, awkward and stilted. But telling someone not to cry is as fruitless as telling a boiling kettle not to whistle. We stand there for who knows how long before his cries peter down to whimpers.

"The day after I landed in Australia, your uncle put me straight to work. I was on prep work and the grill, same as you. I did a full twelve-hour shift before I was allowed home. I haven't not worked for more than a day in over twenty-five years, not even when my children were born. When your ma and I were married in Hong Kong, our honeymoon was overnight to Macau only."

Though I know Baba has never taken a day off unless he's had to, this still comes as a surprise.

"It was your uncle who introduced me to your mother in Hong Kong. She was shy but sharp and she didn't ask about my car or my house. She asked me about my family in China, if I missed them. She asked about working in a restaurant, if it was hard for my body because of all the lifting, carrying large sacks of rice and things. I was surprised, because most people don't think about lifting in the restaurant, they only consider the cooking. I thought your mother was unlike any other girl, not that I knew very many of them. But she was special."

I smile inwardly, listening to my father reminisce. I know he cares about Ma a great deal, but I have never heard him speak this way before. It makes my insides swell into a soppy mess and tumble back down when I remember why we're here.

"Ma will be okay." I say this with as much confidence as I can muster. "The hospital will help her."

"It's not that easy, Anna." And he looks me square in the eye. "There's no cure for crazy."

Chapter Twenty-Two
Ji6 sap6 ji6

BABA GETS US UP EARLY.

"Hei2 san1, hei2 san2." *Wake up, wake up.* He flicks the light switch on and off, so it hurts to open my eyes.

"What time is it?" Lily moans.

"It's already seven. I have to be at the restaurant. You go to school."

I'm stunned. I can't believe that after last night, Baba is trying to round us up like ducklings.

"Are you sure that's a good idea?" I ask.

"Of course it is. Things happen, and we need to do the jobs," Baba replies. "No lazing about. I pay bills, you go to school. I do my job, you do yours."

Lily grumbles and Michael cries when Baba wakes him, but he's too scared of Baba to make a big fuss.

We sit at the breakfast table, bleary-eyed. Baba has made a huge pot of congee, enough to feed the weekend buffet-goers.

He plops huge portions of gloopy rice into bowls, and it spills over the sides. "You all go to school today, okay? Do good, study hard."

"What happened to Ma?" Michael whispers. "Is she coming home?"

"Of course she's coming home! What nonsense is this?" he barks in Cantonese.

"Would it be so bad if she didn't?" Lily gripes under her breath, but I definitely hear her.

"Your mother is fine!" Baba roars. "There's nothing wrong. Your ma is fine. She was just playing around." He frowns at his son, whose lower lip has started to wobble. "No crying. You're a man. Men don't cry." He wags his finger and scowls, and I know he's reprimanding himself for last night as much as he's scolding Michael now.

We eat silently but with fervor, our ceramic spoons clinking against the bowls. Baba's cooking is top-notch, but the congee's hot and I'm too weary to taste it.

"Hurry up, eat. Then off to school, all of you." He claps his hands and starts to clear the table, stacking the bowls together until they're teetering high.

"Baba, I'll do that." I jump to my feet.

"No! I'm fine. I can take care of my own family," he snaps. We watch as he struggles to load up the dishwasher and finally gives up and leaves the bowls in the sink.

"Time for school. I can drop you off on my way to the restaurant. Hurry up."

"Baba," I say carefully. "Are you going to visit Ma at the hospital in Gosford? Visiting hours are just before the lunch shift."

My father scowls. "Why would I do that? There are doctors and nurses to look after her."

"But someone has to bring Ma her things. For the hospital."

Baba turns to me.

"Neoi5, *daughter*. You need to go to the hospital for your mother. Bring her things . . . I just can't leave the restaurant."

His excuse irritates me. After all that fuss about us doing our jobs, isn't it his job to look after Ma?

I shrug and say, "I guess so."

"Good, good." He nods. "Get the boy to give you a ride. Tell him I'll pay him extra."

Boy? Something inside me snaps. "His name is Rory," I say indignantly. "Why don't you call him by his name? He's not just your employee, you know."

"What you mean?" Baba asks. "Rory. Troy. Albert. What the different?"

"Because he's my boyfriend."

The kitchen falls still. Lily and Michael turn to stare. The IKEA clock ticks too loudly.

I've said it. No going back now. Not how I would have planned it, but these things don't work out the way you think they will.

Baba looks at me, the vein in his forehead bulging. I meet his gaze. Daring him, waiting for him to react, complain, forbid me from seeing him again, anything. I know Ma would have choice words on the subject.

But in typical Baba fashion, he just shakes his head and pretends I hadn't said anything.

"Get ready for school," he tells my siblings without looking at me.

Lily and Michael rush to obey. I stand my ground, but Baba won't meet my eyes. His silence is too uncomfortable. I can't read him.

"Baba," I finally say. "About Rory . . ."

"Enough," Baba snaps. "Do what you want, Anna. I don't have the energy to stop you." And he goes into the living room.

My heart crumbles. *He doesn't even care.*

But another part of me realizes that Baba is right; there are other priorities for us as a family.

After Baba, Lily, and Michael leave, I stack the dishes and text Rory for a lift to the hospital. Right now, I have to focus on Ma.

I go to her room to pack the things she'll need. The shadows on the wall are gone. There are no signs to read. I have no idea what's to come.

I pull out the list that Dr. Patel gave me. There are two sheets. The first is a list of dos and don'ts—which I realize is mostly don'ts. The second sheet lists out visitation rules and once again, a lot of don'ts.

Psychiatric Ward Visitation Rules

1. *Visiting hours are strictly between 10:00 a.m.–12:00 p.m. Monday to Friday,*

and 2:00 p.m.–4:00 p.m. Saturday and
Sunday ONLY.

2. All personal items must be stowed in the
    provided lockers throughout the duration of
    the visit. NO EXCEPTIONS.

3. Please have any items ready to be inspected by
    the staff before they are passed to the patient.
    This includes ANY food items and sundries
    (e.g., sanitary products, etc.).

4. The following items are strictly forbidden on
    the ward and will be confiscated by staff. NO
    EXCEPTIONS.
    • Tank tops
    • Leggings
    • Skirts or shorts above knee length
    • Any drawstring clothing
    • Computers
    • Cameras
    • iPods
    • Radio
    • Mobile phones
    • Shoelaces
    • Belts
    • Sharp items/glass items

- *Razors*
- *Cords*
- *Chemical hair removers*
- *Aerosol containers/products, including hairspray*
- *Alcohol-based products*
- *Bar soap*
- *Dental floss*
- *Mirrors/glass products*
- *Stuffed animals*
- *Jewelry*
- *Money/wallet*
- *Other valuables*
- *Illegal drugs/alcohol*
- *Lighters/matches*
- *Musical instruments*
- *Knitting needles/crochet hooks/yarn*
- *Hair dryers/curling irons/any other items with cords*
- *All makeup*
- *Saline solutions*

I scan the specific items one by one, wondering what in the world could have transpired to make them be so specific. iPod? Just how old are these guides?

My hands are sweaty as I try to figure out the list of things I'm supposed to bring.

Clothing for the duration of patient stay.

Duration of her stay. There had been no mention of how long she would be there, only Baba's exclamation when he realized it could be longer than three days. *What did that mean?* Rory said he was in hospital for three weeks. Is that what we need to prepare for? Surely there are laundry facilities?

I pull out three pairs of clean white underwear from her drawers, billowy and supportive despite the elastic wearing off. I tuck in one more pair, and then another fistful and one more after that, just in case.

Next, I move to shirts and pants, but this proves tricky as I have to cross-reference them against the list of forbidden items. The forbiddens are twice as long as the list of requirements. No shoes with laces, no strings or belts, but other forbiddens leave me scratching my head. No hats or head coverings (religious garments excepted, if deemed safe). I throw some comfy-looking shirts and stretchy pants into the bag and move on to the bathroom.

The list of toiletries is even harder, as there's a footnote that says no items containing alcohol will be allowed in the patient's room with the big bold *No Exceptions* trailing after it. I'm really starting to hate those words. Worse still, every single bottle of shampoo and conditioner we own is oversized, all family packs bought in bulk. I wonder if I have time to nip to the store, maybe get some travel-sized items, but I give up and just put them in the bag.

There are so many more forbidden items—Q-tips, nail scissors, balloons (balloons!), dental floss, razors—the list goes on. Finally, when I have double-checked everything for the seventeenth time,

I zip it all up in a duffel bag. I add a blanket and pillow from the winter linens; Ma is always complaining about being cold, and the hospital seemed chilly.

Just as I'm about to leave the room, there's a soft popcorn *ping*. Ma's phone is on the bedside table, tethered to its charger. Lily must have plugged it in yesterday. I go to switch it off—technology is definitely on the forbidden list.

I see the notifications on her screen and almost drop the phone.

There are ten, fifteen of them. All of them WhatsApp. All of them notifications saying the messages were undeliverable.

And every single one of the messages is addressed to me.

I deleted my WhatsApp months ago, trying to clear space off my phone. I'd told Ma this, because she was the only person I knew who used the app to chat to friends and leave voice messages to our family. I asked her to text or call me instead. But apparently, she's been sending me messages that have failed to arrive anyway.

I retrieve my phone and wait for WhatsApp to reinstall. It takes a while to sync up, but one by one, the messages from Ma ping in.

She's been sending them since the beginning of the year. They're a bit long-winded and rambling and I read them carefully, looking for signs. Some are reminiscing about life when we first moved to Sydney. I shudder when I read the one about the black dog from months back. *All these signs and I never noticed.*

Then I get to the ones from the past couple of days. Whispers and secrets, people listening in the wall, on the phone. The last one is from yesterday. It's all gibberish. A sob escapes and I wonder what Ma had seen in my eyes last night. If only I had known. I could have stopped it, maybe. If I had my app, I could have known. But she seemed fine. Angry, but fine. I had no idea what was really going on in her head.

How did I not realize?

A horn blares twice outside. I go to the window and see the mop of brown hair from the Audi convertible. Rory looks up and gives a meek little wave.

I shoulder the bag I've packed for Ma and shut the door to her room.

Rory seems nervous and uneasy when I get in the car. I chalk it up to the weirdness from yesterday. I still don't know what to say, how to thank him.

There's no emoji for *I'm sorry you had to watch my mother maim a fish*.

We drive in silence for a while. Desperate to kill the awkwardness, I tell him about the WhatsApp messages from Ma's phone. I don't mention that I called him my boyfriend in front of my father.

"I'm sorry. That's horrible." He doesn't sound surprised or more put-off.

"The doctor said it's a psychotic delusion." I don't go into the unbearably awkward conversation with Dr. Patel and Baba's denial.

Rory winces. "Delusion is the hardest thing. Your poor mother."

I sigh heavily. "I just wish I knew what was going on in her mind." I pause, not sure if I'm allowed to ask this, but I do anyway. "What was the hospital like?"

Rory doesn't say anything for the longest time, drumming his fingers against the steering wheel.

"It was pretty horrible. When I wasn't feeling all doped up and woozy, I was bored out of my skull. People were . . . I don't know. You feel weird because you see how messed up everything can get and then wonder how far away you are from being that. Or maybe you're already there." He shakes his head. "I hated every minute of it."

I don't want to know anymore. I finger the strap of Ma's bag with its permitted items. If easygoing Rory hated the hospital, I'm not sure how Ma is going to fare.

The hospital parking lot is full, and we can't find a spot. Rory is jittery, his fingers drumming against the steering wheel, and he keeps looking around. It takes me a second to realize how uncomfortable he is. *Of course, the last time he was here would have been . . .*

"You don't have to come with me," I say quickly.

The color returns to his face, and he looks visibly relieved. "Really? Are you sure . . . 'cause . . . ?"

I want to say no and ask him to come in, to take my hand and show me the way, but the look on his face tells me it's too much. Even being here, stopped by the entrance of this painful place, seems more than he can take.

"I'm fine," I lie. There are no caterpillars or pleasant flutterings in my stomach anymore, just deep pockets of fear and dread.

"Call me if you want a lift later." He gives my hand a squeeze. The second I'm out of the car, he pulls away, the fresh wheels squealing against the worn tarmac.

There's no one at reception, so I'm left to figure out the direction to the wards on my own. I stare up at the giant board with the stick-on letters until I see it.

Psychiatric ward, Level 4.

It takes a while to find an elevator. I push the button and wait for an eternity before the doors part to reveal a tiny gray woman in a lavender sweater. I smile at the woman and my hands shake a little as I press the number four.

"Are you visiting family, dear?" my elevator companion asks.

"Um. Sort of. Just checking things out." I try to be as noncommittal as possible.

The elevator rumbles and groans. I know it's built to fit at least two stretchers and life-saving equipment, but right now, it doesn't seem to comply with the task of transporting a tiny old woman and me. I swallow, aware of the parchedness of my throat. Maybe I should have gotten a vending machine coffee.

Finally, the box judders to a stop and the doors churn. I let the old woman hobble out a few steps, just enough to be polite, before hurrying out in front of her and bustling down the corridor.

"Have a nice day," she calls after me.

The psych ward is in a different section from where the elevator is, and the signs up here are a lot harder to decipher than at the entrance. I can hear my heart thumping and the squeak of my shoes on the waxed floors. It's so eerily quiet except for the electronic hums coming from inside the rooms. I shudder, imagining the equipment that gives off those sounds, tracking life in those sick, frail bodies. I start to feel a bit woozy.

But I push on and finally see the large block letters that read PSYCHIATRIC WARD. The smell of antiseptic is stronger here, and it clings to the inside of my nostrils, to the roots of my nose hairs. I stagger toward the double doors.

They don't budge.

"You have to wait," a voice says beside me. A middle-aged woman in a burgundy velour tracksuit gives me a wry smile. She points to the clock overhead. "You have to wait. They're strict about the time."

She's right. There's still three minutes to the top of the hour. I glance around and realize there are a few other people milling about the hall, reading posters or on their phones, looking bored.

"Oh, thanks." I return what I hope is a friendly smile.

"First time?" Velour Suit nods toward my heavy duffel. I nod back. "You check the list? They're strict about the list." I nod again.

"That's good." She leans forward and lowers her voice. "It's good to visit. It's hard in there and we're all they got. That's why I keep coming back."

I grimace and try not to recoil in horror. I know she's just trying to make conversation, but the whole exchange makes me want to throw up.

The doors crack open and an orderly emerges dressed in maroon scrubs and wearing a thick silver nose ring. Before she begins to speak, the people gather their belongings to head inside. I shoulder my heavy bag to follow.

"Personal belongings, including mobile phones, must be placed in the lockers. Anything to be left with the patient will be inspected." Nose Ring holds up a hand when I get to the front of the door. "Who you here for?"

My mouth is so dry, but I don't want to clear my throat. "Uh, Chiu. Siuling Chiu," I rasp.

"Who?"

I cough twice and try again. "SOO Ling Chew?" I try to make Ma's name as Anglo-sounding as possible.

Her eyes light up as she makes the connection. "Oh. Goldfish." I wince and wonder if that's Ma's nickname. The urge to barf thickens.

"What's in the duffel?" Nose Ring barks.

"Um, clothes?" I squeak. "And shampoo. Things."

"No bags are to be left with the patient. You'll have to take everything out and stow it in the locker."

Crap. I hadn't thought about the bag itself. With its thick straps and metal buckles, it's definitely on the no-go list.

Velour Suit hands me a small plastic bag. "Plastic means you can throw it away when they check what's inside."

"Oh, thanks." I drop to the ground and undo the zip and start laying Ma's clothes out on the floor, trying to stack them up as neatly as I can. The underwear I had painstakingly folded, her pajama bottoms, and toiletries are rearranged into mounds that I then try to awkwardly gather up and cram into the flimsy plastic bag.

"No keys or wallets, chains or belts." The orderly taps the sign next to the door with its long, and now familiar, list of forbiddens. I shake my head and she nods toward my messenger bag. I fish out my own belongings and jam it into the now-empty duffel bag. Nose

Ring glances down and gestures toward a stack of metal lockers in the corner. It's apparently BYO lock, which I don't have, so I shove my stuff into a spare compartment and pray it's safe until I return.

I'm at the back of the queue to sign in. The nurse behind the desk takes her time checking the items presented to her. She shakes her head at the wrapped-up piece of cake in Velour Suit's own plastic bag.

"It's her daughter's birthday cake from her party on the weekend," Velour Suit offers by way of explanation.

"Madam, you know the rules." The nurse points again to what I assume must be "the list" taped to the reception table. "I'll leave it here. You can collect it on the way out."

Velour Suit sighs and signs the clipboard in front of her. "The staff can have it. Enjoy. You're doing a good job looking after her." The heaviness of her voice makes me wonder if she means it.

"Next." The nurse beckons to me. I inch forward, clutching the plastic clothing bundle tightly to my chest. "Last name?"

"Chiu. Siuling Chiu."

The nurse's face softens with recognition. "Oh, from the restaurant." She doesn't mention anything about the goldfish, and I'm grateful. I read the name tag pinned to her faded scrubs. *Mary.* I like her more than Nose Ring.

"You're her daughter? This is your first time here?" Nurse Mary turns around and pulls out a set of papers.

I nod.

"It must be hard," she says with sympathy. "But don't worry, we're going to take good care of your mother." She taps her pen on the clipboard. "You know the rules? What you can't bring in? Make sure you read it carefully."

And once again, I'm presented with the catalogue of contraband that I suspect I know by heart now. Except this sheet has a spot for me to sign.

"All good," I say in the most confident voice I can muster. I figure it's a good idea to make a friend in Ma's nursing staff. But Nurse Mary doesn't return my winning smile as I sign on the dotted line.

"Let's see what you've got." And she proceeds to inspect the mountain of clothing and toiletry items. As she picks through it, I realize I've packed a lot. *How long will Ma be here?* Nurse Mary is diligently sorting things into piles, and I blush when the nurse lifts up a thick woolen sweater that's probably more suited for skiing than a hospital stay.

"She gets cold easily," I try to explain. Nurse Mary cocks an eyebrow and moves it deftly into a pile.

From behind us comes a chorus of loud moaning and wet noises. A figure shrouded in a gown emerges from one of the rooms. Her white hair is kind of flat against her wrinkled face like she's been sleeping on it, and her thin glasses are askew. She must be someone's nanna.

The nanna hikes her gown up around her waist and sticks her tongue out to blow raspberries at us.

"Okay, Doris. You know you're on two strikes already." Nurse Mary doesn't even look up to see who it is. "One more and we're taking away your TV privileges."

The nanna turns back to her room. The urge to vomit is back, and I hold my stomach to stave it off.

"Okay. This pile you can hand to your mother." Nurse Mary puts her hand on a small mound of clothes that include most of Ma's underthings, a few light shirts and trousers, as well as the blanket and pillow. "She can keep these in her room. These—" She gestures to the oversized bottles of shampoo, conditioner, and other toiletries, as well as the few books I had grabbed. "We'll keep behind the nurse's station and give some to her when she needs it, but she'll need to come and ask. And this lot—" She points to the final pile of clothes that includes the woolly sweater and what I now realize is a set of snow pants. "You can pick up on your way out and take home with you."

My throat is parched again, my words all clogged up, so I nod and scoop the bundle of nurse-approved clothes into my arms.

"Now, some more housekeeping." The rules never end. "Please be mindful of noise and activity, as there are other families visiting. You must be respectful of all patients here. Absolutely no verbal or physical aggression against anyone will be tolerated. And absolutely no going into the patients' rooms. There's the common lounge or the kitchen, which has chairs and a table. Do you understand?"

I nod again.

Now Nurse Mary leans forward and looks me square in the eye. "I know this is your first time, so you might be surprised by what you see. Your mother is on a strong dosage of lithium and a couple of other mood stabilizers and antipsychotics that were prescribed by Dr. Patel. We're monitoring her response to them and adjusting her meds accordingly. So she might seem a little . . . different. Not quite herself. But don't worry, it's a normal part of her treatment."

"Different? How so?" I reel back in alarm.

"Patients respond differently to the medication. Some might be extra active and chatty while others might feel sluggish or lethargic. It's all a matter of adjustment, and that's why it's important your mother gets the care she needs here so she can feel better and manage her condition at home."

"C-condition?" I'm trying to remember what Dr. Patel said.

Nurse Mary murmurs sympathetically. "We don't have very much information and that's not uncommon at this stage. Over time, as she undergoes therapy and long-term treatment, we'll get a better understanding of the full picture and a more specific diagnosis. Now do you have any questions before you see your mother?"

I want to ask more, but my brain has locked down, so I shake my head no. Nurse Mary smiles. "Great; why don't you go wait in the kitchen and I'll have someone find your mother for you?"

I thank Nurse Mary before making my way to the kitchen. *Kitchen* is a generous term; there isn't much in here, not even a kettle or microwave to make tea. Instead there's a water cooler, some paper cups, and a sad roll of soggy paper towels in an otherwise-bare cupboard.

Another family is already visiting at the end of the large table that takes up most of the space in the room.

Nose Ring is standing beside a middle-aged woman who I think is a patient. She has thick glasses and unruly hair. Her visitors are a young couple, maybe her children, but that doesn't quite seem age-appropriate. I'm trying hard not to pay too much attention to them when the patient suddenly jumps up and screams. "You're a bitch. You're stupid. Shameful. Idiot. Bitch." Nose Ring doesn't move, and the couple tell the patient to calm down. Fortunately, the woman listens. She sits back with her head bowed and her arms folded around her. The young woman speaks to her in soft dulcet tones. The man sees me hovering by the doorway and gives me a sheepish shrug.

I'm embarrassed, like I'm eavesdropping, and I'm just about to go wait outside when I hear Nurse Mary call out.

"All right, Mrs. Chiu. Straight through here. There you go."

I forget my embarrassment and stand up, eager to see my mother. I want to hug her, hold her. The whole goldfish saga seems like eons ago, a distant memory. I just want to be my mother's daughter again. To curl up into her arms and feel safe and warm.

But the woman who comes into the room is not my mother.

Chapter Twenty-Three
Ji6 sap6 saam1

THE WOMAN WHO COMES INTO the room wears Ma's face, with the same weathered crease in her brow that always makes her look cross. She has the same splotchy skin, shiny on her fat apple cheeks but dry and a bit flaky along her forehead where she scrubs too hard with the washcloth. She wears the same short bobbed hair, the raven-black strands swirling together with gray and white hairs like marble frosting. She has the same ears with their tiny unpierced lobes.

But the woman who walks into the room has none of Ma's fire. Her eyes are unfocused, half-closed, like her lids can't be bothered. She moves in slow, halting, jagged steps, a robotic arm on its last bit of battery. She doesn't smile, doesn't frown, doesn't scream, doesn't scold. She doesn't even see me. She moves with her weird staccato steps toward an empty chair and drags it out. She's wearing an oversized hospital gown that hangs on her tiny body like a heavy sea monster.

She sits down. I stare. She stares back, unblinking.

"Mommy?" I approach her gingerly, like a rabid dog. She squints at me and after a long while, her jaw opens as if to say something, but she doesn't do more than that. She just looks, her mouth yawning open like the water balloon clowns waiting to be shot at the funfair.

I hug her from the side. Ma has no reaction. It takes everything in me to keep it together as I survey the kitchenette looking for something, anything. Finally, I go to the cooler and get a cup of water.

"Ma. Jam2 seoi2." *Drink water.* I've stepped into caretaker mode, serving tea, trying to bring some normal into this. I kneel on one knee and try to look Ma in the eye. She looks back, but if she recognizes me or what's going on, I can't see it in her expression. Her hands reach out automatically to take the cup. They're shaking badly and most of the water spills down her gown before it makes it to her cracked lips.

She doesn't say anything, not a word, and I wipe the corner of her mouth with the side of my sleeve.

Drugs. It's the drugs, that's all. I tell myself to be calm and matter-of-fact, but I can't stop the heartbeat hooves in my chest. *Of course, it's the drugs,* my brain insists, but the rest of my being won't believe it.

The other family are standing up to leave. "Excuse me." I stop Nose Ring, who's about to go with them. "My mother, what— what is she on?"

She shakes her head. "I'm sorry, you'll have to speak to her treating doctor. I don't know anything about that."

"Well, Dr. Patel then, is she in?"

Again with the headshake. "I'm sorry, Dr. Patel has seen the patients today, so she won't be back until tomorrow." And she goes out.

Ma and I sit alone in the kitchen. She doesn't say or do anything else. I want to ask her about the WhatsApp messages, the fish in the tank, but I don't want to talk to the zombie creature in front of me. I want to talk to my mother.

I don't know what to do, so I give her more water. I keep checking the clock, hoping maybe Baba has changed his mind and decided he could come after all. The restaurant is only a few minutes away, surely he can step away for just a bit?

When Nose Ring comes to get us, we've been sitting in near-silence and sipping from cups of water for over forty minutes.

"All right, Miss Ping. Time to go back to your room."

Out of nowhere, my mother looks up and smiles directly at Nose Ring. I'm taken aback—no one has ever addressed Ma as Miss Ping before. It's not even *close* to her name. She'll respond to a stranger calling her by the wrong name but not to her own daughter speaking to her?

Even more ridiculous, Nose Ring goes on to say, "You gonna give us a smile, Miss Ping?" And Ma bares her teeth, her lower lip pulling down so we can see her gums. "That's a good pretty smile, Miss Ping."

Behind the zombie mask, Ma looks pleased and follows the orderly out without so much as a goodbye.

I'm left sitting in the kitchenette, completely alone and bewildered.

Nurse Mary signs me out. "Simone told me you want to speak to Dr. Patel?"

Simone. Nose Ring. I nod and Nurse Mary pulls out a clipboard.

"Let's see, Dr. Patel is here on Saturday from ten to two. So if you come during visiting hours, I can book in some time for you to chat."

After today, I'm not sure I can bear to come back.

Nurse Mary appears to read my thoughts. "It's hard, I know," she says kindly. "It's hard for the families. But she's lucky to have you. Some of the others aren't so lucky. They haven't had a visitor in weeks."

Now I'm brimming with guilt, but I thank Nurse Mary and go to retrieve my things from the locker.

The parking lot has emptied a bit when I step outside. I think about texting Rory or maybe even heading to the restaurant, but right now, I can't stomach the idea of going back there after last night.

I just want to be alone, so I head toward Gosford station.

"The train on platform three terminates here. Please do not board this train."

I jerk awake. Somehow, I managed to fall asleep on the train, the rocking motion and my exhausted body seizing my consciousness.

I've missed my stop and have ended up a few suburbs over in Burwood.

I move groggily off the train as the announcement bells and the computerized voice drones on. The indicator boards show another train to Ashfield is in twenty minutes.

Great. I still have Ma's duffel bag with the woolly sweater and ski pants, so I find an empty bench and wait. I check my phone, but it's dead. I rummage through my bag for something to read and pull out a couple of thick pamphlets Nurse Mary gave me.

The Family Guide to Mental Illness. The first one shows a distressed-looking teen in a hospital gown sitting on the floor with her head in her hands. I wonder if that was Rory, melancholy and tragic with his worried parents hovering over him. It's definitely not what Ma was like today.

I look around for a trash can to chuck it away.

"Wang tiu bao dong goo geung hee sui lew."

The scratchy voice tickles my brain, itching to be remembered. I spin around and I see her, an old Asian woman sitting a bench away, her hair pulled back into a crisp bun. It takes me a moment to recognize her, but it's definitely her, the woman who was talking to herself at the bus stop near Michael's school.

Her hair is neat but her face is bare today, and I see she is much older than I first imagined, with deep folds and pockets of doughy flesh hanging from her eyes.

"Luk cza fong ngam diu hao hao." She shakes her head and walks over to the trash can. I watch her sniff and peer inside, then reach in and pull out a McDonald's sandwich. She sniffs it again, unwraps it, and takes a bite.

I watch in horror as she eats the sandwich before me, then puts the wrapper in her bag. I want to say something, tell her to stop, but I'm hot glued to the seat as she pulls out a squished coffee cup. It drips down her dappled blue blouse. She turns around and her words register loud and clear.

"Soda is bad. Too much caffeine. No good for brain."

The old woman's form warps before me. She's still hunched over the trash, her face is all a wrinkled blob, but her features are familiar, her eyes shrewd. It's the face of my mother, and it pulls into a sneer.

I swallow the scream lodged in my throat and bolt from the bench.

"Ma! What are you doing?" The Cantonese pronunciation is frantically bad. A balding man in a beige zip-up jacket hurries over to the woman, who's still stooped over the trash, pawing through its contents. "Ma, leave that alone. That's disgusting."

The woman ignores him, but she lets him steer her toward the bench again. He grabs a used napkin from his pants pocket and hastily starts to wipe the woman's hands, muttering all the way. Her eyes are vacant now, no longer watching me. I watch them from the platform, trying not to appear too obvious. The woman goes on with her random wellness offerings, her voice clear and distinct, but this time she's not speaking to anyone in particular.

"Kun czoi see kun guang het ngac." *Celery helps lower blood pressure*. Ma was big on this one, too, like the walnuts. The woman's son doesn't say anything, just slumps on the bench beside her, his eyes darting about. He catches me watching and glares darkly. I duck my head quickly and pretend to be absorbed with my dead phone. But I keep them in my gaze.

They sit side by side, silent except for the woman's occasional outbursts and advice. At some point, the son buries his head in his hands, rubbing the bald spot over and over in tighter and tighter circles.

I stand and wait, my legs aching, but they don't move. The man looks in my direction a couple more times, suspicious still. I fiddle with my phone and pretend to be immersed somehow with the blank screen.

They sit quietly, unmoving, until finally the woman turns to her son and says, "Jon wut ka?" *Let's go.*

He nods, resigned, and she stands, ignoring his hand of help. He casts a final glance in my direction, and this time I don't pretend I wasn't watching. I give him the smallest nod that he returns.

"Dad! You found her," a girl's voice calls from the top of the stairs.

I know that voice. It's Wei.

She hurries down the steps to meet the older woman, offering an arm for her to lean on. They move slowly up the stairs, Wei speaking rapidly in clipped Cantonese. The man follows behind. They seem like any family out for the day. I watch them, unable to look away.

At the top of the stairs, Wei finally glances over and sees me staring. Her eyes widen, blinded with panic when she recognizes me. But she turns away quickly and disappears into the station.

My train pulls in and the doors slide open. I hesitate for a moment, staring after Wei. I feel stuck, uneasy, unhinged.

The whistle blows and I board.

Chapter Twenty-Four
Ji6 sap6 sei3

THE HALLWAY OUTSIDE our apartment smells like charcoal barbecue and I can hear the smoke alarm going off inside. I quickly open the door and plumes of smoke assault my nostrils.

"Lily! Michael!" I cough against the inside of my elbow.

"It's okay. Just a bit of smoke. These gas ovens are so hard to handle," the familiar male voice calls from inside. I walk into the hazy kitchen.

Ah-Jeff is standing beside our oven door, waving a tea towel.

"Uncle Jeff, here!" Lily has found one of Baba's broadsheet newspapers and uses the pages to quickly fan the smoke away. "Phew! Oh, hey, Anna."

"Ah-Jeff. What are you doing here?"

"Where else would I be?" He gives me a crooked grin. "I hope you like charred pizza."

I smile and get plates.

* * *

Ah-Jeff makes us personal pizzas for dinner. He shows Michael how to toss the dough in the air like mini Frisbees. It's nice to have him around, even if it takes twice as long to clean up the mess of flour in the kitchen. Afterward, Lily goes to our room to study. I can't concentrate on my own schoolwork—or I just can't bring myself to care—so I pull out the *Family Guide to Mental Illness* and try to read as Ah-Jeff teaches Michael about subtraction.

Ah-Jeff helps me put Michael to bed. "Thanks for coming over," I say as we're making tea in the kitchen.

"Of course. I told you, my main job is to look after your dad. And if this is how I help out, then I'm happy to do it."

"I sort of told Baba Rory was my boyfriend."

Ah-Jeff's eyes widen as he hands me a cup. "How did he take it?"

I shrug. "He didn't say anything. But I could tell he was angry."

Ah-Jeff nods. "Your father is the old-fashioned Chinese. Strict. No feeling. Just hardworking." He makes a mean face that so closely resembles Baba that I choke on my tea. Ah-Jeff laughs.

"I hope he doesn't kill Rory," I lament.

"Give your father some time. He's a reasonable man and Rory is a good boy. He will see that."

I feel a little pleased that Rory's won Ah-Jeff's approval. "You should go home," I say. "It's almost midnight. We'll be okay."

He shrugs. "I can wait for your father."

I look around nervously. "I don't think Baba is coming home tonight. Even after everything with Ma, he'd still rather stay at the bloody restaurant. He can't even take twenty minutes to see her at the hospital." The tears I've been fighting all day threaten to overwhelm me, but I force them back down.

"You should go easy on your father. It's hard for him," Ah-Jeff says.

"He won't even admit anything's wrong. Ma was sad and stayed in bed and he just stopped coming home—" I can't hold back the tears anymore.

Ah-Jeff sighs heavily. "Anna, has your father ever told you about his cousin Rongrong?"

"No, Baba doesn't talk about his family in China except that his parents passed away and he was an only child."

"You're right, your father was an only child and Rongrong was like a sister to him. Growing up, she spent a lot of time at your grandma's house because her own mother was a bit—the English way is to say—touched in the head. She talked and sang to herself in public and the whole village whispered."

"Judgmental much?" I huff.

"It was, but that was the way things were. Rongrong grew up and met a boy working in a factory and they were going to get married. Your father was going to act as the older brother in the ceremony; he was so proud. But at the last minute, the wedding was called off. Rongrong's fiancé's family found out about her mother."

"That's horrible."

"Yes, it's the way things were. His family were worried about passing on bad genes. Rongrong was devastated. She tried to kill herself and your father stopped her, fortunately. In the end,

Rongrong joined a convent and became a nun. She cut off all ties to her mother and your father as well. Her mother was put in an institution and to this day, her daughter hasn't gone to visit."

"But it wasn't her mother's fault," I say. "And seriously, why would she want to marry a guy who doesn't approve of her family?"

Ah-Jeff sighs. "Like I said, it's the way things were. It's the way things *are*. Look at the newspaper and TV. In the US, they'd rather blame mass shootings on mental illness, not guns. It's not easy."

"Baba says there's no cure for crazy." I hate how crass that word sounds. *Crazy.*

"He's not wrong."

"But there's medicine and therapy and ways to help." I wave the thick hospital pamphlet in front of him. "There are lots of ways to manage it. Ma doesn't have to be so sad or upset or angry all the time. If Baba would just accept that she needs help, give her the support she needs, things can be better for all of us. But he's too stubborn and bullheaded for his own good. It's laai4 ngau4 soeng5 syu6." *Dragging cows up trees.*

My butchered Cantonese makes Ah-Jeff laugh. "You're very wise, Anna," he muses. "Give your father some time. Just have a little patience."

Lily is hunched over her laptop.

"How was school?" I ask.

She shrugs but doesn't look up. I figure she's busy writing an essay or doing a problem set, but then I see she's looking at

WebMD. She's also drawn up a giant table on a thick piece of paper, the columns filled with neat, precise handwriting.

"What are you doing?"

She clicks on a link and opens a page on personality disorders. "I made a list of every single time Ma was in bed or had a blowup or something. Maybe you can remember more than I can? I've got how long each episode lasted; I had to guess a lot based on emails and school assignments, but I think it's pretty close. I'm sure it'll help them."

"Help who?" For some reason, I have the urge to reach over and slam her laptop screen down.

"The doctors at the hospital. They need to know her symptoms so they can help her." She turns back to her screen. "Based on what I can tell, her highs and lows, it could be bipolar or maybe extreme anxiety. I think the timeline will help."

I see she's color-coded her columns. Ma in bed is highlighted in blue, her shouting-screaming nights are done in yellow, and then there are other things, streaks of greens and pinks.

"What are those?"

She points to the green. "People she cut off. Remember Mrs. Huang? They were friends and then out of nowhere they stopped talking." The pink: "The stories she tells. She tells them a lot. The same ones over and over about how people did this or that to her, how they slighted her. She kept us up for hours talking about them."

That sickening feeling is back in my stomach. I can't believe how much Lily remembers, how she's putting it all down, writing it all out like a problem set. I hate seeing it all laid out in front of me, screaming the obvious. *Something is wrong with your mother. This is not normal.*

I want to tear the chart into pieces.

But maybe, maybe this is a good idea, maybe it will help like Lily says. She's so lost in her documenting, writing furiously and drawing deliberate neon streaks. There are more colored boxes than not. So, so, so many bad days. Where are the good ones?

"Anna." Lily cocks her head to the side. "Do you remember the convenience store that Ma stopped going to 'cause she said the owner was snobby? Was that on Thomas or Elizabeth?"

I force myself to think of the words she's saying. Ma's changed her route, changed her routine so many times, it's hard to keep track. But just because she changes her behavior, it doesn't need to be color-coded, does it?

Thinking about Ma, about her erratic behavior, fills me with an icky guilt. Like I'm being a bad daughter with just my thoughts. I'm committing the ultimate Chinese daughter crime. M4 haau3 seon6. *Not filial pious.*

I realize I can't help Lily with her chart. So I go to bed.

I wake up to a strange, low buzzing. The room is pitch-black. The buzzing is my phone on my desk. I pick it up. *Unknown number.*

"Hello?"

"Anna! Anna!" The voice on the other end is high-pitched and energetic. *Ma.*

"Mommy?" The tears flow. "It's good to hear your voice. You must be feeling better."

"Oh, Anna, it's amazing. I have never felt so alive." She sing-songs the words, a little off-key. "Anna, we were playing a game before. I pretended you were someone I didn't know to trick her."

"Game?" I sit up, shaking off sleep. "When I was there? You didn't say anything about a game."

"It was a good game. We tricked her good."

"Tricked who?"

"Simone. I didn't want her to know you are my daughter. Shhh. That will be our secret, okay?"

"Ma." I wipe my eyes with the back of my arm. *Was that why she was being so weird at the hospital today?*

"Why would you do that?"

"I don't want her to know my secret. She's a spy for government. I've seen her talking on the phone on her break. She's telling them the patients' secrets. I'm sure she'll get fired soon."

Her voice has a pitch. And she's not making sense. *Is this her psychosis? Maybe the hospital isn't making her better. Maybe she's worse.* My chest shudders as I try to weep as silently as possible.

"Oh, Anna, you sound like you are crying. Don't cry. Shh. It's okay. Your mother is happy again. So nothing to worry about. You tell them your mother can come home now, okay?"

"You can't, Ma. You have to get better."

But she doesn't hear me. "Oh, Anna. I hate it here so much. It's boring, and the people are strange. There's a lady here who won't stop crying. She's so sad. I tell her not to be so sad, but she is always crying. Anna, don't cry, okay?"

"Okay, Ma." I choke back a sob.

"Anna, I'll draw you a picture, okay? I'll draw a beautiful picture with amazing birds. Wah, Anna, I am so amazed. I have never drawn anything so perfect before. I'll give it to you tomorrow, okay? And then we can go home together. Okay?"

"Okay, Ma." I realize I can hide the sobbing by forcing myself to smile, but nothing can stop the tears.

"Anna, come get me tomorrow. I miss you, baby girl. You and Lily, too."

"Okay, Ma." This comes out as no more than a whisper.

"She's calling my name. The horrible nurse. Don't tell her our secret, okay? She can't know you are my daughter. Just tell her you are my friend. No, tell her you're my sister, okay?"

I can't force any more words, so I nod even though she can't see.

"I have to go now. They listen to the phone calls." And she hangs up abruptly without a goodbye.

The wails burst from my chest. I blubber and howl, pushing my face into my blanket.

"Anna?" I feel a weight on my bed and thin arms wrap around me.

"Lily." I clutch her to my chest and bawl until my lungs feel raw and my cheeks sting. Lily curls around me, the same way I did to her the night Ma came into our room.

"Shh, it's okay, Anna."

We hold each other until we fall asleep.

Chapter Twenty-Five

Ji6 sap6 ng5

I CAN'T BRING MYSELF TO go back to the hospital. Baba rings while I'm in class, and he never calls from the restaurant. He leaves a hurried message.

Neoi5, daughter, *where are you? Hospital called.*

Your mother needs you.

I delete it and don't ring back.

The next couple of days, I'm a zombie. I make myself go to school and do my homework, trying to put Ma and the hospital out of my mind. Rory and I send each other memes.

How are you doing?

I'm okay. 😔

I know he's worried. I know he wants to talk more. I know I

should try. Try to talk about Ma. But I don't want to. I just need to pretend to be normal. Just for once.

But it's far from normal. Ma calls me every night. She asks me to bring Michael.

"When will you come see your mama, Anna?"

"I have to go to bed, Ma. I have school." I can't bring myself to just hang up.

When she finally gets off the phone, Lily crawls into bed with me, stroking my hair like she's the big sister.

"It's okay, Anna. It'll be okay." Her soothing words lull me into a dreamless sleep.

On Friday afternoon, I'm called into Miss Kennedy's office.

"Have a seat, Anna." Miss Kennedy's pink paper clips are gone, replaced with cherry red. I try not to think of the watery rivers of goldfish blood running down Ma's wrists.

"How are you doing today?" She smiles without showing her teeth.

I shrug. "All right, I guess." I try to smile the same way, but it feels wrong.

"We're well into Term Three now. Have you had a chance to think about what we discussed? Maybe picked up some additional extracurriculars?"

"Um, not really," I mutter, refusing to meet her eyes. "Things got a little . . . busy this term."

"Anna, we talked about you reaching your potential. I know you're a smart girl, and you've done enough to get by. But your grades are mediocre at best, and with the HSCs coming up, you're going to find it tough to keep up with your fellow classmates . . ."

Something inside me snaps. "Maybe I'm just fine with being mediocre. Maybe I don't care to tick these arbitrary boxes for you to see me as a functioning human being."

Miss Kennedy looks taken aback, wounded even, and I feel a little bad for my outburst—but only a little bit.

"I see." She pulls up in her chair and starts to stack her folders. "Well, that's fine—it's *your* future, after all." She doesn't meet my eye. Her polished nails click against the laminate surface. "I'm just here to help *you*. But I think you should rethink your priorities, Anna, and treat people who are looking out for you with a bit more respect."

I squeeze my hands into fists. I could storm out, but I'm conditioned to respect elders. "I'm sorry, Miss Kennedy. I've . . . had a very trying week. I lost my temper." I force a tense smile.

She finally looks up. "Well, Anna, it's important to learn a bit of self-control. We can't just throw tantrums."

You're telling me. "Of course not," I say through gritted teeth.

She gives me a fake smile. "Let's put it on your list for personal development." She taps my file three times like she's casting a charm on it. "How about you mull over that a bit, and we'll schedule another appointment before the end of the year?"

"Of course." I resist the urge to add a sardonic *miss* and curtsy. I hightail it out of her now-suffocating office and run smack into another student.

"Watch it!" I look up to see who I've almost mowed over.

It's Wei. We haven't seen each other since that incident at Burwood station.

She looks horrified, guilty, like I've caught her pilfering from a collection tin. She tries to push past me.

"Wait, Wei." I grab her by the arm. "Was that your grandmother?"

"What's it to you?" Her eyes narrow into needles.

"I just—I just wanted to see if you wanted to talk about it?" I gulp. "I—I saw your dad. And it—it must be hard."

She looks like she wants to answer, but another voice calls out to her.

"Wei, what are you doing?" Connie is walking toward us, her highlighted hair floating behind her like a veil. "Why are you talking to her?"

I drop Wei's arm. "This isn't your business, Connie." I look to Wei for affirmation, but she shakes her head.

"Oh my god, Anna. You're as wacko as your mother," Connie sneers.

A tingling terror spreads upward, starting from the base of my skull. "What do you mean?"

She shrugs. "My dad told me about the 'incident' at the restaurant." Her air quotes make me want to scream. "But come on—the walnuts, my family's party. Everyone knows your mother should be committed."

She grabs Wei's arm and the two of them stalk off. I think I see Wei looking back toward me, but I can't be sure through the blurriness of my tears.

I have to get out of here. The bell rings for the last class, but there's no way I'm sitting in that room with Connie and Wei.

I reach for my phone.

> **What are you up to? I need to get out of here.**

It feels like eons before Rory replies.

> **I have to work, remember.**

> **Call in sick. Please??**

> **I need to do something normal.**

A long wait.

> **Your dad's going to kill me.**

He probably will, but right now I don't care.

> **I'll meet you at Hornsby.**

I've been waiting at the station for a good thirty minutes and Rory hasn't come. Clusters of dark green, blue, maroon, brown, and gray uniforms have passed through as kids come out of school. They always come in distinct waves, never intermingling, never a brown skirt mixed in with a bunch of maroon blazers. I don't really stick out much, a lone navy skirt who keeps staring at her phone.

> **Where are you??**

Rory hasn't texted back and I wonder if he's bailed, or maybe Baba wouldn't let him call in sick. Come to think of it, outside of Rory's mental health day, I don't remember anyone ever calling in sick in the years that Baba's owned the place. Loyalty and a relentless work ethic—it's the only way Chinese restaurants like Baba's stay solid.

Finally, I hear the loud purr and the throttle of the Audi engine. Rory has the top down and he's wearing his sunglasses. I want to hop coolly over the side, launch myself into the seat, but I know that's asking for disaster, so I just open the door.

"What took you so long?" I'm grateful to see him even if I sound a little snappish.

"Sorry, I was getting supplies." He pushes the sunglasses up on top of his head and puts the roof up before we drive away from the station.

"Supplies?" I ask.

"You'll see." He pulls into an empty parking lot and reaches into the back seat. With a wink, he hands me a giant plastic bag. "Anna's Emergency Normal Kit."

I frown and peer inside the bag. Then I burst out laughing.

"This is what you think I meant by doing something 'normal'?" I pull out bottles of neon nail polish and copies of *Cosmopolitan* and *Vogue*. "What am I, a Real Housewife?"

Rory shrugs. "Don't forget the Taylor Swift album. Oh, and here." He retrieves a giant Starbucks cup out of his cup holder. The black marker scrawl says *ANN*. "This is for you."

"Thanks." I feel ridiculous and better. "You know, I bet Miss Kennedy would think this is totally me on my way to personal development." I tell him about my second Pathways meeting.

"Rough. My guidance counselor was like that. She was all positivity and focus, believe, achieve. Like somehow it was just my mind-set and attitude. And if I just 'fixed my outlook' I could simply snap myself out of my shit." He shakes his head.

"I thought I should tell her about Ma," I say. "So she'd lay off me. But it would just raise questions."

"You should talk to *someone* about it. If not me, someone at school?"

I shake my head, thinking of my encounter with Connie and Wei.

"I'm serious, Anna. It'll be good for you to get this stuff off your chest. You can't keep it bottled up inside."

My stubbornness softens. I know Rory wants to help. I want to trust him; I know I can trust him. But even when I think about opening my mouth, to let go of the terror, angst, and sadness inside, the worries I have for Ma still in the hospital, for Baba, who still hasn't come home, for Lily and her giant spreadsheet charting Ma's moods, and how desperate I am for a sign, any sign that this will all be okay, the words themselves are stuck somewhere and won't come out. I ponder this for a bit.

"I—I guess I don't really know how to talk about it. The language is missing."

Rory chews his lip, his fingers drumming the steering wheel for a bit. Then he breaks into a smile. "I have an idea."

Rory exits the freeway and pulls onto a small road. We're somewhere near the national park, Ku-ring-gai I think. The roads are steep and windy, lined with trees.

We come to a dead end, fenced by low barriers made of logs and tree stumps. Beyond them is a slump of white buildings, identical and discrete.

Rory pulls up the glossy black handbrake and opens his door.

"Where are we going?"

He points toward the buildings and I hesitate.

"Come on." He slams his door shut, and we head beyond the barriers. My heart feels like it's squeezing up into my vocal box. Rory takes my hand.

We have to go sideways through the narrow gap between the buildings. I shiver and hug my arms. It's a few degrees cooler here; the concrete walls hardly ever see the sun. There are vines clinging to the rough gray surfaces and tiny leaves and green tendrils tickle my skin, along my legs and even next to my face. It's amazing to think that in this tiny chasm, practically forgotten by humanity, life still thrives.

On the other side is a weathered wooden fence. Rory turns, his steps unerring as he tramples through the overgrown grass. There are cigarette butts littered all over, and I spot the glint of a broken bottle.

"Through here." Rory wedges his fingers beneath a timber slat and moves it to the side so that the top rests against the tips of some bent rusty nails. I clamber through the opening and catch my shoelace on a sliver of wood.

When I emerge from the opening, I see two dirt paths, one wide and well-trodden that swings to the left, and to the right, a small strip of trampled weeds hint at a walkway beneath it. I turn automatically to the left but Rory grabs my hand.

"This way," he says, and leads me through the weeds. I smile when he keeps hold of my hand.

Two roads diverged in a wood, and I—

"I took the one less traveled by." Rory finishes the Robert Frost quote without me saying a word. He looks back and smiles. He leads me deeper into the line of trees, sure-footed. He's been here before.

Finally, we are standing on a steep embankment. Rory leads me up another windy path. We walk for a while, close to the edge, until we come to a clearing. There's nothing but wilderness stretched out before us and I take a deep breath. My lungs sting with the clean, crisp air. We are nowhere and anywhere in the same moment.

"This—this is incredible." I spin around, slowly, taking in the view.

Rory is standing at the base of an old tree. It's an oak of some sort, gnarly and misshapen. He points to a hole in the middle of the trunk.

"Do you know Wong Kar-Wai?" he asks.

I nod and walk toward him. Wong Kar-Wai is one of those infamous Hong Kong directors who made a big name overseas.

"There's that movie, with the hotel room . . ."

"*2046,*" I say. I liked the movie but mostly because I could watch it without the English subtitles. I tried to draw deep cinematic insights with my broken Cantonese.

Rory smiles. "That's right. And in the movie, the protagonist has a secret he can't tell anyone . . ."

"So he whispers it into a tree," I finish. My heart is racing and my palms are sweaty. Rory takes my hand.

"Yeah." He looks down at our interlaced fingers. "After I was in the hospital, I started seeing my therapist, and in the beginning, I was all closed up. I just didn't know how to . . . how to talk. Then I thought of the movie. So I drove around to find the perfect spot."

He drops my hand and I feel the loss until he guides his arm around my waist and turns me toward the tree. "I thought perhaps you might find your words here."

He guides me to the trunk, bringing my hand upward. I lean forward. The hole is no bigger than a tennis ball. It doesn't seem very deep; I wonder how many secrets it can contain. But it looks comfortable, the rounded edges are well-handled and smooth; I can picture many a wanderer gripping it by the sides as they whisper their weary thoughts.

I step toward it and put my face up to the knot. It smells warm, musty in an aged way. I put my ear to it, but the tree is loyal to its purpose. Rory's secrets are safely tucked away. I turn back to him, feeling a bit ridiculous. "You want me to talk to a tree?"

But there's no mistaking the dead seriousness of his face. "Go on," he says. "Take as long as you need. I'll wait at the car." And he heads back the way we came.

I turn back to the knot. *This is so ridiculous.* If Wei or Connie could see me now, they'd definitely think I've lost my marbles.

But Rory thinks it will help. And there is something irresistibly inviting about the worn edges, like clasped fingers forming a shallow cup.

Here goes nothing.

I teeter onto my toes, seeking my voice.

I emerge from the bushland, the leaves and gravel giving a satisfying crunch beneath my feet.

The car is idling and Rory has his eyes closed, mouthing along to some unheard lyrics. I'm not an expert lip reader, but I swear it's Aretha Franklin. He looks so animated, his hair flopping about, neck loose and shoulders shaking, lost in his cocoon of music. My body surges with warm fuzzies and caterpillars of affection.

He spots me and reaches for the volume knob as I open the door and I catch the last bars of the song. "How'd you go?" he asks.

"Um." I choose my words carefully. "It was a bit awkward?" I didn't really get very far spilling my secrets, and I don't want to seem ungrateful for everything he's shown me.

He nods thoughtfully. "All right, I guess tree talking isn't for everyone." He looks pensive for a long while. "What about journaling instead?" he suggests.

"Oh." I consider this for a bit. I used to keep a diary when I was little, one with bright purple hearts and a tiny metal key. I stopped when five-year-old Lily figured out how to break in. But thinking about it now, a notebook with my thoughts, my worries, my fears . . . "I can try that. I think it'll work better than a tree," I say.

"If you want to, when you feel ready, you can make an appointment with Cindy. She's really awesome and easy to talk to."

I hesitate. "I don't know. I mean, I'm sure she has other patients with bigger problems . . ."

Rory huffs. "That's the thing. Everyone thinks therapy is for when things get too bad, but really we all could use someone to talk to. Or even a tree."

I definitely hadn't considered talking to a professional before. At school, they encourage us to talk to the guidance counselor, but there is no way I'm booking more time with Miss Kennedy.

"You have to find someone you're comfortable talking to," Rory says, like he's reading my mind. "So if Cindy doesn't work out, you can find another therapist. It's all about finding the right match for you."

"Hmm. And what if . . . I wanted to talk to my therapist about you?" I ask playfully.

Rory is unfazed. "That's fine. It's all professional courtesy. But let me warn you, Cindy already knows how awesome I am."

I laugh and punch him on the shoulder. It's like a curtain has been lifted. The air feels lighter and I have to admit, even though talking to a tree felt ridiculous, I *do* feel better.

"Thank you. For everything," I say.

Rory grins and starts the car. The radio comes back on.

"'Natural Woman'?"

He smiles and winks. "You know it."

And then he leans over and kisses me, and I feel a deep pulling inside me. I drag him closer, feel the tiny hairs on the back of his neck, the base of his throat, taste the inside of his mouth. My legs and hips move, and I'm climbing out of my seat and into his lap.

His hands roam over my uniform, large enough to cover most of my back. I feel light-headed and finally pull back to breathe. My glasses are askew and he looks a little wonky through them, but I hardly register it.

"How's this for normal?" he whispers.

I answer with a kiss.

"I'm worried about my mom." We're lying on the hood of the car watching the sky pinken. After a lot of making out, talking seems easier. Maybe it's all the blood rushing away from my head.

Rory nudges my ribs. "Elaborate?"

"I'm worried the hospital isn't making her any better. She calls me every night and she doesn't make sense."

"Hospitals are shit." Rory's bluntness startles me, and I turn to him. He's staring up at the clouds. From this angle, his eyes are golden half-moons, smooth and hard like marbles.

"Hospitals are shit," he says again. "But they do their job." He falls silent for a while. "When was the last time you saw her?"

"That day you drove me," I say. "I hated seeing her there. I hate waiting for nothing."

"Maybe you should give it another try."

I turn back to the sky. The clouds are fluffy purple and lavender hues. I think I see a goldfish and catch myself thinking it's a sign.

"I just wish I knew what's wrong with her. So I can fix it."

Rory turns toward me. His brow wrinkles and those sleek marbles glint in the almost-twilight. "So you think I need to be fixed?"

I reach for him and cup the side of his jaw, feeling a prickling of whiskers. "No, that's not what I mean." He smiles, so I know he believes me. "I just don't know what to do. How to act. I don't know who she is anymore."

"She's your mother. And I'm sure she misses you."

I kiss him again. I'm done with talking for a while.

Chapter Twenty-Six
Ji6 sap6 luk2

I DON'T WANT TO BE HERE. The hallway smells like antiseptic and musk that makes me gag. My breaths are short and ragged, and I can't stop pacing and wringing my hands over and over.

I'm back at the hospital for visiting hours, Michael and Lily at my side. It's been more than a week since Ma was first admitted. Since then, she's been calling me every day, asking us to come. Some nights she sounded happy, just wanting a chat; other times she was sinister and angry, whispering about Simone, the patients, and staff. Every time I picked up the phone, I'd check the time. An even minute meant she'd be normal, loving, and chatty, and an odd minute meant she'd be on the edge. The signs didn't work, but I needed them to guide me.

I didn't want Michael or Lily to see Ma all drugged up and not knowing her own family. I asked Baba what we should do. He was still at the restaurant; he said it was up to us.

I knew we couldn't put it off forever. This morning, after Ah-Jeff left us, the shadows by Ma's door looked like happy children, plump and lively. There was no point putting off the inevitable.

"How about we go visit Ma today?" I asked brightly.

Lily was hesitant, but Michael was overjoyed. I knew he missed Ma terribly, the trauma of the aquarium forgotten in his young mind.

We're here now, loitering outside the ward, waiting for the clock to tick over. I keep an eye out for Velour Suit, but she's nowhere to be seen.

"Anna, are you okay?" Michael asks.

"I'm fine," I snap, and he looks alarmed. I'm horrified at myself, as I try to never ever yell at him.

"I'm sorry," I add quickly, and give him a hug. "I didn't mean to snap at you."

"It's okay. You're just worried about Ma." He's so matter-of-fact and genuine. He's six now and he seems older and wiser, even though I can't see past the fact that he's my baby brother. I reach down and hug him tighter.

"That's right."

The double doors swing open and Simone steps out. She sees me right away. "You're back. I wasn't sure if you would be." I can't tell if she's being sarcastic or sincere.

"Um, yeah, I'm back. This is my sister and brother." Lily and Michael give shy waves. Simone's presence has me on guard, but I do my best to smile and look friendly for Ma's benefit.

"Dr. Patel wants to talk to you." I've forgotten that I had asked to speak to Ma's doctor. I should have come prepared, made a list of questions, but it's too late.

"I got this," Lily whispers beside me, and pulls out a neatly rolled tube of paper. Her color-coded chart. I smile, feeling grateful that she's forever the lovable, studious nerd.

We put our belongings in a locker, and once again I've forgotten a lock. Nurse Mary signs us in.

"Anna." She remembers me. "Your mother has said such wonderful things. And this must be Lily and Michael." I squirm under her kind gaze. I wonder what exactly Ma has been saying in her state. "She's already waiting in the kitchen. She'll be so happy to see you."

My Chinese guilt hangs heavy. I can't believe she's been waiting for us and we never came. *What a terrible daughter.*

Mary points the way. My insides belly flop.

I can see her sitting at the table, facing the door. I notice that she's gained weight; her cheeks look plump and filled out. She stands up eagerly when she sees us.

"Lai4 lai4 lai4." *Come here.*

Michael stops in the doorway. He gawks at Ma, unsure of what to do. She waves him over.

"Bou2 bou2, come to your mother. Look at how you've grown." There are tears in her eyes.

And all at once, we rush forward and hug our mother.

Ma cries. Michael cries. I cry. Lily sniffles. We hug and sob and rock together. Ma looks like Ma again; she feels and sounds real and warm. She's not a distant voice on the phone or a zombie that answers to Miss Ping. She's Ma.

And she's back.

Eventually, we pull apart and sit down around the table. Ma won't let go of us, so we all have our hands in the middle, like a stacking game. Her eyes are still wet and she's beaming.

"I'm so warm and happy. I'm so, so happy," she says. I nod with her and we ugly-cry, letting our tears fall, because we don't want to use our hands to wipe them away.

"Michael, you look taller now. You still do art in school?" He nods and goes to cuddle her. "I'm so proud of you. I do art here, too." She pulls out a folded piece of paper from her pocket and smooths it out carefully on the table.

"Look, I drew this for you. Isn't it beautiful?" The large looping scrawls are green and gold, streaks of red cutting through. Ma beams and points. "So beautiful, right?" she says in English. And she flaps her hands like giant wings.

It's the drawing she mentioned on the phone after I first visited. The birds. But all I see are whirly winds and giant tick marks that if I squinted could be wings. It's not anything close to what I'd call a bird at all.

But Ma looks so happy, so proud, so all I say is "It's beautiful." Lily makes a face.

Ma beams like a kindergartner receiving praise, then carefully pockets the page. "I want you to go to art program, become good artist," she tells Michael. "Art makes people happy. Art is good. Happy life is good."

"It's too late now," Michael says, but he doesn't sound too upset about it.

"Next year. I tell your teacher you can go for next year, okay? I want you to go." He wraps his arms around Ma's neck, and she pulls him into her lap.

"Lily, my beautiful, intelligent daughter." She reaches for Lily's hand. "You are smarter and always study so hard. You are going to grow up to be so beautiful and clever and will get a good job and your husband will love you because you are so special."

Lily doesn't say anything, but her expressive face can't hide her surprise. I don't think she's ever thought these things or heard them spoken aloud from our mother. I can see her analytical brain working to process it. And then, finally, I see her smile and my whole heart smiles as she hugs our mother.

Ma laughs and strokes her younger daughter's back and turns to me.

"Anna, my darling Anna. You are such a good sister. Such a good daughter. How is the boy? He good to you?"

Oh no, did Baba say something? I feel bad about the whole Rory boyfriend business now. "He—he's okay." I feel the heat on my face.

"He's good boy. I can tell. Very kind. Kind heart. He makes you happy. You look so happy, Anna. It's love. Love is the good thing. Love and happy." And she reaches out a thumb to brush at tears still running down my face.

I'm stunned. I don't know what to say. Lily looks the way I feel, her mouth slack and hanging wide open. Ma knows I have a boyfriend, and she seems . . . *okay* with it? I reach up to hold her hand to my face.

"I want to sing you a song. I have a good song. Makes me very happy. So I sing it all the time."

"Sing it, Mommy," Michael demands. "I like your voice."

Ma smiles. "Okay, we sing together?" She looks at us and sucks in a deep breath and begins in warbling Mandarin.

"Shi shang zhi you Mama hao.
You Ma de hai zi xiang ge bao.
Tou jin le Mama de huai bao,
Xing fu xiang bu liao!"
Mommy is the best in the world.
With a mom you have the most valuable treasure.
Jump into your mom's heart,
And you will find happiness!

It's a kids' nursery rhyme. I don't remember Ma ever singing it, not to me, not to Lily, not to Michael. I think I might have heard it on TV once, or maybe on YouTube or the radio. Ma sings it, belts it with gusto, her eyes wet and teary as she turns to all three of us.

The words are easy enough, even for my really awful Mandarin. After a few bars, very very softly, I join in. Michael hums along, not sure of the lyrics but catching the melody. Lily stays mute, watching us, probably judging or wondering and processing the signs that are unfolding before her.

I can't read the signs myself. I'm baffled by Ma's song choice; is it more of her suspicion of us or is it something else?

But Ma is singing, loud and clear and strong. She's Ma with all her fire, all her rage, all her love that is sometimes too fierce. I sing with her and Michael and as our voices start to fade on the last bar, even Lily finally joins in.

"*Xing fun na li zhao?*"
Where will you find happiness?

There's a slow clapping behind us, and we all turn.
Baba is standing in the doorway, wiping tears from his eyes.

Chapter Twenty-Seven
Ji2 sap2 cat1

"BABA, YOU'RE HERE."

My father doesn't hear me as he approaches the table, his eyes locked on Ma's. They gaze adoringly at each other, like a courting couple. I can glimpse a moment from their past, what they would have been like years younger, before Sydney, before the restaurant, before any of us were in the picture.

"Lou5 po4, how are you today?" He surveys the table. "Our darling children have come to see you."

"Hoi1 sam1 saai3 le!" *Extremely happy.* "You didn't wear a jacket today; are you cold?"

He didn't bring a jacket today. Which means he's been before. I'm surprised. I thought after that first day, when he sent me to bring Ma's things to her, that Baba had stayed away. He hasn't come home, sending Ah-Jeff in his stead. Could it be that he's been caring for Ma all this time?

Baba takes a seat at the table and stretches out to join our pinwheel of hands, smiling warmly. "I'm so glad you came. My beautiful family all together. This is a happy day."

My heart is heavy with guilt. I've been the one staying away. I've been the bad daughter.

"I'll be back." I excuse myself from the table and go into the corridor. I lean my forehead against the wall, feeling the little bumps and textures of paint press against my skin, soaking in the coolness. A roar of laughter comes from inside the kitchen; Ma and Baba's voices ring like a symphony. They sound young and happy.

"Anna." I'm startled out of my reverie by Lily. She has that fierce wrinkle between her eyebrows, clutching her paper tube in her hands. "Remember. We have to talk to the doctor."

"Right." I scratch my head. "Dr. Patel."

"Yes?" a voice answers from the check-in station, and we hurry over. Dr. Patel is peering down at the notes on her clipboard and finally raises her head.

"Ah, Anna, right? Nurse Mary said you wanted to speak with me." She registers Lily standing beside me. "I assume this is your sister."

"Yes." Lily offers a very adult handshake. "I'm Lily Chiu. Nice to meet you."

Dr. Patel smiles kindly, but there's a cool demeanor about her gaze. "I have a few minutes before my next appointment. Shall we step into my office?"

*   *   *

Dr. Patel's office is packed with three neat desks, file folders, and papers. In the middle of the room are two identical pod-like chairs with mint-green cushions. The large whiteboard on the wall shows that Dr. Patel shares this space with a Dr. Fitzgerald and a Dr. Adelaide.

"Have a seat." She gestures to one of the pods, and Lily and I perch on the edge of the sagging seat, shifting to make room for both of us. I wonder if this is where Ma sits when she's treated, or if that's all done in her room that I'm not allowed in.

"So what can I do for you today, ladies?" She's all business, and I resist the urge to neaten my jeans and T-shirt. I feel like I'm being interviewed for a scholarship or placement, though I've never sat through one of those interactions before either. *Is this what Rory does with his therapist, Cindy?* She doesn't wait for us to answer. "Nurse Mary says that you have some questions about your mom's treatment?"

"Well—" I'm stalling, but Lily jabs me in the side. "I, ah—we just wanted to know more about all of this. What is she on? Is she getting better?"

Dr. Patel jots down some notes. "Sure."

She proceeds to describe Ma's treatment plan, rattling off drug names, terms, and dosages. Her voice is fast and clipped, and I struggle to keep up, catching only a few words. Lithium. Sleep aid. Mood stabilizer. It swirls into a giant mess.

Lily's brow is deeply furrowed in concentration, but the rest of her face is set in a scowl.

I try to remember what I read in the pamphlet. "Um. But the lithium—so that's, like, for depression, right?"

"I think we need to consider all possibilities in addition to depression," Lily butts in. She unravels her chart and gestures to the fluorescent marks across the page. "See, her moods are up and down all the time. That could be bipolar. Bits of dissociative personality, maybe."

"I see." Dr. Patel studies the page, her eyes scrutinizing Lily's work. She gives my sister a half smirk. "You've put a lot of work into this, haven't you?"

"The chart covers three years. There are some gaps because I couldn't remember. Up and down. Happy. Sad. Like a yo-yo. See?"

That aching ickiness is back. Lily sounds so crass and matter-of-fact about Ma's moods, and she doesn't blink an eye. I feel like we're betraying her somehow. *We're talking about what we're not supposed to discuss.*

But Dr. Patel looks impressed. She takes Lily's chart and studies it carefully. "This is very good, Lily. This will definitely help us plan your mother's care."

Ever the perfect student, Lily beams with pride.

But Dr. Patel isn't finished. "Your mother has had a psychotic delusion, which means she's having some problems telling what's real and what's not. It's going to take some time for us to understand the best way to treat her."

I recall Rory recounting his path to treatment. "What happens now?"

"Our main focus at the moment is to get the brain chemistry back in balance and reduce the psychotic symptoms. As part of the program here she's been participating in group therapy as well as social art."

"But—but Ma can't do group therapy." Lily looks appalled. "She doesn't like speaking English to strangers. She can't."

I'm trying to picture Ma talking about her feelings in her broken English and everyone laughing at her. I have to agree with Lily. How will she get better this way?

Dr. Patel sits back and clasps Ma's folder to her knees. "Girls, I understand you're worried about your mother. And I promise that we will take good care of her. You have to trust us. She's doing well."

"Well? How is she doing well?" Lily explodes. "She's singing weird songs, and did you know that she's calling Anna at all hours of the night? That's not normal." She can't stop the tears from cascading down her fiery red cheeks. "You're the doctors! Why aren't you doing anything to *help* her?"

"Lily . . ." I put a hand on her knee, but she jerks free. She leaps up onto her feet, and before I can say anything, she grabs her chart from Dr. Patel's hands and rips the page in two. She throws them to the ground and storms out of the room, knocking over some papers on one of the desks in her haste to exit.

"Lily!" I call out after her, but it's no use. She's gone. Dr. Patel hasn't moved, hasn't even flinched. Red-faced, I try to offer some wayward explanation. "I'm so sorry about that. This has all been really hard for her."

"Of course." She gives me a serene smile. "It's not at all

uncommon, and you shouldn't apologize for your emotional response to the situation. It's a very difficult circumstance, and your family is under a lot of stress."

I toy with a frayed thread on my shirt, trying to find the words for what I want to say. "Lily, Lily's always had a harder time dealing with our mother. She—she can make things worse sometimes. They butt heads a lot."

It's a struggle, but I manage to find some of the words to express my thoughts. I've been writing a bit in a journal now, trying to understand how I feel about Ma, our family, and everything that's happened. "Ma always finds some reason to be angry with us. I used to think it was because we did something wrong, but maybe—maybe now I realize—it's really no one's fault?"

Dr. Patel gives me a reassuring smile. "Family dynamics are always challenging, and mental well-being can definitely throw a wrench in the works, especially when cultural elements are involved." I am so relieved. She gets it. She's easy to talk to, nonjudgmental and sage. I wonder if maybe I should speak to her more, remembering what Rory said about talking to someone professional. Maybe someone like Dr. Patel could be a real help for me, someday.

"So, what happens next?" I ask. "How long will she have to be here?"

Her thick eyebrows draw in. "It's hard to say at this stage. We don't want to rush things. She needs routine and support in a stable environment that we can provide here." She leans forward again. "You miss her, don't you?"

"I—" *Do I miss Ma? Does Lily miss Ma? Do I miss the good*

days and the bad days and the guessing and the unpredictability? I'm not sure. "I just want her to be okay." That's the truest thing I can say.

"Your mother is very lucky. Not all of our patients have family to help. She's going to need your ongoing support. This is the beginning of the journey." She reaches out and folds her hand over mine. They are surprisingly calloused, but her grip is warm, firm, and reassuring. "But we'll do it together. You can trust me."

There it is again. That word. *Trust.* It's a funny word that tries to roll off your tongue but doesn't quite make it, caught on the tight curl of the tip. The air hisses out between your teeth when you finally say it, all sinister-sounding, like a serpent's word.

Trust.

It's a heavy word, that can make and break us. Help or hurt us.

Trust.

For so long, I didn't feel like I could trust anyone. Could I trust a doctor I've only met once before with my mother's condition, even if that doctor seems sympathetic and easy to talk to?

Ma seems better today; she speaks like Ma, even if she's singing strange songs. And she seems happy. Giddily so, but happy. It's not what I would have ever called "normal," but I'm starting to see that maybe what I call "normal" is just a state of mind.

I look the kind doctor in the eyes and finally say, "Okay."

She nods approvingly.

I find Lily locked in a stall in the visitors' bathroom, drawing out long sobs. My heart breaks for her.

"Lily. We have to go."

There's a long pause and then a roaring flush. The door opens and Lily steps out. Her eyes are red and inflamed, her cheeks raw. She avoids my gaze in her reflection as she splashes water on her face.

"Lily." I know I need to say something reassuring, bright, and hopeful in a good big sister way. "It's going to be okay."

She ignores me as she soaps up her hands, staring intently at the suds as the water runs over them.

"The doctors know what they're doing," I go on. "They're going to help Ma—"

"You know the first thing I thought when I heard Ma was in the hospital?" she blurts out, whipping around to face me with all her angry energy. I can only shake my head.

"The first thing I thought . . ." She tilts her head up toward the ceiling as the tears flow again. "I was bloody *relieved*." Her sobs come. "Can you believe that? I was relieved that my own mother was in the hospital. What is wrong with me?"

"Oh, Lily." I fold my arms around her. My poor, brilliant little sister carries the weight of the world on her tiny shoulders, and I always forget she's barely a teen. I bury my nose into her thick mess of hair. "Of course you felt relieved. I did, too, a little." It's true. After everything we'd been through, bending and twisting to Ma's moods, hiding everything and pretending everything was just normal, this had been the brutal snap we'd all been waiting for. *And now we can finally move forward.*

"I'm a terrible, horrible person," Lily wails into my chest.

"Lily. Look at me." I make her lift her sniveling face and peer over the tops of my glasses so there's nothing coming between our gaze. "Lily. You are amazing and strong and passionate. And Ma loves you. I know she does. And she is so damn lucky to have you as her daughter."

I can tell she doesn't believe me. *She needs more.*

"And most of all, you're an incredible sister." My own vision is blurring now. "And I'm the luckiest of all to have you by my side."

Her bottom lip trembles, and we both start to cry. We hug and hold each other until we're gasping and then suddenly we're giggling hysterically, big belly guffaws, like the whole room's filled with laughing gas. Love is like that sometimes, all-encompassing, nonsensical, and beyond our control.

Finally, I wipe the last of the tears from my eyes.

"Come on. They must be worried about us."

Lily reaches for my hand. Her slender fingers slide between my own. Of all our features, our hands are the most similar; the same size, the same shape, the pairs of them made to work together.

She squeezes my hand and I squeeze back. We give each other strength.

"Ready to face the music?" She nods. "Let's go."

The four of us leave the hospital together—Baba, Michael, Lily, and me. Ma seems a little sad as Simone calls her away, but she hugs us all in turn, even Baba. "Be good. Mama loves you all so much." She blows us all kisses.

"All right, Miss Ping, they can come back tomorrow." I notice Ma scowl at the orderly and I can't help but smile. Ma is Ma.

"Come back to the restaurant," Baba says as we head to the parking lot. "You think your boyfriend, *Rory*, will mind driving you home?" He looks me squarely in the eye. It's the first time he's mentioned the subject since I let it out.

"I—I'm sure he'll be fine with it," I stammer. Baba grunts and gets in the car as I hide my smile.

Not quite a conversation, but it's something.

It takes just a few minutes to get to the Jade Palace. Baba calls me into his office. Lily and Michael play a game with Miss Chen in the dining room. I haven't been back since *the incident* and the atmosphere of the restaurant feels surprisingly relaxed. I can't believe how much I've missed it. I'm also pleased to see that the aquarium is gone and in its place is a nondescript print of brushstroke calligraphy.

"Come, sit. I want to show you something." Baba takes out a clear page protector that is jammed full of paper.

He pulls out the top sheet and hands it to me. It's a crinkled black-and-white printout of a commercial real estate pamphlet. A thick white fold line runs through the middle of a tiny shopfront on a familiar-looking street. I peer at the address. *Liverpool Road, Ashfield.*

"Baba, what is this?"

"It's little, takeaway only, I suspect. I've done the math. The margins will be tight and the overheads are more expensive, but we save on staff. Ah-Jeff said he will come and work with me. With your help, and maybe even Lily for a bit on the weekends, we ought to be able to cover it." He gives me a tired but hopeful smile and takes a deep breath. "I'm selling the Jade Palace to Uncle Bob."

I'm speechless, stunned. The words are there, but they sound Greek or German. *Baba is selling the restaurant.* In all my life, I never ever thought he could give it up.

"What about the staff? Miss Chen, Chef Lim . . ."

"I spoke to Bob already. He told me everything will be the same, everyone can keep their jobs, and Miss Chen will step up as manager to run it. The name, the staff all the same. The only thing different, I guess, is no one will be sleeping here." He jerks his head toward the corner where the cot sits.

"But the restaurant's your life!" I blurt out. "The buffet is booming and you wanted to get more tours. And what about your plans to move out of Ashfield, buy a house in Roseville or the Northern Beaches . . ."

Baba waves my protests aside. "Those things, they—they are not important." He sounds pained as he presses on. "I started the restaurant for my family, to give my wife and my children a good life in Australia. I worked hard, earned money for my family. I always think this is my job, what I must do to take care of my family."

He sighs deeply and looks me in the eye. "Anna, I'm sorry. I was only halfway right. When I was always here at the restaurant, every night, doing numbers, planning menus, and working around the clock, it wasn't me who was taking care of my wife and my family. It was you."

My eyes are wet and I see Baba's are the same. Knowing how

much my father hates to see tears, I try to not let them fall. "Baba," I whisper.

Baba wipes his eyes with the back of his arm. "It's okay, Anna," he says. "I fix it now. I sell the restaurant and I come home. We have takeaway restaurant in Ashfield, and who knows? Maybe tour buses will go there one day. Maybe they come by rocket ship, you know?" He shrugs. "Or the teenagers with their phone, they come and take pictures and put on the YouTube and our restaurant can go, how do they say, many people see—go sick?"

I laugh. "Viral, Baba. It goes viral."

He shakes his head. "There you go. Maybe we get virus. We don't know." He offers me a broad smile and taps the crinkled page on the desk. "And you've always said we should be making the real Chinese food, not the Chinese Western stuff. Maybe we can now."

"Really?" My ears perk up.

Baba nods and says confidently, "I want to hear your ideas, Anna. Because I want you to help me run it."

I'm speechless again for the second time in as many minutes. A part of me is terrified. But another part of my brain is running wild with the possibilities. Maybe we could make xiao long bao or BBQ pork buns. A yum cha–style takeaway? For dinner! And Baba's right, maybe we could appeal to teens and hipsters and make the place Insta-famous.

Now I know I'm smiling. "Baba." And I reach out and hug my father. He stiffens but laughs.

"Okay. Good. It's settled, then." Despite his new softness, he's still a long way from being outwardly affectionate, but that's just him. *No, that's* us, I remind myself. And there's nothing wrong with that.

"Baba, what are you going to name it?" I ask. "The new restaurant, I mean. It can't be Jade Palace."

"I hadn't thought of this yet." He takes a moment to consider the options. "What about 'Anna's House of Dumpling'?" he asks in English.

I stick out my tongue and pretend to gag.

"Well, why don't I let that be your first task as my partner?"

"I like 'Anna's House of Dumpling.'" There are four of us in the car on the way back to Ashfield. Michael and Rory have both given Baba's new name the thumbs-up.

"No way." Lily agrees with me. "It makes it sound like an angry-old-lady place where they wave feather dusters at you." I don't think anyone except the two of us will fully understand her reference. *And that's perfect.*

"I can't believe your father's really selling the place," Rory says. "What's this Uncle Bob like?" I can tell he's wondering about his future delivery boy prospects.

"He's all right. Chinese businessman, big on profit. But he promised everything would stay the same, so I'm sure you could stick around."

"I hope so." He gives me a tiny nod. I don't want to mention the giant elephant squished in my mind: If Baba sells the Gosford restaurant, Rory and I won't see each other as much.

The butterflies in my heart are drooping.

Chapter Twenty-Eight
Ji6 sap6 baat3

October

MA COMES HOME FROM the hospital during school break. She's all smiles, hugs, sunshine, and positivity. It's like she's been at a Disney resort and come back as a newly indoctrinated Mouseketeer.

"No more bad thinking," she tells us. "Bad thoughts in the head poison the brain. From now on, only happy Mommy, okay?"

"Mommy, welcome home." Lily wraps her in a tight hug, and Ma hugs her back. There's a tugging deep inside me as I watch the two of them healing before me. It's all surreal.

That evening, Baba makes us an elaborate meal at home with all of Ma's favorites. The table is piled high with ceramic plates and platters of steamed fish, stir-fried beef, and thick gravy and ma po tofu, not too hot but just spicy enough, just the way Ma likes it. We all sit around the dining room table, which is covered in newspaper so we can spit out the fish bones. I can't remember the last time we were together for dinner like this. Maybe Chinese New Year, a couple of years back.

It's almost like we're a normal family. Almost.

We're all quiet, not sure of what to say. The only noises are the sounds of us all sucking the meat off our fish bones. We pretend to ignore the constant trembling of Ma's fingers. She can't hold her chopsticks steady. We try not to stare as time and time again, the silky pieces of tofu fail to make it into her mouth, dribbling down her chin and onto her blouse.

"Ma, have some fish belly," I say, picking some up into Ma's bowl. I'm doing the Chinese daughter thing, giving my mother the best piece of the meat. Ma smiles and I see the gratitude and pride in her eyes, which makes me feel a million times better. The chopsticks ting against the ceramic bowl as she tries to pick up the slippery fish. Finally, she gives up and sets the utensils down. She eats straight out of the bowl, slurping noisily, like some kind of animal.

"Hou2 mei6," she says when she's done. *Good taste.* "Your father is always a good cook. One hundred percent." She beams lovingly at her husband. He forces a smile and tries not to stare at the grains of rice stuck to her face like pockmarks.

Ma says she's tired after dinner. Michael demands to be tucked in. Poor little guy has missed Ma. Baba goes to help put them both to bed, leaving Lily and me to clear the table.

"It's a side effect from the medication," Lily says as we wash and dry, side by side. I know she's thinking about Ma's trembling, the same as I was.

"But does she seem . . . different to you?" I ask carefully. I recall that first time I saw Ma at the hospital. She recognizes us and calls us by name, but I can't help thinking that the Ma that's come home is closer to that zombie version of Ma, the one Simone called Miss Ping, than the mother we know.

"Give it some time," my little sister says. "It's the medication. And everything's still new."

Of course, Lily is right. As the days go on, Ma seems more like herself. She smiles and laughs, soft and breathlessly. She sleeps in a lot, but she's up and about by lunch. Not bad days, not good days, all medium days. She starts taking Michael to school in the mornings and picking him up in the afternoons. Her hands still shake, but she manages to get through most meals using a spoon. Once a week, she takes the train into the city to see a therapist who speaks Chinese. And at the end of the month, she visits a separate psychiatrist who prescribes her medication that she picks up from the chemist in Ashfield Mall.

Eventually, it feels like we reach some semblance of normal.

Chapter Twenty-Nine
Ji6 sap6 gau2

November

IT'S OUR LAST WEEKEND as the official owners of the Jade Palace. Uncle Bob has tucked away a banner in the office, ready to be unfurled in the morning.

UNDER NEW MANAGEMENT

The dining room is jam-packed, not a spare table in sight. Many of the locals that Baba has served through the years have come to see him off and enjoy a last meal. Baba looks happy, chatting idly with the big tables, offering free servings of spring rolls and egg drop soup. I'm proud to see how much Baba means to the people here.

A portly man pats his full belly, satisfied after his fifth helping of spring rolls. "Well, good luck with the new restaurant, Roger," he says, calling Baba by his selected English name. "Why, we might even stop by when the missus and I head into the city. What's the new place called?"

Baba beams. "Mama Hao." *Mother is good.*

It was Michael who suggested the final name when Ma came out of hospital. Ma was so proud. I liked it, too. It seemed fitting.

The man wipes his chin. "Sounds like a lovely place."

The staff all stay after work, and Ah-Jeff pours out tumblers of Hennessy and Coke. He gives Rory a drink first, and then nonchalantly slides a glass over to me with a wink. I glance over at Baba, but he's laughing and joshing with Lim, slapping his thigh while nursing his own glass of dark amber liquid.

"Cheers." Ah-Jeff, Rory, and I clink glasses. I take a careful whiff. It's much stronger than beer and burns a bit going down but not in an entirely bad way. Rory and Ah-Jeff are watching me, and I somehow manage to keep my face neutral.

"Not bad."

We stay and drink into the wee hours of the morning. Everyone toasts Baba over and over and then someone raises a glass to Ah-Jeff.

"What about Anna?" Lim cries as he pours yet another drink. "She's the best Chinese fry cook I've ever seen."

"And the smartest one to boot," Ah-Jeff adds. My face is already red-hot from the alcohol, so I don't know if I feel embarrassed or damn happy to be called out this way.

"To Anna!" And we clink glasses again.

Baba is in no state to go home, so we pull the cot out for him one last time and help him out of his chair. He turns to my boyfriend.

"Rory," he murmurs drunkenly, his arm slung over Lim's shoulder. "You take care my daughter. She good girl, you hear?"

"Ah—yes," Rory stammers. "Yes, sir." I laugh as Miss Chen and Lim maneuver Baba into his empty office.

It's just a few hours before sunrise. Rory takes my hand as we stand in the parking lot. The dark Jade Palace looms over us, a misplaced silhouette from another time.

"I can't believe it's really over," I say. "In so many ways, this place has been home. The staff are my family, too, you know."

"Yeah, I know what you mean. I feel it, too," he says. "I think your dad approves of me. You think he'll ever call me son?"

"Hah! You know nothing about Asian parents," I say.

"Maybe son-in-law, then," he muses. I have to chuckle, because he's technically not wrong. But I'm not in the mood for cultural semantics as I snuggle into his side.

"I wonder how you'll like working for Uncle Bob," I muse, my eyes feeling a little heavy from all the liquor. "Maybe you can ask him for a raise."

"That might be a bit hard if I'm not on his payroll," Rory says.

It takes a moment to register. "Wait, what do you mean?" I pull away.

Rory looks sheepish as he rubs the back of his neck. "I—ah— I'm going back to school. I'm taking my HSC exam at TAFE."

"Really? Oh my god, Rory, that's amazing!" I throw my arms around him and hug him tight. I savor the sensation of his hands around me. "Wait, are you sure? I mean, are you ready for it?"

"I think so. My parents were worried, too. But it won't be like before. It's an adult learning environment so it's not going to be all the Year Twelve stuff. And my sister said she'd be there to look out for me, with moving to the big city and all . . ."

My ears prick up. "Wait, moving to the city? Does . . . does that mean what I think it means?"

"Yeah, I mean, I love driving you around and all, but don't you think it's high time you just took the damn train?"

I smile so wide, I think my face will break. "Where are you living?"

"Stacey and Daria are looking for a place in Newtown," he says. "It's only three stops away from Ashfield."

The good news keeps on coming. I squeal, like a girl or a pig, I'm not sure, and hug him again.

"I guess you take this as good news?" He threads his fingers through my hair.

I answer with a kiss.

When I finally stop squealing, we go for a walk amid the empty streets.

The air feels cool against my skin in a deliciously new and dewy way. Rory sees me shiver and gives me his hoodie, all warmed up and cozy from his skin. The stars look even brighter now, set against their ink-black canvas. I guess they're right about it being darkest before the dawn.

"That's my house. Well, my parents' house." Rory points it out in the dark. It's a two-story beige structure, and I can make out a balcony and glass front. There are definitely no dollar-store window shields being used to block out the western sun. It's by far the nicest house on the tiny street full of nice-looking houses.

Rory is waiting for me to say something.

"It's cute. You won't find something like that in Newtown. You sure you're ready to give this all up?" I tease.

He squeezes my hand as his answer.

We stand on the street just outside the front gate, full of anticipation.

"You want to come in?" he whispers.

I lick my suddenly parched lips. They still have the syrupy thick sweetness of cognac and Coke.

"Okay."

Sex is that thing that hangs in our heads like a catnip toy. As teens, we're told to ignore it, there are tomes of scriptures and hours of lectures to tell us repeatedly to turn away, don't look. We are civilized beings, modern intellectuals who can, nay *should*, ignore our primal impulses that call us to bat at this thing that dangles so obviously.

I have to be honest, I haven't really thought about sex *that much*; definitely not as much as adults think teens think about sex. Don't get me wrong—I've felt things, lots of things and often, but I don't think I've *thought* about it. Before the beginning of this year, it was little more than an idle daydream, a high-concept manifestation of the perfect boyfriend, the perfect moment, the perfect experience, the details scant. Mostly, I thought it would just happen, an elegant footnote in the story of my life.

Sex with Rory isn't a footnote. It's not a soliloquy or a sonnet or some over-the-top ballad to be sung for generations to come. And it's definitely not as perverse as Whitman's "Song of Myself."

It's nice.

When Rory hovers over me and I can feel his skin pressing up against the bits of my skin that have never felt someone else before, it's *nice*. I feel sated, protected, and exhilarated all at the same time. And when it's over, he kisses me and a whole new sensation blossoms through me, warm and endlessly satisfying.

I fall asleep with his hand on my hip and my head resting in the crook of his arm.

Chapter Thirty

Saam1 sap6

December

MAMA HAO IS OFFICIALLY OPENED. There were no lion dance troupes, no big ceremony to mark the occasion, though Uncle Bob sent a couple of dressed-up citrus plants to deliver good business fortune. These take prime position at the front door, next to the rickety chair and table that serve as our single outdoor dining table.

Business is slow for a while, which is just as well, with finals rapidly approaching. I spend my evenings at the restaurant with *Macbeth*, Whitman, and countless problem sets propped up next to the giant stovetop where I'm steaming dumplings to order.

Every night, Baba and I close up shop together around ten and I go back to the apartment to study more until my eyes refuse to stay open. My body feels wrecked and I miss my stop going to school a few times because I keep falling asleep on the bus.

But it all feels good. It all feels normal.

                    *   *   *

"Anna. Caa4."

Ma hovers by the doorway, holding a cup of tea. Since she's come back from the hospital, she's been hesitant about coming into our room. She's uncertain about a lot of things, skittish, like she's not sure how to act around us; like an invisible barrier was erected between her old self and her new self.

I pull my headphones out of my ears (dollar-shop replacements that leak sound, but what can you do?) and smile, which she takes as a clear invitation to enter. She approaches my desk and surveys the books and problem sets and clears a space to set down the teacup. The liquid is murky and thick.

"Haa6 ful cou2." *Prunella.* "Calms the internal fires. Not enough sleep. You study too hard." Her look is stern and tired.

I try not to grimace and pick up the cup. As far as herbal teas go, prunella is not the worst; it's made with rock sugar so it's not too bitter, and has a woody aftertaste, like liquid branches, which is tolerable. Ma's cooled it down with ice, so it's actually refreshing, especially with the summer heat and no AC in our apartment. I take a sip as Ma watches.

"It's good," I say as I set down the cup. It's the thank-you that she's after, and she gives a satisfied nod.

"Chinese medicine is the best. Natural. Not like the Western medicines, pill for this. Pill for that."

I frown. "But pills work, Ma." Lately, I've noticed she's not really taking her medication. She's insisted she doesn't need them, that

300

eating "brain foods" like fish and nuts will do the job; she's eaten most of the walnuts already. *I'm better now*, she says whenever I mention it. *I don't need medicine. Do you keep taking aspirin when you have no more fever?*

Ma waves aside my comment and sits down on my bed to watch me as I drink the prunella tea.

There's no tea for Lily. She's studying at a friend's house for the night—the "no sleepovers" rule has been relaxed or just not mentioned. A few more rules have fallen by the wayside.

Like no boyfriends.

Ma picks up the picture of me and Rory that I've stuck to the wall next to the one of the family. It's a selfie we took the afternoon Jade Palace closed. The wind is whipping my hair around, and I'm squinting. Rory stares into the camera, his lips pressed against my temple in a half kiss. It's a classic, dorky couple shot, and Rory's made it his profile pic on Facebook.

"Are you happy, Anna?" she asks as she stares at the photo. "Rory make you happy?"

"Of course, Ma," I answer. "He's a good boyfriend."

She presses her lips together and stares at the picture and says in English, "This picture, you not happy face. Your mouth is smiling, but not the eyes."

I cringe. "It was windy, there was sun," I try to explain.

She switches to Chinese. "The first time I saw you and Rory together, you looked so happy, Anna. So radiant in the face. In this picture, there is no radiance. You look flat."

I don't say anything. The first time Ma saw Rory was that night in the restaurant with the aquarium and the fish, and it's not something I'm keen to relive.

"I don't mean at the restaurant," she says softly. "I mean the first time, when he drove you home. I watched you from the window."

Normally, I'd feel all kinds of mortified and uncomfortable digging into me. Internal fires making my face go red-hot. But I don't. Maybe something about the tea?

"I know why your face so unhappy," she says in English, and points to the photo again. I wince, ready for some hypercritical lecture of how Rory is the wrong boy, a distraction, that I shouldn't be dating, I should be focused on my studies like Lily or thinking about the family. That I'm a bad Chinese daughter.

"You're unhappy because your heart is broken and fixed together. Many, many times you hurt inside so it shows on your face. Too much heartbreak cannot be erased."

"But Rory's not like that, Ma," I start to protest, but she shushes me and reaches over and touches my forehead, brushing stray hairs aside.

"I know. I know Rory is a good boy and he help you a lot. I don't mean he is the one who break your heart. I think your mother break your heart too much," she whispers.

She bows her head forward and says, "Deoi3 m4 zyu6." *I'm sorry.* "Ngo5 zi1 dou3 zou5 ngo5 neio5 m4 jung4 ji6." *I know it's not easy to be my daughter.*

"It's okay, Ma." My eyes get misty, and I swallow the large lump bubbling up from my chest. I don't want to cry.

"No more bad thinking," she says. "Your mother will take care of her mental health. And take care of her daughters, too."

She uses the back of her hand to brush away the tears. "Okay. Don't stay up too late." She picks up the empty cup and leaves, trying to covertly dry her eyes.

I take off my glasses and wipe at my own. Ma's left the picture of me and Rory on the desk. I pick it up. My eyes in the photo are a bit tired, and my smile looks a little ragged. I stare at the photo, willing myself to feel the drama and overwhelming emotion of Romeo and Juliet or Edward and Bella. But it doesn't come. My eyes are too tired, and I have to stifle a yawn.

My phone buzzes. It's Rory wishing me good night.

Go to bed. 😴

The caterpillars rouse. It's not Romeo and Juliet, but it feels pretty darn good.

Exams are brutal. But I survive. I don't slay them, but I hope I've done enough.

"Marked improvement." Mr. Murray hands back my last Whitman assignment with the note scrawled over the top. "Some insightful observations, Anna," he tells me. "I hope you'll consider taking Advanced English next year?"

"It's actually in my plan. They're studying the Australian poet,

Eileen Chong," I reply, and he looks pleasantly surprised. I don't say anything more. I still have my last meeting with Miss Kennedy, and I need her to sign off on my Year Twelve schedule and not blow everything to pieces.

Miss Kennedy's smile tightens when I walk into her office. I try not to let it bother me as I take a seat. I'm surprised to find the paper clips are a jumble of pink, blue, and red—even a few plain silver ones thrown in.

"Miss Chiu. Last time you were in here, you stormed off—rather abruptly, I must add. Have you had time to adjust your attitude and approach to this process?"

I nod eagerly, which catches her by surprise. "Absolutely, Miss Kennedy. In fact, I want to apologize. I'm—I'm ready to make the most of my . . . pathways." I smile sweetly as I hand her my proposed schedule.

She lifts an eyebrow when she unfolds the paper. "This is . . . quite ambitious." She taps a nail against the table as she reads. "Advanced English," she murmurs approvingly. "Hmm, but psychology is only a three/four level, so it won't count toward your required course load."

"I know. I'm—I'm hoping it'll help me decide what I want to do for uni."

She frowns. "Bachelor of Psychology programs are *quite* competitive, Miss Chiu. Frankly, I'm not sure your grades are going to be strong enough for them."

"I—I know that," I say. "And I'm not really expecting to get in. But there are other tracks, like UNSW has Psychological Science, which is easier and has similar classes. I'm just really interested in psych, so I want to study it. I don't really care how I do it." I lift my chin as I say this, confident and assured. Miss Kennedy doesn't take notice.

"Well, that's nice that you've finally discovered some *interests* in your future, Anna. A career in psychology will be challenging but rewarding."

"The thing is, I've been helping out a lot more at my dad's place. We're running the restaurant together. So I'd like to keep doing that."

She flashes that fake smile. "That's nice, Anna. But restaurant work can be very demanding; you don't want it to take away your focus. The whole purpose of Pathways is to ensure you have the foundations in place to pursue a solid career of your choice."

"With all due respect, Miss Kennedy, the system is broken if I have to give up other things, things I'm passionate about, just so 'the system' can tick a box that says I'm moving toward some socially acceptable career path." I don't know where this has come from, but I can't stop. "Maybe I will be a psychologist, or maybe I'll be a real estate agent or start my own company. Or maybe I'll take over my dad's restaurant and just know a lot about psychology. I don't think I need to figure this all out now just because I'm heading into Year Twelve."

"Anna," Miss Kennedy says evenly, "I know lots of things seem unfair, but we just want what's best for your future."

"And what's best for my future is for you to sign off on my schedule, Miss Kennedy."

She taps her finger on the desk. I'm noticing that her folders are looking a little crinkled in the corners. Something's happened to her immaculate order. I'm dying of curiosity, but I know it's not my place to ask.

"That's fine." She takes my paper and adds it to a pile. "I'll sign off. At the end of the day, it's *your* future, isn't it?"

"It *is* my future, Miss Kennedy." My voice is clear. "And I'm looking forward to it."

She stops shuffling her pages, and I hold her gaze for a long moment before I stand and take my own leave.

Wei is outside waiting her turn. I give her a nod, but she doesn't meet my eye. I'm used to it by now. I don't want to push us to be friends. But I still hold on to the hope that we can be.

So I'm not expecting it when she calls out my name.

"Anna."

I turn.

Wei looks a bit sheepish. "How, um, how's your mom doing?" she asks.

"She—she seems to be doing okay," I say.

"Is she on medication?" Wei's question is probing, but I can tell she's genuinely curious.

"Um, she was. I mean, I think she is. She says she's better and doesn't need it now?" *No more bad thinking*, Ma has promised. I've taken her at her word.

I want to change the subject, so I ask, "Um, how's your grandmother?"

Wei winces with the same discomfort but then says, "She—she, ah, they put her in a home for a bit. They say it's better—like, for her to have a routine and stuff."

I nod. "Yeah, Mom's therapist says that's good for her, too. Rou-routine." These words feel like a foreign language coming out of my mouth. This is the first time I'm talking about Ma to someone other than family, a doctor, or Rory.

Wei's eyes spark on the word *therapist*. "Oh, so she's still talking to someone?"

"Yeah," I say enthusiastically. "She has a therapist who speaks Chinese, so that helps a lot."

"That's good. My grandma doesn't really understand what's going on and that scares her."

"You—you could talk to my mom's therapist, maybe? She speaks Mandarin, but it's still Chinese. I can get a number for you."

"That would be great." She gives me a grateful nod and even though this whole interaction feels so awkward, I'm glad we're having it.

She turns to go but then quickly spins back around. "Hey, your dad, is he running that new dumpling restaurant, Mama Hao?"

I perk up. "Yeah. I'm kind of his partner. I made up a few dumpling recipes myself."

"Wow, really?" Her eyes light up. "That's cool. I—I'll be sure to come by over summer. I love dumplings."

"Definitely. I'll keep an eye out for you." We part ways with mutual nods and I can't help smiling.

I'll never cease to be amazed by the surprising power of a good dumpling.

Chapter Thirty-One

Saam1 sap6 jat1

Six Months Later

"ANNA. ANNA, ARE YOU AWAKE?"

My eyes crack open to the bright light streaming in from the hallway. Ma is hovering over my bed.

"What time is it?" I whisper.

"Anna. Anna, the man is outside. He's coming for us. I heard him say he would take you, Lily, and Michael away from me. Anna, he has a van. He is ready to put you all in the van with him."

Her words come out fevered and fast. I sit up and briefly rub the sleep from my eyes, then go to the window.

There's nothing outside.

"Ma, there's no one there." My heart hammers in my chest as I look again, hoping I've just missed something around the corner or some shadow that Ma could have seen that has spooked her badly.

"He's there, Anna. I saw him. I heard him talking on the phone, like the kind they have for the secret service. In the ear. He makes plans with the president. They are coming to take you away. I heard them making the plan. They just have to find the van. The van will come."

She's babbling. She paces the floor of our room, turning her hands over and over and rubbing them like Lady Macbeth.

My insides are ripping apart. "Ma, please. You're not making sense. Go back to bed. It'll be better in the morning." *She's still seeing a therapist every week. How could this happen?*

This isn't supposed to happen.

"The government wants to take the children. They need the children for the wars."

"Ma, please." I'm on the brink of tears. Everything is spiraling, spinning too fast, like a Gravitron at the fair. I'm going to throw up.

"Lou5 po4." Baba appears at my doorway, dressed in an undershirt and gym shorts. "Anna."

"Lou5 gung1. Don't let them come. Quick, we have to hide the children. Take everything out of the closet." She goes to my and Lily's shared wardrobe and starts to pull things aside.

"Ma," I plead. The tears are flowing thick and fast. *She was okay. She was okay. She was better.* It's like a wrecking ball slamming into my chest, cracking the cage that protects my insides to pieces.

"Lou5 po4, please. Go back to bed," Baba pleads. But Ma is

frantic and scurrying, throwing clothing about. Lily is sitting up, the blanket clutched to her face, and sobbing.

I look at my father through blurry eyes. "What do we do?"

Royal Prince Alfred Hospital is a ten-minute drive away. We struggle to get Ma outside—she insists the man with the van is hidden in the bushes or behind the rubbish bins. She shrieks when Michael, Lily, and I are out of her line of sight, convinced that we will be whisked away. Her harrowing voice and panicked sobs have me jumping out of my skin. My body starts to believe that someone really is after me.

Somehow, we manage to get her into the car. The lights in our apartment block have all winked on, and I see the residents peering out at us from behind their thick curtains.

"Shaddup!" an angry male voice screams into the night. Someone's dog is barking, which sets off another group of dogs. Ma is screeching and crying and sobbing.

"Please don't take my babies."

There's nowhere to hide.

Michael gives her Tux to carry, and she clutches the little toy to her chest, stroking its worn fur, her eyes darting to and fro. The roads are pretty much empty, but that doesn't stop Ma from pointing and wailing hysterically at the few cars we pass.

"They're coming to get you! All of you!"

"Ma, stop it!" I scream desperately. "There's nothing there. What's wrong with you? Why can't you see that? There's nothing there!"

"Stop yelling, Anna! You're not helping. She's just scared," Lily scolds. To Ma she says, "Cover your eyes, Ma. Then you can't see them."

Ma squeezes her eyes shut like she's about to jump out of a plane. She puts her head down in my lap and covers her ears. She actually seems calmer. We manage to drive the rest of the way.

But the second we pull into the Emergency Bay, she's flailing again at the sight of the ambulances.

"The van. That's the van. Look at them. All of them. No, don't look. Goodness, Anna, don't look." And she tries to shield my eyes. She thrashes about and won't come out of the car. Baba and I work to drag her, and she kicks my father in the shoulder.

Eventually, a pair of hospital orderlies emerge with a gurney and they manage to strap her down and take her inside.

It takes eons to get Ma checked in. The waiting room is empty, and the chairs are cushy and new compared to Gosford Hospital, so we try to make ourselves as comfortable as we can. Except for Baba, who won't stop pacing the hospital floor and muttering to himself. I'm worried that he's going to be committed next.

Rory arrives. "Sorry it took me so long. The trains stopped running, so I had to take an Uber."

I hug him so tight, afraid he'll disappear.

"You okay?" he asks.

I nod. I'm just so relieved and happy to see him. The past hour has had me so on edge that when he reaches out to hold me by the shoulders, I immediately fall down like a sack of rice and need to be propped up.

We sit on the carpeted floor, me leaning against Rory with Michael's head in my lap. Lily and Baba are at the vending machines, unable to sit still.

"How come Ma is broken again?" Michael's words are slightly muffled with Tux pressed against his face.

"She's not broken. She'll get better." I lift up bits of his hair and watch them cascade between my fingertips. They fall neatly, perfectly back into place.

"I hope they fix her right this time." He hugs the penguin tighter and squeezes his eyes shut like he's trying not to cry.

I don't know how to tell him that maybe our mother can't be fixed.

"Siuling Chiu."

I've managed to doze off a little and wake with a start when they call Ma's name. I rouse Michael and Rory helps me to my feet.

The doctor is young and cute. I read the name tag. Dr. Wong.

"Hi, hello. We're here. We're all here." I'm announcing us like we have a restaurant booking.

"Good. I'm sure this wasn't how you were planning to spend your evening." Dr. Wong gives us a wry smile.

"How's our mother?" Lily asks.

"She's quite agitated and doesn't seem to want to cooperate with the staff. We've managed to get her sedated, so she's sleeping for now, but if this continues, we might have more of a problem." He looks at the clipboard in his hand. "Now, it says she's been admitted before? Is she still receiving treatment?"

"Yes, yes. I take her to appointment every week," Baba says without hesitation. He's keen to cooperate this time.

"Okay, well, that's good. Has she taken any drugs, marijuana or alcohol or anything that could affect her mood?"

"No, no, nothing," Baba insists. "We listen to the doctors from the other hospital. She come home, they say she's fine. How did this happen again?" Baba has his hands in his hair, and I'm worried he's going to tear it out.

"I'm sorry, sir. Where mental health is concerned, relapses can happen." Dr. Wong's voice is soothing. "Now, I understand she's on medication. Who's her prescribing physician?"

"Dr. Patel. From Gosford Hospital," I tell him.

Dr. Wong raises his eyebrow. "That's a bit far. When was the last time she had a prescription filled?"

Lily and I look at each other. "Maybe last month?"

The doctor clicks his pen. "Right. And what about her meds? Is she taking them regularly?"

"She take the medicine," Baba insists. "She take medicine doctor give her." He looks to us to back him up.

My mouth is so dry, it's hard to speak.

The truth—the one Baba doesn't know—is that getting Ma to take her pills is hard. "They make my hands shake. Make my skin dry," she claimed. "I'm better now. No more bad thinking. No medicine."

Lily was better than I was. She insisted on watching Ma after dinner, even counting the pills left in the tube. But Lily wasn't there every night, and I was often stuck at the restaurant.

It's our fault. We should have known better.

"I'm sorry, Baba," I whisper.

My father shakes his head. "It's my fault. I come home, look after my wife. But this still happen," Baba moans in English, his head in his hands. Dr. Wong gently touches my father's arm.

"It's okay, Mr. Chiu. These things do happen. The important thing is, you've brought her in and she's here in our care now. We'll look after her, I promise." He gives Lily and me a reassuring smile.

"What happens next?" I ask.

"RPA has a brand-new, state-of-the-art mental health hospital, but there are no beds available at the moment. I've put in a request to move your mother there as soon as we can."

"She has to stay in the psych ward again?" I feel like I've been hit with a sack of iron fillings. "For how long?"

"We'll have to see."

We go home, and Baba makes tea for all of us, even Rory. I feel the exhaustion in my bones. My emotions have flatlined. I'm raw and numb. Michael has fallen asleep curled up on the couch. Lily disappears into Ma's room and Baba clinks and clanks in the kitchen, his face stoic and serene. I wonder what he's thinking. But more so I wonder, *How can our family go through this again?*

"Anna, I'm going to put a sign in the restaurant. *Closed for family emergency.*" Baba eyes the three of us on the couch. "You should put your brother to bed," he adds.

I watch Michael breathing. He looks peaceful. I almost want to wake him up, hear him howl and cry so I can comfort him. So his tears will drown out the sorrow that's my own.

"I'll take him," Rory offers, and once again, I'm incredibly grateful. I hope he knows just how much. He bundles Michael's dangling limbs and carries him to his room. I close my eyes, letting the quiet wash over me. Savoring the nothing.

Rory comes out of Michael's room and flops onto the couch beside me. He looks like he's been through the wars, his hair matted and half-slept-on. I snuggle up against him, and he plays with a strand of my hair.

"Thanks for coming," I say. "You didn't have to."

"Of course I did."

"I don't know if I can do this again."

"Of course you can, Anna. You're a tough cookie, Anna Cookie," he adds with a smirk.

We sit in silence and I savor his scent. He smells warm like cinnamon and sweet biscuits.

"I should go," he says.

"Stay," I murmur into his chest. I don't want him to go. I need to hang on to the tiny bit of my life that feels in control and normal.

He raises an eyebrow and I swat him lightly. "On the couch, I mean." Even with the relaxing of the rules, there is no way Baba would let a boy into my room.

"Okay." He kisses me on the top of my head.

I go to the linen closet to get sheets for the couch. There's a soft thud coming from Ma's room. I shuffle down the dark hall. I can hear drawers sliding and shutting and near-silent murmuring. I open the door.

"What are you doing?" I ask my sister.

She looks surprised to see me. "Packing. We have to get shampoo—there's a list and ours is on the don'ts."

I'm all too familiar with the list. "Let me help you."

We pack in silence. Without me saying anything, she's already packed a plastic bag inside the duffel bag. "It'll be easier to carry to the hospital this way." She's pleased with herself, and I chuckle at her perfectionism. *She's ever so smart.*

"How did you know to tell Ma to shut her eyes?" I ask. "How did you know she would calm down a little?"

"I could tell she was just scared," she says with a shrug. "Remember when Michael wouldn't sleep in his own bed because he was afraid of the dark?"

I do remember that. "And no matter how much we tried to explain that there was nothing to be scared of, he wouldn't believe us."

"And it was only when you suggested we use monster spray under his bed he was finally able to sleep."

"But Michael's a kid," I say. "Ma's an adult. She should know what's real and not real."

"Is the point that we need Ma to know what's real?" Lily muses. "Or do we just want her to be okay?"

We finish packing in silence and when we're done, the two of us stare at the duffel bag on the bed. Tomorrow we will have to bring it to Ma. Tomorrow, we'll be meeting a new Nurse Mary, a new Nurse Simone. Tomorrow, I don't know if Ma will be all drugged up or if she'll be singing again.

My heart sinks.

"After everything . . . this wasn't supposed to happen," I whisper. "It's supposed to be okay now. Why can't it just be normal again?"

Lily cocks her head to the side. "Anna, life isn't some fairy tale or movie. We don't get whisked into the sunset or try on fifteen outfits before the school dance. This *is* normal," she finishes.

Her words echo over and over when I shut the door to Ma's room. *This is normal.*

I find Rory stretched out on the couch. He looks innocent and cherubic, like Michael. When we were first going out, I was obsessed with being a normal teen, doing normal teen things. I felt ridiculously out of place. Because I wasn't "normal."

But Rory isn't either. He battles his demons every day, and he still finds the time, energy, and heart to help me. To help us.

That's not normal, that's amazing.

I lay the blanket on top of him and switch off the lights.

Chapter Thirty-Two
Saam1 sap6 ji6

THERE ARE HORSES in my room. Their hooves are thunderous and loud, vibrating me off the bed.

Actually, it's my phone clattering on the floor. I fumble for it in the dark. *Unknown number.* It's four a.m. I answer it with dread.

"Hello."

"Anna, it's me! It's ME!" *Ma.*

I swallow and try to smile, even though there's no one to see it. "Hi, Ma. It's late, you should be asleep."

"Anna, this place is terrible. You have to get me out of here." Her whisper is frantic and feverish. "The doctors here, they are bad people. They have bad ideas. There's the Chinese one, the boy."

"Dr. Wong," I say.

"He is so snooty. He waves his hand around, showing me his wedding ring. So what? Big deal. He thinks he's better than me? Anna, you have to get me out of here. You have to save your mother."

The tears are hot against my face. "I can't." *I'm sorry.* "You have to stay there for a while."

Ma doesn't seem to hear me. "There's someone outside my window. He's shouting, can you hear him? He's saying I'm no good. I'm a bad mother. My children hate me. He has dark red eyes and his face is all squished. Anna, his face is like the dog! A big black dog outside my window. Anna, I'm scared," my mother whispers.

Lily's words come back to me. *This is normal.*

And we just want Ma to be okay.

I grit my teeth and suck in a deep breath.

"Anna, are you there?"

"Ma, listen to me. I love you. No matter what happens, no matter anything in the world, I love you. Lily loves you. Michael loves you and Baba loves you. We love you so, so much."

"Anna. My precious daughter. Ma loves you so much, you are my everything." I can hear her crying through her words. I swallow hard.

"No matter what you hear," I say, "no matter what bad things they say. Remember that we love you and we are here to fight for you. We will fight the bad things, we will fight the shadows together. We are your family."

"Anna." Ma is sobbing now and I keep going.

"So next time you see the man outside, next time you see the big black dog and he says bad things about you, remember we are there with you to fight them together. Okay? Don't be scared. Be brave for me, okay?" I wipe at the tears on my cheek.

"Anna."

I want to reach through the phone and hug her. Wrap her in my arms so we can cry together. I want to reach into her head and squash the demons, the bad things and the bad thoughts and the voices and ideas that make her stay up in the night. To fight the things that make her scared.

Because she is my mother.

"Anna. I have to go. They say I can't be on the phone anymore."

I nod through my tears and then remember to speak. "Okay. Remember, we're all here for you."

The phone goes dead, and I can't stop crying.

This is normal.

It's heartbreaking. And it's true.

"Anna."

There's a weight on my bed. Lily reaches her arms around me, and we both sit and cry. After a while, the door to our room opens. Rory comes in and joins us on the bed. Michael and Baba follow shortly after, woken up by our sobs. There are tears and hugs and holding. We all miss Ma.

She'll come home soon.

Mom
Maa1

ANNA. ANNA, YOU WON'T BELIEVE. *I will tell you a story and you will not believe it.*

Anna, you were right.

I try to go to sleep, but the dog man at the window was back. He had a chain around his neck and he was snapping his jaws so his teeth made loud clacking, like the pop cap gun.

SNAP SNAP SNAP

He doesn't bark like a dog, but maybe he is part crocodile. He tells me I'm a bad mother. My kids hate me. He tells me they will run away. He will take them from me. He said he will find you and he will take you away.

SNAP SNAP SNAP

But then Anna, it was a miracle. Because I hear your voice, Anna. You are standing outside with him. I can't see you, but I can hear your voice and you are yelling back.

"Go away, dog man. You don't scare us. You are nothing. We are family. Family is everything, you are nothing."

The dog man whimpered, and he became a small puppy. So cute. You pick him up and play with him. You always liked dogs, Anna.

Anna, I love you. Your mama loves you. And I want to get better. I want to come home. I will take the medication. I will look after you and take care of you. And I will take care of Lily and Michael. And your father, too.

I'm not scared anymore.

I love you, Anna.

I love you.

Helpful Resources

The **National Suicide Prevention Lifeline** provides free and confidential emotional support to people in suicidal crisis or emotional distress twenty-four hours a day, seven days a week, across the United States. **suicidepreventionlifeline.org | 1-800-273-8255**

The **National Alliance on Mental Illness** is the nation's largest grassroots self-help, support, and advocacy organization for individuals who have experienced mental illness and their families. Their website provides educational information on mental disorders, online support groups, and a video resource library. **nami.org | notalone.nami.org**

Mental Health America is a community-based nonprofit organization dedicated to addressing the needs of those living with mental illness and to promoting the overall mental health of all Americans. **mhanational.org**

The **Jed Foundation** is a nonprofit organization committed to supporting the mental and emotional health of young adults that provides free resource programs to help prevent suicide among college students. **jedfoundation.org | halfofus.com**

Active Minds is a nonprofit organization dedicated to utilizing the student voice to raise mental health awareness among young adults ages 14–25 and empowering students to speak openly about mental health. **activeminds.org**

Acknowledgments

I am indebted to many families in the creation of this book.

First and foremost, to my parents, who have taught me everything about love, hard work, and kindness. They have rallied behind me and supported me with the utmost care and trust.

To my extended family, aunts, uncles, and dear cousins—we go through so much together because we are family.

To my amazing husband, Phil, thank you for always being my first reader, my best love, and for keeping me alive and cared for. Thank you to the extended Towers clan: Barbara and Tony, Greg and Alana, and Penny and Ben.

To my early readers, Wendy Chen and Kylie Westaway, thank you so much for your time and attention and for your beautiful brains and support.

To my bestest friends, Kay Wong (who helped me come up with the final title), Roger Lee, and Ann-maree Kaufmann for being there for laughs, tears, drinks, and silly comments.

To my off-the-charts-amazing publishing family, Anna McFarlane (the one true Anna!), Nicola Santilli, Sophie Eaton, and all of the A&U crew. Lovelovelove Romina Panetta Edwards's amazing work with the *Dumpling* cover!

So much love for Radhiah Chowdhury—you are AWESOME and this is as much your baby as it is mine.

To my writing fam, Australia truly has the bestest and coolest people in YA! To Justine Larbalestier for being the most amazing supporter and kick-ass guide. To Alice Pung, first for letting me fangirl her and then for being a bountiful source of inspiration and spirit. And to all my dear author friends who give the shout-outs, support, and virtual hugs that are always, always needed; thank you Pip Harry, Erin Gough, Tim Sinclair, Tara Eglington, Emily Gale, Sarah Ayoub, Gabrielle Tozer, Leanne Hall, and more.

Special mention to Subtle Asian Traits and the SAT fam; your daily memes helped boost the ABG, boba, and K-pop appreciation throughout the book. :D Thanks for making me smile. Also thanks to Brian Cook and a special shout-out to Starlight—may you always SHINE on.

And of course, none of this would be possible without the beautiful community that is #LoveOzYA. So many of you have helped me get this far. This place—this space—is full of the most incredible people on the planet, I'm sure of it.

About the Author

Wai Chim is a first-generation Chinese American from New York City. She grew up speaking Cantonese at home and absorbing Western culture through books, TV, and school. She spent some time living in Japan before making Sydney, Australia, her permanent home. Learn more about her at waichim.com.